THE EARL OF EXCESS

The Rakes of Mayhem
Book 1

Anna St. Claire

© Copyright 2021 by Anna St. Claire
Text by Anna St. Claire
Cover by Wicked Smart Designs

Dragonblade Publishing, Inc. is an imprint of Kathryn Le Veque Novels, Inc.
P.O. Box 7968
La Verne CA 91750
ceo@dragonbladepublishing.com

Produced in the United States of America

First Edition July 2021
Trade Paperback Edition

Reproduction of any kind except where it pertains to short quotes in relation to advertising or promotion is strictly prohibited.

All Rights Reserved.

The characters and events portrayed in this book are fictitious. Any similarity to real persons, living or dead, is purely coincidental and not intended by the author.

ARE YOU SIGNED UP FOR DRAGONBLADE'S BLOG?

You'll get the latest news and information on exclusive giveaways, exclusive excerpts, coming releases, sales, free books, cover reveals and more.

Check out our complete list of authors, too!

No spam, no junk. That's a promise!

Sign Up Here

www.dragonbladepublishing.com

Dearest Reader;

Thank you for your support of a small press. At Dragonblade Publishing, we strive to bring you the highest quality Historical Romance from some of the best authors in the business. Without your support, there is no 'us', so we sincerely hope you adore these stories and find some new favorite authors along the way.

Happy Reading!

CEO, Dragonblade Publishing

Additional Dragonblade books by Author Anna St. Claire

The Rakes of Mayhem Series
The Earl of Excess (Book 1)

The Lyon's Den Connected World
Lyon's Prey

Foreword

The Battle of New Orleans took place in Louisiana, an area rich in many dialects, including (US) Southern dialects, French, English, and variations of these. The French influence in the area's vernaculars was strong, particularly in both Creole and Cajun languages. Bethany Phillips is of Creole and Acadian heritage and fluently speaks the French of her ancestors, with a sharp understanding of surrounding dialects.

Please note that Southern dialects vary depending on geography and I attempted to represent a flavor of that diction.

As a final aside, leprosy had established itself in the area, and since much was unknown about the disease in these early years, those afflicted with the disease were often relegated into smaller colonies away from the general population until later in the nineteenth century, when sanitoriums became more prevalent. They also generally knew leprosy as Hanson's disease. However, I used the more common term *leprosy*.

Thank you for reading *The Earl of Excess*. I hope you enjoy Matthew and Bethany's story. Please connect with me at any of these places.

www.annastclaire.com
amazon.com/Anna-St.-Claire/e/B078WMRHHF
facebook.com/authorannastclaire

Chapter One

Chalmette
Near New Orleans, Louisiana
January 8, 1815

THE THICK MORNING mist had quickly given way to daybreak, which had pushed through the fog only minutes earlier. On its heels, dark sulfuric clouds of black rose everywhere as cannon fire erupted, camouflaging the musket balls and grapeshot which were cutting down bodies everywhere Colonel Matthew Romney looked and slashing holes in the defenses. Surely, Hell had risen. The bright blue sky had lasted only moments before the fighting began.

Matthew hated mosquitos, had grown tired of this war, and would never comprehend the military's refusal to adapt to the guerrilla warfare they faced in the American wilderness. He considered the ungodly number of fallen men, who would never see their families again. He thought of his own family and wondered how they were doing—*what they were doing*. His younger brother, Jason, would soon be eleven. Matthew left his family and everyone important to him over two years ago; his only connection to his world was the sparse letters he received from home.

A rider skidded to a stop in front of him. "Colonel." He slid from his horse and saluted. "Can you point me to the general, sir? I have urgent news."

Already? The battle was ten minutes old. "General Pakenham is in the house." Matthew turned and pointed toward the white Villeré plantation house a hundred yards behind him, where command had set up days before.

"Thank you, sir," the messenger replied, just before a musket ball hit him square in the head and knocked him to the ground.

Matthew's heart lurched and for a moment, he felt lightheaded, almost weightless. He looked down and saw a scrawled note in the messenger's hand. He retrieved it and ran to the house, weaving through bodies and praying he would not have the same fate.

Running up the steps, he pushed past the sentry at the door and into the office Pakenham occupied, handing him the note before leaning down to catch his breath.

"Thank you, Romney." Pakenham perused the scribble, suddenly pacing. "Jesus! Where did you get this?"

"A messenger, sir. He died after asking for you. I saw the note and grabbed it. The man said it was urgent." Romney struggled to get his heart under control as he pulled himself up to stand at attention.

"Colonel Rennie is dead, and most of his men perished trying to retreat. The messenger may have been part of his regiment. Dedicated man. The ladder unit is still behind us. I wish to heaven it had made it through," he murmured. "We have to move toward Line Jackson and check these dirty shirts without them. Assemble our men," he said, examining his saber and snatching his hat. "No time to lose."

"Yes, sir." Matthew raced to follow orders, with the general on his heels. Within what seemed like only minutes, the surrounding eight-thousand men assembled and began their march toward Line Jackson.

The American line was a canal widened into a defensive trench and strengthened by a seven-foot earthen and timber rampart. Large bales of cotton covered with mud hid and protected cannons, blending them into the embankment.

Red-clad bodies from previous assaults lay everywhere as they got closer, forcing the men to step over and around fallen comrades as they pushed through. On their way, they got word that Major General Samuel Gibbs had also been killed. Gibbs's assault had also failed, and it had decimated his men in the torrent of battle. The surge of American fire had been like none they had ever seen before—almost surgical with precision. The plan had been to annihilate Jackson's men in a net of crossfire, but with Rennie's demise and their other setbacks, that strategy had failed. Ahead of them the rampart emitted what looked to be the devil's flames moving toward them.

"Bayonets, ready," Matthew commanded the surrounding men, pushing down the cold fissure traveling up his spine. *Everything feels wrong.* He felt for his saber for assurance, but its presence made little difference.

Within sight of the line, Pakenham gave the order to attack, answered immediately by cannon fire and a volley of shots that cleared almost all the men in the lines ahead. Chaos ensued as stunned men continued to push forward, only to be blown into the air, body parts flying. The potent smell of sulfur, excrement, and bile assaulted them. Men tried to retreat, cut down in red waves by grapeshot and musket balls.

The oppressive sounds of terror roared in his ears—explosions, cries, laughter, virtually every noise he could imagine overwhelmed the senses. In his peripheral vision, Matthew thought he saw Pakenham go down. Before he could check, a wave of red ignited the ridge ahead of him. A moment later, he felt a sharp pain hit his lower abdomen. Stunned, he fell from his horse. His mare screamed, struggling to detach herself from him. "Run, girl," he whispered. He wanted to run himself, but could no longer move. His mother's face floated in front of him. *Stay strong, Son. Come home to us.* He wanted to go home. It was his last thought before blackness swallowed him.

The battle sounds gradually faded into voices. The realization he had lived stirred him to consciousness. He could feel the sun warm his face but could not open his eyes. Was he blind? He willed them to open, but saw nothing. Everything hurt, especially his head and his gut. Men spoke around him. How long had he been here?

"We need to find the officers. Look for General Pakenham. He was said to have fallen near here," a husky voice said. "I would not want to explain to Wellington that we left an officer's body behind."

"Over here," a second man shouted. "I think this is 'im. They must have pulled 'im away from the middle of the battlefield. Did ye know Pakenham was Wellington's brother-in-law?"

"I did not know, and I do not care. Hurry," the one with the husky voice commanded. "I can feel them watching us, giving us time to gather our dead. Stack them in piles once we peel the uniforms. It's impossible to know how long we have."

Matthew could barely breathe. He was underneath something heavy. It smelled awful. The metallic scent of blood assaulted him. *The dead had not been here long enough to rot, had they?*

Am I dead? Matthew tried to move an arm. Nothing moved. Nothing worked. The men were there to retrieve the living and bury the dead. He could hear grunting and thuds, unsure either sound meant help for him. It mattered not. He could not save himself. This was surely the end. Warm tears formed and rolled from the corners of his eyes.

Matt, are you mad? They could have seen you. You take the wildest chances. Evan Clarendon's excited voice sounded in his head. *You locked the door, and they cannot get back into the residences.*

He must have been dreaming or hallucinating. Evan Clarendon was across the Atlantic, not in this mosquito-ridden hellhole.

A scene from years past rose in his mind. He and his friends had spied a group of older bullies known to torment the younger boys. On this night, the older bullies were swimming in a nearby pond and had removed their clothing. His friend Evan had taken the added measure of locking the doors to the halls, so the unclothed victims would have to wake people up to be allowed back inside. It had been a perfect crime. Rather than knock, the group of naked boys tried to scale the residence halls to get into the windows and were caught. The headmaster had not been amused. The older bullies had stepped into trouble for the prank, and Matt and his friends had laughed for a week.

A lump formed in his throat. *I will never see my friends or family again.* "Please do not let me perish here, Lord," he heard himself murmur.

Matthew, open your eyes. You are wasting valuable time. You must do something. Save yourself, Lucas's voice prodded him. Lucas Pemberton would know what to do. His friend was resourceful and rarely panicked.

Have a care, Matt! You pledged a blood oath to always be part of our foursome, I will not lose you. Come home to us. You simply cannot give up. I will not accept it. Wake up! Evan Clarendon's voice chided him—*goading* him to move, just like he did that day in the woods when they had taken a blood oath. Evan had used a small pocketknife to prick their hands. The four of them had rubbed the blood together and swore to be there for each other. God, he missed his friends. He tried to groan but even to his own ears, it was barely audible. *I have to try harder.*

Right! Come on, Matt. There is more we need to do together. Stay focused. You will get through this. We are waiting for you, Christopher Anglesey's voice pleaded in his ear. *You can do this, Matt.*

If he ever made it out of this Hell, he would tell everyone he held dear how much they meant to him.

Muffled footsteps and a soft whimper to the left of him pulled him from the vision. *Please, God, let someone be here.*

"Help," he moaned, but his voice sounded more like a whisper. Would his plea bring help or danger? Matthew decided he had to try. *I am so thirsty.*

He heard panting. Surely, he would not perish by being eaten by a wild animal.

An alligator does not pant. Calm yourself.

"Dandie, the groan came from this direction." It was a woman's voice.

A woman? What would a woman be doing on this godforsaken battlefield?

"Come here, girl."

The thud of a body being dropped sounded behind him.

"No, it wasn't him. This one is dead. Yet I know I heard someone. We must be quick; find him before the men with boats come back." The woman's voice was low, almost a whisper. She seemed to talk to someone . . . her dog? A soft bark answered.

A man's moan sounded. He realized it was his.

"Here! Dandie, do you hear that?"

Another body gave a soft thud as it fell back to the ground. Footsteps approached his head.

"Dandie, here." Her voice was close. Matthew heard a small dog move in his direction before feeling its wet nose sniff his face.

"Help . . ." he moaned again.

He felt pulling, then sheer pain shot through him. His moan became a scream.

"Shh! Sir, we are trying to help. You are under other men, and I must pull you free. This may hurt, but please stay as silent as you can," the soft female voice said.

"Who? Who?" he said, struggling to talk.

"My name is Bethany. My dog's name is Dandie. I hate to rush; however, I am afraid fighting will resume. From what I have witnessed, we will need to leave quickly. Please try your best to help me with what strength you can muster. We must hurry," she pleaded. "Lead the way, girl," she encouraged her pet.

Matthew was unsure of who "they" were—the British or the Americans. He nodded, or at least thought he did. A few minutes later, he was out from under the body. He heard it thump, taking the space he had once filled.

"Cannot see," he whispered hoarsely, frightened but grateful to live.

"I think you can walk. You have your legs, which is a miracle. I hate to ask this of you, but you need to help me get you out of here," Bethany whispered. Her voice broke. "Be glad you cannot see," she added. "I will never unsee this horror."

She tugged on his arms, pulling him up, and pain ripped through his side. His head throbbed and he felt dizzy, forcing him to lean into her smaller, soft body. Her pace was quick, and soon he heard the shrubs rustling. Matthew could hear, and he could smell. He wondered at his ability to differentiate the surrounding sounds.

The soft smell of honeysuckle and water helped clear his senses. He heard the soft ripples of water. They had to be on the riverside of the plantation. He tried to visualize the layout.

Leaning him against a tree, Bethany propped his limp body up to assess their situation.

"My boat is small, but I think I can get you in it with us."

"You and . . . your dog." His voice croaked the words. He was parched.

"My canteen is in the boat with clean water. You can have all of it if you wait here. I will be back."

"Where are you going?" Matthew asked, his gravelly voice strained with each word. His mind screamed with questions. Piercing pain reminded him he lived. *Perhaps being reminded I am alive is what I need, but the pain is not what I would have chosen.*

"To my boat. It is hidden. I must secure it before trying to put you in it. Your injuries are such that we must go to my home in order for me to help. I will be back. I promise. Stay quiet," she ordered softly. "I will not leave you here to die."

A few minutes later, she was back and helped him up. "They are returning. We must hurry."

Chapter Two

BETHANY PHILLIPS HAD sorely miscalculated the time needed to gather the last of the winter vegetables and herbs when she left home that morning. Usually, the chore took twenty minutes once she landed at the Villeré Plantation. The plantation had the best gardens around, and Major Villeré, its owner, had encouraged her to take as she needed.

Troops, both British and American, had gathered around the mouth of the Mississippi for weeks, raising tensions and making everyone nervous. Without warning, the British had overrun the plantation, taking the men guarding it by surprise. It had become a makeshift headquarters with bivouacking in the house and on the grounds.

Skirmishes between the forces had occurred repeatedly, and as a result, General Andrew Jackson placed everything under martial law—adding to the isolation and wariness everyone felt.

Still, she had rationalized her visit to the plantation. She needed more herbs to carry her through the winter. The garden was secluded, and Bethany had planned to slip in and out without being noticed, certain the British encamped there would be asleep.

Instead, she found herself with a wounded British officer—and a handsome one, at that. *British and an officer*. Her penchant for finding trouble was well-established. When she was twelve, two neighbor boys had swum close, not realizing she was fishing. Taking the opportunity to spy on them, she had laid down her fishing pole and climbed a tree. However, the tree limb she chose had failed to hold her weight. It cracked and sent her into the creek. Tobias Smith, the oldest boy, had rescued her and brought her home. And he had never let her forget she owed him. He reminded her each time she went into the Trading Post, his family's business.

Bethany would have to keep the man hidden until he healed and could leave. If discovered, she could face treason charges. It would be hard to explain his presence. Bethany should be afraid. She regarded herself as having sound judgment and common sense, yet she had shown little good judgment that morning. She waited for a sense of foreboding or fear overtaking her but felt nothing, even knowing she stood as much a chance of getting in trouble with the Americans as she did with the British. He needed help, and the least she could do was provide it. She had seen too much senseless bloodshed, and saving a life was worth the risk.

She glanced down at the soldier sleeping on the floor of her small boat. She watched the rise and fall of his chest, assuring herself he still lived. The musket ball in his side had to come out. Hopefully, it had stayed in one piece and had not splintered, buried itself in the bone, or worse, an organ. Her grandmère had spoken often about that complication; she had come across it many times. Bethany herself had not performed surgery but had assisted Grandmère twice and possessed copies of her grandmother's remedy recipes to guide her. Grandmère was visiting her sister, Bethany's great-aunt Theodosia, who was sick and needed her. Based on her letters, she should be back soon. She wished Grandmère was back already, so she would not be alone with him.

That he could not open his eyes worried her. *What if he is blind?* "No," she said aloud. "His eyes just have debris or dirt in them." Sorrow filled her as she thought about his challenges. She only had herself to count on with this. No physician would be available should she need help. Mentally, she laid out the surgical area she would use in the house. It would have to be the kitchen table. And brandy. She needed lots of brandy.

If only I had found him before the burial crew arrived on the battlefield. He might not have lost as much blood. Those men were more like thieves. She had watched two men plunder pockets as they stripped the dead from their uniforms. It was barbaric. She had heard what happened to the dead soldiers but seeing it still shocked her.

"I'm not sure how you escaped losing your clothing," she whispered in his direction, "but I am glad." Perhaps it held information about his family. Bethany would search his pockets and send word to them, praying her efforts would aid him in making it home.

Dandie curled up next to him. There was no man in Bethany's life, and those she had met, even in town, were greeted with a growl from her pet. Yet Dandie liked this one. Her pup had even attempted to soothe him by licking his face. She felt grateful for Dandie, recalling how the dog had heard the man's groan and had run onto the battlefield to find him.

Her dog was all she had. The gangly little white terrier had been a gift from Mama two years before and had been her only salvation when Mama had died from consumption the previous winter. Even Grandmère's magic herbs had failed to help. A familiar pain gripped her heart. She prayed her grandmother's medicine could help this man.

"You like him, Dandie?" she whispered to her pup.

The dog's head popped up and she smiled, parting her shiny black lips to show a perfect under-bite, her row of small white teeth displayed like an upside-down grin, with a crooked lower fang. She gave a wag, thumping her tail on the floor of the boat. It was a cheery smile. She put her furry head down and nudged his sleeping one.

Is she trying to tell me something? Has he become worse?

Bethany mused as she kept her skiff toward the center of the river. Her bag of produce and herbs sat at her feet with her canteen. "The major will not appreciate what they did to his home," she said out loud to no one in particular. "We may get winter vegetables again, but it will be a while." She looked at the soldier. *Who is he?*

Her dock came into sight, and she rowed the boat up to it, wrapping the rope around the cleat and placing the bag of vegetables on the deck. Getting out, she grabbed the rope from the cleat and pulled it toward the shore.

"We are home," she said, peering through the brush on the riverbank. Her house appeared as she had left it. It was a common enough style. A one-story gray wooden house, it had a wide front. Windows lined the walls on the front and back, giving good airflow through the house on warmer days. A wraparound porch surrounded the entrance. She had fastened the outside shutters of deep green from the inside. Squinting, she spotted the stick she had carefully set above the door. *Good.* It was still there, and the windows looked untouched. Relief flooded through her.

Dandie licked the man's face, rousing him from his slumber. He smiled, trying to evade the dog's long tongue. Bethany noticed his smile immediately; it was a kind smile. His eyes fluttered, but remained closed. Perhaps her small egg cup would help flush the debris out of his eyes if she could open them.

His square, chiseled jaw and strong nose gave her the feeling he belonged to the British aristocracy. His dark brown wavy locks barely touched the top of his regimental collar. He was the most handsome man she recalled seeing.

I bet his eyes are blue.

Silly woman! I need to save him, or I will never know the color of his eyes.

"Sir, we are at my dock now." She shook the boat to wake him. "I pulled the boat as far up on the sand as I could. It may be a little rocky as you stand. Go slow and reach for my hand." She stretched her arm out to him.

"I will endeavor to stand." He grimaced, holding on to his

side and easing himself up. His bleeding had increased again.

"Careful. Take one step at a time until you feel my hand," she urged. She needed to come out later and throw a bucket of water over where he had been lying to wash the blood out of the boat, in case someone came upon it.

The boat wobbled but righted itself as he grabbed her hand. When their hands touched, tiny tremors raced up her arm and down her spine. The feeling shocked her, and she nearly released his hand but held it fast. *Not sure what that was, but it was nice.*

"Perfect," she said. "Now slowly walk toward my voice," she urged, trying to dismiss the flutter which had settled in her stomach.

Dandie waited patiently until he got out of the boat before she leaped around him and jumped onto the grassy surface. Once Bethany got him onto the shore, she pushed the boat under the dock and secured it with her rope. Grabbing a large tree limb nearby, she covered the small dock, hoping to keep her boat covered. So many flatboats had gone missing during the past months. She needed hers.

"You are hiding your boat?" His voice sounded pained.

She was astounded he could tell what she was doing without his sight. "Yes. This war has given people license to steal," she responded with conviction. "It seems even the most mundane things find their way gone." She paused and added, "It might be nice to know your name. It feels awkward not knowing what to call you."

"Colonel Matthew Romney," he rasped.

"Oh goodness," she exclaimed, recognizing the dryness in his voice. "I let you sleep and forgot to give you water. I am sorry. You are thirsty." She reached into her vegetable bag and brought out her canteen, handing it to him. "Here. Drink."

He grabbed the water bottle and turned it up, drinking heartily.

"*Matthew.* It agrees with you. It is a very nice name." She smiled. "We should settle down before a patrol boat, or worse—a nosey neighbor—sees us."

"Agreed."

The three of them moved into the house. Once inside, Bethany walked Matthew to her bedroom.

"You sleep here. It will be more comfortable for you," she said with a note of firmness in her voice. He needed a comfortable bed to sleep in if he was to recover. She would make up a pallet on the floor. "We need to take this uniform off in case we have visitors. I can clean it and hide it for when you are ready to wear it again. We need to hide your accent, but that could be hard. Perhaps, we should keep conversation with others to a minimum. I should not like to explain a British officer's presence to anyone," she added with a smile in her voice. "Do you think you can get your clothes off on your own?"

"Yes . . . well, except for the boots. My batman . . ." His voice faltered.

"Did he die?" she asked softly.

"Yes," his voice cracked. "Bart had been with me as my batman during the entire campaign." His pain was palpable.

"Oh." She stayed quiet for a moment. "I will be glad to help with the boots."

He sat down on the edge of the bed and pushed his foot forward. It barely moved. Bethany picked up his leg and tugged on his boot, pulling it toward her as much as she could until it finally popped off, sending her tumbling backward, laughing. She quickly pulled the other boot off. "Let me know if you need me to help with anything else," she said, glad for the moment he could not see her face coloring.

"I will. Thank you," he returned. His face had paled, probably from the pain. "Wait."

Bethany turned back. She could not help but notice the sprig of black hair revealed by his opened collar, propelling even more heat to rise her neck. "I need to get the bullet out of your side. You also have injuries to your arm, although they do not appear as serious."

He tugged off his jacket and removed his shirt. "My family's address in my pocket . . . on a letter. Would you help me write a letter to them?"

"I will." She had planned to do that, anyway. It warmed her heart that he thought of his family. She would look for the address later, feeling better that he had asked her to look.

Matthew's head pitched slightly before he fell back on the bed. Bethany flew to his side and checked on him. *Good. He is still breathing.* "Looks like I will have to finish this myself." She grimaced. At roughly five feet tall, she was not sure she could handle his much taller frame. Satisfied he had not hurt himself more, she decided she could work where he lay.

She heated the water while she gathered candles and supplies. Opening her cabinet, she reached for the small bottle of brandy her mother had saved for special occasions. If she were to describe a special need, it would be this, although Matthew had passed out for the moment.

Bethany studied Matthew's face closely, looking for any sign she was being too harsh as she cleaned and probed his wound. Seeing pus and smelling an odor, she knew the surrounding skin might already be festering. She strived to pick off as much of the nasty stuff as she could. He grimaced and cried out, though he appeared to be in a deep, tortured sleep. Perhaps he dreamed of the battle. He did not move. Bethany worked quickly, determined not to stop.

Moving her forceps close, she picked up long tweezers and a probe, needing to first look for the ball. When she hit metal, she held her spot and grabbed with the tweezers, pulling gently until she tugged it from beneath his rib. She held it up, flushing it with water and examining it to make sure it had not broken off. It appeared whole.

Thank you, Lord.

Hurriedly, she picked out bits of debris—cotton from the uniform and pieces of things she could not identify—then cleaned up the blood. Satisfied she had done her best, Bethany poured water and small amounts of brandy on the wound, flushing it and making sure it was clean before she sewed it closed. With no movement from Matthew, she heated her needle with her candle flame, threaded it with silk, and stitched his wound. To ensure it would stay closed, she secured it from the inside and then added a surface level of stitches, like her grandmother had taught her to do with these deeper wounds. Pleased with the stitches, Bethany mixed mashed up bread, water, ground linseed, and ground oatmeal and put the warm poultice over the wound as Grandmère had taught her, hoping this would stem any further infection.

Weary, she took a long cleansing sigh before she examined his arm. The wound was much less threatening, so she cleaned it and applied the same poultice as she had on his side before searching for anything else she might have missed.

He had only removed his shirt and jacket before passing out. Worrying her lower lip, Bethany stepped back from the bed, trying to decide what to do next. Rest was the best thing for him. When he woke, she would try to get him to drink linseed and licorice tea as a preventative for fever. If needed, she had willow bark as well.

She stoked the small fire in the fireplace, then made sure the blankets covered him before she blew out the candle. Leaving the room, Bethany spied his jacket on the floor where he had thrown it and checked its pockets. Finding the letter he had mentioned earlier, she folded his jacket and hid it in her closet. She would stitch it where he had been wounded and clean it tomorrow. For now, she would make good on her promise.

Taking a seat at her small escritoire in the family room, she read the return address on the envelope. *This must be from his family.* Carefully, she opened it and looked for a name, checking it against the name he had given her. Taking a clean sheet of paper, she dipped her pen in the ink and wrote.

8 January 1815

Mr. Romney.

I write to you to let you know I came across your son, Colonel Matthew Romney, after the battle this morning in New Orleans. Your son was badly injured, but my dog and I brought him off the field to my home before they buried the dead. I was afraid he would not have lived otherwise. It was a gruesome battle.

I removed a musket ball and sewed him up. He also complains of not being able to see. I hope it is temporary. Matthew told me how important you were to him and asked me to write you. I will do my best to care for him. If he survives this injury, I will try to help him find his way back to England. I do not know what kind of communication you might receive from the battle, but I thought it important to let you know he was not killed.

No one knows we are caring for your son. It could cause trouble if they knew, but we were more concerned you knew your son was all right.

Respectfully,
Bethany Phillips
New Orleans, Louisiana

After sanding the letter and securing the ink, Bethany folded and sealed it. In her best handwriting, she carefully addressed it, using what appeared to be his father's address on the back of the paper. Somehow this would work out for both of them. *I will have to be careful not to let anyone know I am caring for him alone.* She looked up and prayed Grandmère would return soon. People on both sides of the ocean felt strongly about propriety, and she had just flaunted it, even though she was only helping him heal.

She would take the letter to town tomorrow and ... then what? It was not like she could just walk him up to a British man of war and say, "Found your man here. Fixed him up. Here's his address." She sniggered.

Good grief! What had she done? She was just trying to save a life, not thinking beyond his survival. No matter. There had to be a way. She would think of something. Perhaps one of Papa's old contacts. Worrying would solve nothing.

As if on cue, a loud moan drew her attention back to her bedroom. She walked in and found Matthew curled up in pain, still asleep. Sweat beaded his forehead and soaked his clothes. From what Grandmère had told her, his body was fighting off a fever and infection. *Best give it time to do its job*, her grandmother would say. Bethany stood next to her bed, pulled the covers back up, and silently sent up a prayer asking that he pull through. While she loved her dog, she relished talking to another human being.

A yawn overtook her. Any further worries would have to wait for tomorrow. Gathering up her spare blanket and pillow, she fashioned a pallet in front of the fireplace for herself and Dandie. As soon as her head hit the pillow, she fell asleep.

CHAPTER THREE

Ten days later

MATTHEW WOKE WITH a headache. He tried to look around, however, all he could see was darkness. *Where am I?* He gave his eyes time to adjust and still, nothing. Reaching out, he touched softness that felt much like a quilt. Abruptly, he recalled a voice, her voice. It had been soft, young, and enchanting. When he recalled a high-pitched bark, memories of the battle and what must have been his rescue flooded him. Then, it hit him. *He was blind.* He had never considered the world through blackness, yet he had been thrust into it.

He smelled the salty scent of the marsh, heard crickets and frogs, whose noise rose above the quiet, and he could differentiate the smells of a nearby kitchen—herbs, pork, cooked fish, and the smell of apple pie. He felt the warmth and heard the crackle and pop of the fireplace across the room. But lost to him was the light of the morning and the sights of nature. *I will never see the faces of my family and friends again. I will never see colors or appreciate the sight of the seasons changing. My parents, my sister, my brother—no one ever again.*

He reached for his eyes, making certain they could not open. This had to be a dream. *I cannot be awake. And if this is a dream, it is a nightmare—just like the ones I had of the battles.* He took the heels of his hands and rubbed his eyes slowly for a minute. Opening them again he faced the source of heat across the room. And saw nothing. *My eyes are useless.*

He laid there thinking back to previous battles—recalling another soldier in his ranks that had been blinded by injury. It had been temporary, even though the surgeon had predicted that the head injury caused by a blow to the head would probably see him blinded for life. Others had lost an eye, but his own hands felt his eyes and they seemed intact.

Scenes of battles haunted him in the darkness. He relived the death of the messenger, who had just arrived with a message for Pakenham. It felt like he had relived them many times over since yesterday's battle.

Matthew struggled against a surge of panic that threatened to consume him and forced himself to think. Pushing his hand through his greasy hair, he was reminded of a bath he most certainly needed.

He recalled the woman that had rescued him and wished he could see her face. She had been selfless and kind. Her voice was sweet and almost melodic. It made him think of warm summer days in a field of daisies and green grass—things he might never see again.

As if summoned from his thoughts, a small wet nose nudged his arm followed by a whimper. Gingerly, he lifted his arm and reached for the source of the cry. That he could feel and hear confirmed he lived. Where was he, though? The last clear memory he had was readying his men for the attack.

Afterward, he remembered only snippets of conversation and pain.

"*Bonjour!*"

A bright, cheerful voice startled him from his musings. *It was her voice.* Was his rescuer French? Perhaps Creole?

"Can you sit up, Colonel Romney?" she asked, not waiting for an answer. "I confess it is not much, but I found some of my grandmother's jam, some bread, and some tea." The sound of a small table scraping across the floor toward him was followed by the soft jangle of ceramic dishes settling next to his bedside.

He heard himself groan as he pulled himself into a sitting position. "I appreciate your efforts on my behalf," he rasped, trying to clear his voice.

"Supplies being what they are lately, I must apologize for not offering a decent tea. I have some leaves and am endeavoring to make you a pot. It is the second time I have used the leaves, so they should be fine. But first, I need you to drink *this* tea. It has been very helpful with the fever."

"I cannot see," he said, simply. An overwhelming need to cry nearly overtook him. He was lost in a land he knew nothing about. His regiment—indeed, his lifeline to home—was most likely lost. Vaguely, he remembered voices of men picking up bodies near him, talking about getting uniforms and anything else they could find from the bodies. They had been looking for General Pakenham's body. *God, was everyone dead? How was he still here?*

"Dandie found you," she responded.

At the sound of her name, the small dog barked.

"That's an unusual name. I rather like it," he said, trying to smile.

"It's short for Dandelion. It suits her since she goes everywhere, just like a wildflower," she said. "I am Bethany. You may call me Beth or Bethany," she said.

"Bethany is a lovely name." Matthew felt the corner of the mattress dip down on the edge as she sat down.

"My mother's name was Bethany." She reached out and touched his hand. "I am going to put some bread in your hand. There is a little bit of mulberry jam on it." She placed the bread in his hand so he could eat. "How are you feeling?" Bethany asked.

He nodded weakly. "Sore. I most likely owe you my life," he said, before biting into the bread.

"I have a pot of tea, which I allowed to cool a little so it would not scald you. Perhaps, try to eat the bread and jam in between sips."

He felt the cup placed up to his lips and opened them, taking a sip. Matthew silently agreed, forcing it down. He usually preferred tea. Obviously, this stuff had been part of a better pot long before this brew. "Thank you," he responded, hoping not to insult the person who had rescued him. *She has a kind voice. I wonder what she looks like.*

"You may have a whopper of a headache," she added. "You passed out from the pain, and I had to dig for the ball. I found it in your side, under your arm. I feared it might have splintered, however was able to extract it whole. It is in a dish on the windowsill in case you might want to feel it and be satisfied nothing was left."

"I have a terrible headache," he agreed. "Perhaps later I might like to feel the ball." If for nothing else, to assure himself he had lived through a nightmare. *He had been hit in the side, for God's sake. Why was he blind?*

"I looked about your temple and saw nothing to show an injury to your head. My grandmother is good with medicines, and I am a poor substitute. Perhaps your blindness is temporary, because of the trauma of the battle you endured," she offered.

It was as if she heard his thoughts. Had she?

"Thank you for assisting me . . . Bethany, I probably owe you my life. You and your dog." He grimaced. "I hope you are right about my eyes. It feels like I have something in them. Perhaps 'tis ash."

"Would you mind if I looked? I used a small cup to flush your eyes and several bits of ash washed off, but nothing of significance. I had hoped they would be better this morning," Bethany added.

He felt her stand and smelled her honeysuckle scent as she came closer. Soft fingers gently pulled his face upward. She was very tender as she opened first one and then the other eye.

"Your eyes look clear. I see no noticeable tears or abrasions. I suppose we must wait for your body to heal. Perhaps stress caused the blindness."

Matthew heard a chair slide next to the bed and could hear her sit down. As she sat, the little dog jumped up on the end of the bed and cautiously walked toward him. He heard Bethany try to shush her.

"It's fine. I enjoy dogs. We always had a dog about the manor as a pet."

"Dandie . . . come off that bed. You can visit the colonel when he feels better." The dog soundlessly jumped down.

"Please, call me Matthew. I believe we are beyond the formalities." He indicated the blanket. "I realized I am without my uniform. Was it beyond hope?"

She was silent for a moment, and he realized he had probably embarrassed her.

"I had to take most of it off to operate on your side. The uniform was full of mud, and I took the pants off as well. I tried not to look beyond what was necessary."

He heard a smile in her voice, and it was his turn to be embarrassed.

"I apologize," Bethany continued. "I should have said something to you about the uniform. There was a burn in it, where you were shot. I mended it this morning and will clean it. However, I found a set of my grandfather's clothing." He felt her lay a packet on the bottom of the bed. "Should someone visit, we cannot let them know you are British, and especially not that you are an officer. They will take you, and they could shoot me for treason. We must get you back to England as soon as we can. I wrote a letter to your family the night you arrived."

"I will do as you suggest. I rather value my neck," he said, trying to make things light as he sipped the tea. "This rather grows on you. May I ask what it is?"

She giggled. There was a twinkling sound to it he enjoyed. "You do not have to make me feel better about the tea. I have several choices, and I thought the most important thing was to keep your body responding and help you heal. It is how my grandmère taught me. This is licorice tea. I thought you would tolerate the taste better than linseed. I can take it if you dislike it. I planned on making some *manglier* tea from the groundsel bush for later this evening. My people use it more than anything else. I want to get something in your stomach and keep that fever from returning. The malaise remedies seem to have broken your fever for now."

"I vaguely remember arriving yesterday, but nothing further."

"It was *a week* ago. You have had a fitful time, mainly sleeping, but you talked in your sleep—to friends, I think." She held up the cup. "I'm glad that you will drink this. I have been spooning it in you these last few days, trying to build your strength. Have you ever had willow bark tea to drink? Perhaps I should give you something for your stomach before pushing that on you. But I do want to keep down the fever. There was a good deal of infection when I cleaned your wound—and you have had a fever until this morning."

She touched his side where he had been injured.

"I found it this morning. It feels like I have an immaculate seam." He chuckled.

"You do, sort of. I had to cauterize much of the wound, as my grandmother taught me. Once that was accomplished, I stitched the top with silk. Hopefully, the stitches will dissolve in time on their own. The wound had been full of debris and puss, which probably accounted for several days of fever. I think Grandmère would have been pleased," she said, with a smile in her voice.

"She must be a smart woman, your grandmother." He had not expected to find someone with any medical training. This woman had undoubtedly saved his life. "I feel extremely fortunate to have been found by you and Dandie." He smiled. "Are you sure I am not dreaming? Surely you are both angels on earth."

"No, not angels," she replied softly. "I did no more than anyone else would have. You were injured, and you needed help."

"I am an enemy soldier," he reminded her. She did not seem to notice.

"Yes, that is true," she returned slowly. "However, you are also an injured man. The battle ended. And the right thing to do was to help you. There were others there who, thankfully, did not find you. They stripped the men of their uniforms and goods and left them for dead. You would not have been aided."

He let that sink in for a moment or two. "Thank you for everything. I will do my best to leave as soon as I am able."

"You are blind. You cannot leave," she reminded him. "My grandmother should be home soon. She may have ideas on how we can get you to the English."

"They may already have departed." The reality struck him as soon as he said it.

"Ruff . . . ruff!"

"What is out there, Dandie?" She jumped up from the chair.

"Where are you going?" he whispered.

"There is a man outside the cabin." She kept her voice in a whisper as she fumbled in a drawer. "Dandie, come with me."

The door clicked shut behind her and he was suddenly alone again. Matthew was not sure he had ever felt so vulnerable in his life as sitting there in the dark, wounded and not able to see. He depended on a woman he had never seen, who had saved his life for which he could only be grateful. Now a stranger was nosing around outside, and he could not help. He heard the front door open and close. Fatigue shrouded him, and he was not sure how long he could keep his eyes open.

"Can I help you?" Matthew heard her say. He heard Dandie answer with a bark and a loud, guttural growl.

"I am looking for a soldier. I have reason to believe he may have traveled in this direction. Word is he could be gravely injured."

Chapter Four

"No, sir. I have not seen one." Bethany spoke up quickly, immediately chiding herself. *She needed to answer only what was asked of her. How many times had Grandmother reminded her of that?* She did not detect a British accent and was not sure this man was telling the truth.

"Are you here alone, Miss…?" he asked.

Bethany grew exasperated at his boldness to find her name. She had not offered it and wanted him gone. She took a deep calming breath. "Mr. . . . ."

"Sinclair," he responded.

"Mr. Sinclair, I find your questions out of line. It is me and my dog, and this." She patted the rifle that Grandmother had trained her to use. "I am trained to use this." Bethany hated to bring *Bessy* into the conversation, but with Matthew in the bedroom, she needed to protect both. Papa had made sure she was a crack shot. "Are you working with the Americans or the British?" she inquired, hoping to gain information. He did not look like an American; however, without uniforms, it was hard to tell Americans from the British.

"I am here on behalf of his family in England. His father hired me to find him, having had nary a word from him in almost a year."

"If the man was involved in the war and was a soldier, would that be unusual?" she asked, still trying to decide about the man.

He cleared his throat. "My sources told me he fought here a week ago, and I had hoped to finally catch up with him. When I heard they did not find him among the British dead, I had hoped..." His sentence waned. "I have received a missive discharging me of my services. But before I left, I wanted to try once more to find him."

"We hear things in these parts. Do you have a name for this man, sir?" Suddenly Bethany was unsure. Matthew needed medical attention, and this man might be referring to him.

"If he was in that battle, he most likely died. The British lost thousands, and many bodies were unidentifiable. Still, he would have been an officer and they would have looked for him. In the hope he lived, I thought to search the surrounding areas within a five-mile radius," he answered, appearing to study her.

Bethany grew more uncomfortable. "His name, sir?" she persisted.

"Colonel, Lord Longueville."

Bethany fought the urge to sigh in relief. "No. I have never heard that name before, sir. It is not one I am likely to forget. If you leave me word on how to get word to you, I will contact you, should I meet the man." Bethany relaxed. *It was not Matthew.* Besides, she reasoned, he was blind. While she hoped it was not permanent, he needed to be stronger before he left, or it would waste her efforts at saving him. And if he could not see, he needed to learn to get around sightlessly. She only knew of one person who could help her with that. *Aunt Theodosia.* The woman had been blind since childhood. She could help Matthew. She needed her grandmother's help if she were to get him healed so he could leave.

"It's just that if he died, the man's body should have been found. Yet they found nothing," he persisted. "The only information I had was that a woman was reported helping a soldier to safety. While the description given was vague, you seem to fit it."

Someone had seen her. Who could it have been? She did not remember seeing anyone there. Flags of truce had signaled a time for the English to secure their dead. She and Dandie had checked and had seen no one in the area. They had been very careful. Bethany was certain, yet they had missed something. She shook her head, suddenly fearful to say another thing.

"Fine. Here is an address," Sinclair said abruptly. "Leave word if you see or hear of him. Tom Morris always knows my whereabouts." He shoved a brown piece of paper in her hand.

He sounded irritated even though she had been cordial to him. Bethany wondered how much of this Matthew could hear inside.

Dandie growled. Her deep guttural sound signaled she had grown tired of the man as well. The small terrier moved closer and sniffed his pants and boots before stepping back to her side.

"Thank you for your help. You should know there are deserters from battlefields," he added before turning and heading back in the battlefield's direction. "They will look for shelter until they are sure that their military units have withdrawn, and they are no longer in danger. Stay aware."

Bethany gave a terse nod. Once the man disappeared, she opened the door and went into the house, closing it behind her. Taking a deep breath and squaring her shoulders, she walked into her bedroom.

"Who was that?" Matthew asked. His voice was faint and raspy.

"I am sorry it took so long. He said he was a tracker. He was looking for a soldier he had been hired to find."

"Probably a deserter. The British take that very seriously. Did he give a name?" he said, barely audibly. "I had almost two thousand men in my command. Perhaps I would know him."

Bethany did not add that the man did not sound British. Matthew did not seem to be concerned about the man at all. "You sound tired. Let us discuss this later. For now, sleep. I will bathe the wound and change the bandages. If you feel comfortable with me doing it, I would like to clean and shave your face. I have my papa's razor."

"I would do anything for a shave. My batman used to shave me . . ." He went silent and pushed his head back down on the pillow.

The two were close, Bethany realized. It was the second time he had referred to his batman. Not a term she was overly familiar with. She surmised it was the person upon whose assistance he counted.

"Dandie, can you bring me the clean bandages?" The little dog wagged her body before turning and going to the basket by her closet. That was the funniest thing about Dandie. When she wanted to wag her tail, her entire body wagged. Bethany let out a soft giggle, watching the dog retrieve a large ball of torn muslin. She needed to make sure his wound stayed clean and dry. "I am waiting for my grandmother to return. She should be back, any day," she said, looking over at Matthew. He was already asleep and snoring.

"'Tis just you and me, Dandie. He has fallen asleep, again. It is probably the best thing for him." Bethany quickly cleansed the wound and felt thrilled to see the tissue was pink and no longer fusty. Very little blood had oozed. Satisfied that he had begun to heal, she put the poultice on the stitches and wrapped it up. Just like the night before, he had turned into dead weight. However, she had figured out how to slide the bandages beneath him and pull them through the other side, allowing him to sleep.

Dandie barked and stood on a chair, nosing open the curtain. Bethany walked back over and peered from the side of the curtain. No one was there. It was not unusual for her dog to hear things she could not. Deciding to watch it for a little while, she made sure she was out of direct view of the window and watched, keeping an eye on the front. If it had been dark, she might have been scared. At least she could see during the daylight. She watched for ten minutes and saw nothing. Perhaps Dandie was seeing something the wind was doing. Something moved, and she looked again. She saw Sinclair step off the dock.

He had been checking by her boat. *The man is determined.* Luckily, she had cleaned it out after they arrived, washing all evidence of blood. He looked frustrated.

This changed her plans. They could not stay. Perhaps she should lock up the cabin and head to Aunt Theodosia's home. Bethany felt sure she would not be followed. If he was going to snoop around here, it would be impossible for Matthew to heal. She needed to hide the uniform, too. He would have to take off the pants and boots. Only the military wore those boots—*British military*. He could have them back when he healed.

Bethany dug into the trunk at the end of her bed, looking for Papa's shoes. She appreciated Grandmère would not get mad if Matthew wore her grandfather's clothing, not for a good cause like this.

"Dandie, we must leave here for a short while. I think we should go to Aunt Theodosia's." She doubted anyone would follow them into the leper colony.

≫✕≪

SHE WAS LYING, and it frustrated him. Why would the girl lie? Edward Sinclair had trailed Colonel Longueville for hundreds of miles, finally determining that Longueville's regiment had headed into New Orleans. He considered the Earl of Romney, the viscount's father, a solid acquaintance and wanted to find his son.

When he reached the site of the battle, hours after the battle had ended, it had horrified him to see so many British dead. He had hunted for any information that could lead him to the colonel or his body. The only plausible information he had gained was the sighting of a young woman helping a soldier to safety. On the chance Longueville still lived, he had sought information until finally finding her.

The woman sounded uncertain and nervous, seeming to judge him with every word. Had he not been so tired, he might have done a better job with his approach. He was certain she knew something she was not telling. She had been too tentative. Harboring an enemy soldier could see her accused of treason and the man she was helping killed under General Jackson's military rule in the area. Sinclair would never harm an innocent woman. He would be careful.

The thought occurred to him. *Perhaps she did not yet know the soldier's name. Perhaps he could not tell her. Or the man had died.* That thought sent a chill to his gut. He owed his friend and would see his son home if there was any way humanly possible.

He watched her house for a few more hours. Seeing nothing change, he finally left to find something to eat. He wanted more information.

SOMETHING WAS WRONG. Bethany had evaded his question. Matthew had heard some of what was asked, but Dandie's sporadic growling had masked the low voices. He could not exactly get up and stand at the window, so he had remained still, straining to hear. The last thing he wanted was for this woman to be accused of betrayal for helping him. He thought he had heard the name Sinclair. Was that the man's name or that of the person he was looking for? There were some men named Sinclair in his regiment, although he would not know what happened to them. He felt his pulse speed up at the thought of his men.

Matthew had rushed to judgment, something his sister, Charlotte, used to accuse him of doing frequently with her. Bethany had been right to defer more talk of the visitor, he conceded. The thought of the battle upset him. He needed his rest, or he would never regain his strength. Bethany had risked her life to save him.

A small knock at the door roused him from his thoughts. "I have given this a lot of thought, Matthew," Bethany began. "I think we should find our way to my Aunt Theodosia's house. My

Grandmère is there, and it would be safe from prying eyes."

"You are worried about the visitor we had earlier?" he asked, trying to sit up.

"No, no. Let me prop you up." She gently pulled him toward her, and he caught a whiff of her honeysuckle scent. He had never fully appreciated that smell until now and hated when she stopped fluffing his pillow. He heard her sit down in the chair near him. "Not that we had a visitor. More. Someone saw you leave with me. That brought him here. I worry for you, and if I am to be honest, I do not want to be accused of treason."

The two of them sat silently for a moment before Matthew finally spoke. "If you feel we need to go to your aunt's house, then we do that. Besides, I cannot make my way to England until I am better—and even then, a blind man may not have much choice in such matters. I cannot imagine it will be easy for me to travel alone. With our countries at war, I do not know when that may be possible," he lamented.

"Please do not think of yourself as permanently blind. My heart tells me it is temporary. Let us believe that," she said, clasping his hands. "I have packed up some provisions. Weather tonight portends rain, and a full moon would be better. It is almost full. If the weather clears, we can leave tomorrow."

"Can you help me with a couple of things?" He dreaded asking for these things.

"Are you hungry, or do you need more tea? I forgot about a wedge of cheese Grandmère had stored, and I also found some dried fruit. Does that appeal?" Bethany asked.

"Perhaps a little later. I require the . . . necessary." Matthew was glad to be blind at this moment, certain that the heat rising from both of their faces warmed the room.

"Oh, dear. I had not thought to remind you. It sits below your bed in a small wooden cabinet. My Papa built the cabinet so that the chamber pots would be out of sight. You have but to reach down and open the cabinet door. It sits at the foot of the bed. I moved it when I moved you in here. You've not been wholly conscious, and I should have remembered to tell you."

"Thank you." He wondered if he could handle this on his own.

"I also placed my grandfather's cane by your bedside." She brought the cane to the side of the bed and wrapped his hand around the top of it.

"You have thought of everything," he said, smiling.

"I tried. I should have introduced you to these things."

"Did you clean my uniform, yet? We should take it with us, somehow, in case it would come in handy. How far will we travel to get to your Aunt Theodosia's?"

"It is about ten miles. We will travel the waterway until we come to a small creek off the bayou. That is where my aunt and grandmother are staying." She cleared her throat. "Your uniform is dry. I have it secured it in a packet, with your boots, so it can be transported, unseen. I must be forthcoming about one thing. My Aunt Theodosia is the caretaker for a small leprosy colony off the bayou. We will be safe there while you heal."

CHAPTER FIVE

THE MAN HAD drawn back and looked horrified, causing Bethany to sit back down in the chair. "I can see the horror on your face, so I should explain," she offered.

"Yes, that might help. I confess I have never seen this . . . disorder they call leprosy. But I have heard it is quite bad," Matthew replied.

"My Aunt Theodosia and my Grandmère are herbal healers. My aunt lives near the colony, but she is not part of it. She helps them and in return, the people care for her. She has been very ill. My grandmother suspects it was her heart. She maintains her distance from the people in the colony, and they give her distance. However, she can supply them with herbs and remedies for their problems. Grandmère doesn't believe that there is a cure for leprosy. She and Aunt Theodosia wear cloth tied over their faces when near the colonists. She tells me that bad breath is well . . . bad, and breathing is something we do. Who knows? But Aunt Theodosia has always been safe. I expect we should do the same."

His eyes were wide open, but his stare was unfocused. She had to keep her hope that he would see one day, soon. She enjoyed the sight of him, she found. And while she had been true to her word when she told him she had averted her eyes when she pulled off his pants, part of her had wanted to look. There was a pull she could never deny.

"I have tea steeping. It's your favorite." She said cheerfully.

He pulled a face. "I cannot argue that it has helped. I do not feel as poorly. Could I have some of the bread and cheese you spoke of?"

He gave her a sheepish smile. With that dimple on his chin, she realized he could ask her for anything. Giving herself a shake, she stood. "I will bring some in, in a moment. And I will bring a small pitcher of water. I boiled it for you, so it should be clean to drink."

"Thank you." His words trailed after her.

Dandie stayed with him. The dog had developed a fondness—or something—for him. She had never known her to like a man. She certainly had not liked the man earlier. A small shudder shook her body at the reminder. Perhaps she should have asked more questions of him. He was looking for a British soldier... *just not Matthew.* He would have no reason to report her for anything suspicious. The thought gave her a small measure of comfort as she placed the tea on a carved wooden tray, along with a small serving of bread and cheese.

"Here you go, Matthew." His name rolled off her lips easily. She liked the sound of it. She had never known a Matthew but knew she would forever think of this man when she heard the name.

"Ruff! Ruff!"

Dandie's bark made her hurry. Reaching the room, she found her soldier trying to stand. "What in the world are you doing? If you fall, you could damage your ribs and restart the bleeding," she scolded, setting the tray on the side-table and hurrying to his side.

"I just wanted to get up, out of the bed. I am used to soldiering, doing things. I cannot have you doing all the work. Surely there is something I can do." His voice was hoarse.

Bethany thought for a minute. "There is."

"What? I would like to help."

"You can listen and familiarize yourself with the sounds of the river. Our travel will be on the river, and while you cannot see, you will be able to hear the splash of a gator or people's voices. We will leave before daybreak. It's not too far, but I want to get there quickly. The camp is a small tributary just off the river."

"I will do that if you do something more for me. Help me sit up and talk to me. Please. I have lain here in this bed too long. I keep reliving the battle in my head. Having someone to talk to would be nice."

She found she would like to have company. It had been a while since Grandmère left, and she loved the idea of talking to someone. "We could practice you speaking, too. If someone asks you a question, you cannot use your accent."

"That makes sense . . . y'all," he finished, wearing a broad grin.

Bethany broke into a giggle. "That's probably perfect. So many southerners down here, it would blend right in. What else do you know?"

He thought a moment. "What'cha talking 'bout?"

Bethany laughed. "You *have* been practicing."

A smile broke out across his tan face, showing perfect white teeth. "I wish I could see you laugh. I love the sound of it," he said, attempting to smile. "Ah aim to please, missus!"

Bethany giggled. A warm feeling shot through her center, and she struggled with unsteadiness of her own, furtively touching a nearby chair back for stability. The man had a dizzying effect on her. "That's an excellent imitation of some of the Southern dialects. How did you pick it up?"

"I find the differences in dialects fascinating and listen to the speaker, trying to detect patterns. It helps with languages."

"Do you know any languages?"

"French was important to know. My governess taught us, and we continued Latin studies at university."

"That should help you with the Creole language. When I was young, they taught me French. While I learned it well enough to speak fluently, I also understand the Creole similarities. We have a mixture of tongues here. It keeps things interesting."

She noticed a sheen on his head. "You are sweating. You probably have another fever." Her hand instantly went to his forehead. It was warm and damp. "I shall make some more tea. It is also a friendly reminder to take it with us. We may need it." Other than the slight perspiration, he appeared slightly better. "Do you feel like standing?"

"I think I will if you help me." Matthew moved his head toward the bed. "I forgot the cane. The cane will help." The sheepish look appeared again.

She liked the way it showed off his dimple. "You are used to being in charge, so this will not be easy for you. Think of getting well as the biggest mission you have ever been a part of," she suggested, handing him the cane.

He stood in front of her, leaning on the cane. "Can I touch your face? I will understand if you would prefer not. I imagine you might want to slap me for even suggesting it. Yet I am longing to know you and I think it is my only way . . . for now."

Her breath caught in her throat. She nodded and realized he could not see. "Yes," she managed.

He leaned on the cane with one hand and moved the other to her face, gently caressing it as his fingertips moved around her face, soothingly touching her chin, her nose, her eyebrows, her hair.

"What color is your hair?" he asked, running his fingers over the tips of her ears and through her hair.

Every touch sent warmth pulsing to the center of her being, a feeling she had never experienced. She silently wished she had a reason to touch him again as his fingers felt her lips, circling them. "Brown with auburn highlights. Grandmère tells me I resemble my mother."

His hand moved slowly. "Perfectly shaped lips. You are very beautiful. I can almost see your cheekbones and flawlessly shaped nose. You have an oval face, and your skin feels so soft, almost porcelain-like." His hand left her face as he picked up her hand. "You are a hard worker. Your fingers are long and dainty."

She almost felt in a stupor. "I have no one to do the chores, and things must be done every day."

He carefully dropped her hand and went to touch her neck and she drew in a sharp breath. "A long neck. The way your hair rests, just so . . ." he touched her hair and pulled it away from her face. "You are beautiful—inside. My fingers tell me that you are such on the outside, too. However, I have seen the beauty of your heart."

"Th . . . thank you," she stammered. Her body pulsed with a strange need for his touch. She stepped closer.

His free arm drew her closer. He seemed so at ease with her. At this moment, it was as if they had known each other before, however impossible that was to consider.

"I . . . would you mind if I touch your face?" she asked. It was as if she was a woman possessed by need.

"Please, I should like you to touch my face." His response came in a hushed tone.

She cradled his face in her hands, feeling its shape, his skin, and his chin. Closing her eyes, Bethany feathered her fingers along his face, trying to see as he did. His eyebrows felt straight and thick, arched near the end. She knew his eyes to be very expressive, even if he could not see. His face showed emotion. She touched his nose. It felt long, straight, patrician. His cheeks were stubbled with several days' worth of growth. And his lips were defined. There was a scent of faint sandalwood, sweat, and a curious sweetness—perhaps clove—a unique scent that she could smell when she neared him. She followed the little dip in the upper lip. Bethany moved to his chin, eager to touch his beautiful dimple. Her thumb rubbed it while her other fingers feathered his lips.

Bethany opened her eyes and looked at the man in front of her. What she had done went against every rule her grandmother had taught her. She found herself close enough to a man to know his scent. She should be shaken, ashamed, or at least frightened of her behavior. But she was not. This man was special.

I want him to kiss me.

The thought came from nowhere. Yet she felt no shame. Leaning closer to him, she inhaled the scent of him again, hearing him draw in a breath through his teeth. She pulled back, rattled and embarrassed. *What was she doing? What was she thinking?*

"You have a fine face," she finally said. *A fine face?* How inadequate. "What I mean is, your face is strong, and . . . handsome." She said, trying fruitlessly to repair her blunder and blushing to her toes. She kept making slipups, and no matter how she tried to check herself, the words flew from her mouth unimpeded.

The two of them stepped back from each other—him holding onto the cane and she rigid, unable to breathe. She dared not speak.

"My sincere apologies, Bethany. I have never spoken thus to a woman, and I have overstepped myself with someone providing me with shelter and aid." His accent was thick. "I apologize for my forwardness. I should never have asked that of you."

In for a penny, in for a pound. "Matthew, there is no need." She swallowed. "I wanted to touch your face, but I cannot explain why." Bethany wanted this moment to never end, but it must. A smile brightened her face. "I had an idea, watching you with the cane. There might be something you can do to help me with my chores."

"You are not upset with me, *yet.*" His chest heaved a sigh. "However, I want to kiss you. *May I?*"

Bethany had never experienced a kiss. She had been living alone with her family. In her eighteen years, she had never gone to a dance, never even drawn a serious glance from a man, all because of the war. She *wanted* to kiss this man. *What could it hurt? It would just be one kiss.*

"Yes," she said in a whisper. "I would like that."

He inclined toward her, taking his one free arm and pulling her closer. Slanting his face, he leaned down, brushing against the top of her forehead as his lips met hers. He feathered her lips with his before kissing her, teasing her lips gently with his tongue. She opened her lips in wonder, and his tongue probed the cavity of her mouth. Warm, gentle, he moved his tongue about her own. She yielded to his kiss and drew closer, placing her arms about his face. Her body knew what it wanted. And it was this man, this kiss, this moment. She fingered the curls at the back of his neck as her breathing picked up. She could hear his breath pulsing against her face. Slowly, she pushed back, breaking the kiss.

They both stood there, chests heaving in frustration, looking at each other. "I should not have done that," he started.

"Shhh!" She placed her finger across his lips. "I know we should forget that happened. I can never overlook it, though. Any kiss I receive the rest of my life will be found lacking against the memory of that one."

CHAPTER SIX

WHAT JUST HAPPENED? Matthew closed his eyes and summoned all the strength he could. While his sight had left him, his other senses had not failed him. They seemed to have heightened. He could not see, yet through his hands, he had seen her. There was no experience in his life to compare this to. The touch and feel of her affected him. Her voice affected him. It was an experience unto itself. He wanted to see the silky hair that entwined his fingers, the perfectly shaped brows, aquiline nose, and bow-shaped lips that summoned to mind a gentle beauty he wanted to caress.

At times he thought he saw slight and shadowed shapes, but it was momentary. He remained quiet about it, unwilling to build her hopes or his own. The only thing that seemed consistent was his ability to differentiate between light and dark. He had not yet resigned himself to being blind—although, he had nothing upon which to base his hope except for a gut feeling he would see again. Finding his way home blind would be more difficult than he could contemplate. As soon as he could see, he would head for home. He needed to. Matthew had never been a despoiler of innocents. He resolved to forget the feel of her skin beneath his fingers and the kiss of her lips. A voice in his head laughed at him. It could never happen.

Several uncomfortable moments of silence passed between

them, both trying to reconcile what had happened. "Perhaps I should lay down for a little while. I feel a bit spent," he finally said.

"Yes, that could be best," she responded, her voice betraying her anxiety. "Let me help you to the room."

"No. I must get used to being blind. This may not be temporary, and I need to adjust." His voice sounded short, even to himself. *I am not upset with her. I am upset with myself.* He had created this situation when he had asked to touch her. Then, he had asked to kiss her. *What the Hell was I thinking?*

You were thinking that you wanted to kiss her, he replied to himself.

He had to figure out this muddle. Pain shot through his side, reminding him that he was not in a good place, health-wise. He needed no reminder. *I cannot see, for God's sake*, he seethed within. *Hell, I cannot sleep without dreaming of the battle. When it was proper time to be awake, I need help to get around, or else I am confined to a bed. What would my friends think of this mess?*

As if summoned, a voice rang through his head. *Matthew, you can do this. You know it is just a matter of time before things improve. You cannot let this get the better of you.* Evan Clarendon's voice resonated in his mind. *Chin up. We will sort this out, Matthew.*

Matthew, you are not dead. I say that would be the worst. You have possibilities. You have to get well, and then you can examine them. Evan's voice gave way to Lucas' voice—he had been the voice of reason.

"I cannot see, men," he murmured. *I cannot see to get home. There must be a way*, he thought. *I cannot stay here alone*, he reasoned. *I will have to go to the colony.* A leper colony.

He had never known a person with leprosy, and knew very little about the disease. However, there had been stories. Yet Bethany said her grandmother and aunt were healers. What kind of healers?

"What kind of healers?" he questioned.

"I heard you say something, but could not make it out. What

did you ask?" she probed.

Bethany's startled voice came from behind him. He had not noticed she had followed him to the bedroom. He was losing his edge—the edge that had saved him.

That doesn't have to be the way of it. *Think, man. You have never been one to throw up your hands in defeat at even a game of cards. Remember who you are, man! You are the Viscount of Excess! You have always had more than you needed . . . believe in yourself.* Christopher's pleading voice rang through his head. He was right.

Matthew had been called this because he always had an ace up his sleeve when it was thought there was no more help or resources. Trouble came, but he always found the way out of it. It had been his idea to steal the bullies' clothing at the lakeside, but not before he had spied a place hidden from view. As it happened—he knew it had been luck—they had found an unused footpath that had taken them back to the hall quicker than they had imagined. They were able to nonchalantly remove themselves to safety and lock the entrances without being seen.

God, he missed his friends. Nothing was impossible when they were together.

Matt, we are here with you. Evan's voice again. Evan was persistent and loyal to a fault.

I miss my friends.

"Your aunt. Your grandmother," he said, recalling that she had answered his questions with her own. "What *kind* of healers?"

"They practice as I have done for you. My Grandmère taught me. We are descendants of the French Acadians. My grandmother's parents came down as children after they expelled the French from Canada. They farmed and traded with the native people and learned remedies. They passed all these things down through the family for generations. They use herbs."

"Ah. They are herbalists. I am familiar with the term. We have similar at home and find them very helpful." He knew the local herbalist in the village near his home helped the doctor with many of the illnesses.

"They use plants and herbs for good, for healing," she said. "They are not feared. People ask them for help. The doctors believe in cutting, bleeding—harsh things. Grandmère believes that the earth has the power to heal itself. The cures are in nature. You only have to know where to look."

"Perhaps they will help me," he said resignedly. He questioned his ability to get past this blindness, and it frightened him. Would he get home?

"You are healing, Matthew. But yes, they may know something that can help your vision. They know far more than the little of which I am aware. My Grandmère taught me to extract certain things . . . the bullet, for instance. I watched her once or twice. That helped when I took out the ball."

He could hear the pride in her voice. She had a genuineness about her.

"You believe heading south on the river is best? I confess I am not wont to get in a boat on the river, not being able to see," he whispered, finally recognizing his fear. "I believe my fear is not being able to see." Admitting it felt better. "I will be of limited use to you."

"Can you swim?" she asked with a lilt to her voice.

"I can." He answered. "I grasp where you are going here."

"I swim as well. Swimming is instinctual, as my Grandmère calls it."

"Yes, I quite agree. Your Grandmère is very clever. I look forward to meeting her," he said, suddenly giving a slight smile. "You must be very much like her." He found the edge of his bed and sat down, placing the cane near the head of it. He heard her take the chair and pull it away from the wall before getting comfortable.

"She has raised me. My mother died when I was much younger, and my father enlisted with the American army. He could not seem to stay put after Mother died. I have not seen him in years. I was lucky to have Grandmère." Her voice was soft.

"She is my best friend—she and Dandie, here." The dog yipped at the mention of her name.

"Yes. You have an indoor dog. I rather like that. Our dogs were relegated to the stables. I always wanted one for myself. I learned to hunt, but never took up the sport."

"We will be fishing for our meals," she said. "There is much to recommend the food supply the Mississippi offers."

"If you feel that we should move to the colony, I am in no position to disagree. However, I wish I knew more about this man that visited. Can you share more?"

"He said he was here at the bequest of a family to find a man who had been missing for a while. He gave me a place to go to ask after him, should I wish to talk further or have something to offer. You are the only missing person of which I am aware. And you went 'missing' this week."

"Nothing else?" Something nagged at him. *What is missing here?* An ache started in the back of his head as he thought of it. Frustrated, he nodded his head in acceptance. "You are right. I have only been missing a few days. Better than dead," he gave a dry chuckle. "Thank you for saving me. Both of you. I had not thanked you, yet. Life is much better than the alternative, in any form," he acknowledged.

"It was that he said they had seen me taking you that makes me need to leave. I cannot in good conscience make you go. But if I stay and am found out for taking in a British soldier, I could face treason charges. I would want to avoid that," she acknowledged.

"I understand." He cleared his throat. "One thing we learn in the military is to pack light and pack tight. I will help you with anything I can. When do you feel we should leave?"

"I think before dawn. We should get an early meal and sleep. I will slip out when it is darker and bring the boat as close to the cabin as I can and hide it beneath the brush. My grandfather built a narrow room on the side of the cabin. You cannot tell a room is there. I will put our things there until it's time to leave. He called it a safe room, although I did not appreciate it until right now. There is a small door hidden from outside view that will allow us to leave the cabin behind a wall of brush, to get away without being seen."

"That sounds fascinating. And sensible. I have noticed a few things," he offered. Matthew felt somehow better about circumstances. "My sense of smell is keener. Is that fish stew I am smelling?"

She swatted him lightly. "You rogue. Yes! It is more of a fish broth at this point. I had dried vegetables. I need to catch the fish. I thought a good meal would be paramount. We shall have bread and cheese. A full belly will do us all good."

"And there is something else. That tea you make," he said with a slight grin. "I remember its scent."

"I had not realized there was one. That's fascinating, Matthew."

He laid his head down. "I apologize. But I have a slight headache from my burst of activity today," he chuckled. "Will you be disappointed if I abandon your company and take a nap?"

"I insist on a nap. Here is your cup of willow tea," she chuckled. "It will help the headache. I am afraid this is in your future until I can be sure the fever and chance of infection are over. Does your side hurt?"

"It does. I think I may have over-indulged," he gave a slow grin.

"I will be back in a moment."

He heard her in the kitchen area fumbling with something. Then, he heard fabric ripping and the scraping of glass from a shelf. His sense of hearing had undeniably become keener than he recalled. He would know if he was right when she returned.

"I have clean bandages, hot water, and the salve," she announced, coming into the room.

Dandie jumped up on his bed and boldly walked around him to his pillow. At the back of his head, the dog settled in and put her paw over his forehead, as if to tell him it would be all right.

He snorted. "Dandie is truly unique."

"Yes, she is quite the personality," Bethany laughed.

He loved her laughter. "You say your mother gave her to you? I had always hoped my parents would gift me one."

"Let me look at the wound," she said, lifting his shirt and pulling back the cloth. "There has been some bleeding. But it's not a heavy color of blood. No signs of infection," she murmured, gliding her fingers around his wound. "This is going to hurt a little, depending on how well it is healing." She placed a pad of hot wet cloth on his wound, forcing him to thrust his side up a little, registering the shock.

"How does it look?" he asked.

"I am quite pleased. For a short time, the wound has shown no more festering. The angry appearance is gone. That does not mean it cannot get worse. We will have to keep it clean." She put a thick smear of warm poultice on it and pressed dry cloths on top. "Sorry for the smell of the dressing. The linseed smells, but it is a must. I should make some more for our trip. It seems to stave off infection."

"I can handle it. Except for the headache, and the lightheaded feeling, I can tell my body is feeling better."

"It could have been worse, and I had feared it would. It looked horrible at first. I prayed the stitching would stem the flow of blood and keep out infection."

He realized she was right. He was lucky that she had found him. Matthew could not let her run and not be with her. After all, it was because of him she had to leave her home. Had she not rescued him, she could wait here for the return of her grandmother. Hopefully, they would get away and make it to the colony without incident. He reached up and patted Dandie's paw with his good arm. "Thank you, girl. You made me feel much better about things," he said.

A soft, guttural sound emerged from the animal.

"She said, 'You're welcome'," laughed Bethany.

Her soft laugh warmed him. He realized that he would have

stayed with her even if he was still sighted. He felt this growing need to know her. In his mind, Matthew pictured her laying on the pillow next to him, her burnished locks spread upon the counterpane of white and a large smile radiating from her face. She had to have green eyes, he reasoned. He felt it.

"Your eyes," he spoke up, without preamble. "What color are they?"

She stopped cleaning the area around his wound. "Green. Why do you ask?"

"I knew it," he said, pleased with himself. "I had imagined them as green."

"And yours are the nicest of blues," she acknowledged. "Can you sit up? Just for a minute. I need to secure this bandage around your chest to hold this in place. It's much easier that way."

It was faint, but he smelled the fishy scent of linseed. He was still amazed at the sharpness of his other senses. It touched him that she was so concerned with his health. Impulsively, Matthew rose to a sitting position and could feel the heat of her breath in his face. He knew he was close to her lips. Without saying a word, he slowly leaned in and kissed her. Wearing a smile on his face, he eased back down on the bed and closed his eyes.

Chapter Seven

Bethany brought her fingers to her lips, startled by his kiss. He had kissed her . . . and she liked it. There would be no turning back from the heart-melting intimacy they had established earlier.

She watched him, sleeping peacefully on her bed as if nothing were amiss. It seemed he fell asleep almost as soon as his head hit the pillow.

There could be no more. She dreaded hearing what her grandmother and aunt would have to say when they found her with an injured soldier, and an English one at that! As if reading her thoughts, Dandie whined at her side.

"It is problematic, girl." She patted the dog and kissed her on the nose. "I am beginning to care for him. You know that will not work out. We are from two different worlds. Yet, I cannot seem to help myself."

Her ancestors were French. She could carry on a conversation in French or English—or even Creole. Instinctively, she felt certain her background would not measure up to anything required by British society and—based on the address of his family—his family was part of that very society.

Dandie presented another concern. She had always been defensive of her—the dog growled at all men. She had growled at the man who had visited. Yet, with this man, she acted as if she had known him all her life. Realizing she should also be grateful, because the dog had a high-pitched bark. If she had disapproved of Matthew, she would surely raise the alarm, and others would be here.

Nothing was going according to plan. In her mind, she would help the man heal and send him on his way. Things were slowly getting out of control. She felt afraid, and she hated being afraid of anything. Navigating the canal and the bayou was not foreign to her, but the dangers presented now frightened her. The man, Sinclair, had mentioned deserters. Then there was the weather to consider. It continued to be overcast, cold, and foggy.

Noticing she was biting her nails, a habit her grandmère shamed her for constantly, Bethany straightened her shoulders and drew a deep breath. *Enough. I must decide.* She also needed to ready them to leave. The small canal where she lived was attached to the Villeré Canal, which ran near the plantation where the battle had raged. They would need to get past that early, before others saw them. Fog could be helpful. And the full moon would be a good guidepost among the clouds. Judging from the weather now, that should not be a problem. Conditions had been as thick as pea soup this morning—most mornings this week.

The colony was hidden in huts just beyond the juncture where the Bayou Mazant started. It had been a while since she had gone by herself to the camp, but Bethany felt sure she remembered the guidepost. She would recognize the jagged tree that had broken off in the middle and leaned out toward the water.

This was not a trip she looked forward to making, but the prospect of being caught and labeled a *traitor* was less appealing. They would leave in the morning—very early. First, she needed to mail the missive to his family. But where? Tobias Smith would help her. Of course, she would owe him again. She laughed to herself. Tobias always made subtle hints toward marriage—never coming out and saying anything. He hinted. That made it easier to stave off his advances. She cared for Tobias as a lifelong friend, but not as someone to marry. She wanted to marry for love. It would be unfair to either of them to consider otherwise.

Gently lifting the edge of the curtain in her room back, she scrutinized the area around the home for any signs of it being watched. Nothing. Hearing only gentle snores from the bedroom, she pulled on her cloak and tucked the letter in her pocket, hoping to make a quick trip to the Trading Post and be back before he woke. It was only around the bend. "Come on Dandie. Let's head to the Trading Post. I'm hoping Tobias can help me with this."

"Grrrrrr . . ."

"Why don't you like Tobias, girl? Even the mention of his name draws ire from you." Dandie's attitude toward her friend puzzled her. Gently, Bethany opened the front door and closed and locked it behind her. She carefully set the stick in place that would tell her if anyone disturbed the door.

It was an overcast day, but signs were that the rain would not appear for hours, and she hoped to be back before that happened. She uncovered the side of the dock where she had hidden the boat and moved the leafy tree limb aside. The leaves had died but had still concealed the small boat. Dandie hopped into the boat and she followed, picking up the oar and making herself comfortable.

Ten minutes later, they pulled up to the small Trading Post dock and a tall, beefy man came out to greet them. "Hello, Bethany. What brings you here today?" Tobias Smith took the rope from her outstretched hand and secured it around the wooden cleat. Holding out an arm, he helped her onto the dock. Dandie waited until Bethany was out of the boat before jumping up from the boat onto the dock. The small dog wiggled her tail and pranced into the store.

"Dandie's in a better mood today. At least she didn't hold her tail in the air and walk around me like she did last week," he said, before spitting tobacco juice into the water.

"She is," Bethany replied, amused at the difference in her dog's mood. "I have a letter to post, and I wanted your help with it."

"Fine, the mail gets picked up tomorrow. Place it in the box over there," he said, motioning toward a wooden box at the end of the counter.

Bethany withdrew the letter and started to place it in the box before pulling it back. "Are we still getting mail out of the country?" she asked, nervously watching Tobias' face. If there was anyone she could trust, it was Tobias, she chastised herself.

He drew up from behind the counter, holding a piece of dried beef for Dandie. "What are you asking, Beth?"

"I . . . I saved a man's life, and I promised him I would let his parents know he is alive is all," she answered, schooling her face to look as carefree as possible.

"You know we have martial law . . . and that we are fighting the Brits, right?" he asked. He grabbed a can and spit the rest of his tobacco into it. Bethany assumed it was so she would hear him. "You aren't speaking of aid'n the enemy, are you?"

She opened her mouth and closed it. "No. I saved a life. It was no more than you would have done, Tobias. He was blind and could not write. He asked me to . . . and I wrote the letter for him."

"I see." Tobias dug around underneath the counter, apparently searching for something. "There was a man in here t'other day. He was asking 'bout you—he described you and Dandie, here. I told him nothin'. He said something about being hired to find a man. What have you gotten yourself into this time?" He blew out a long breath and pulled out a piece of paper. "Mr. Sinclair. He said there was some kind of urgency with needing to find this man."

She remained quiet, processing what he just told her.

"Beth, you gonna owe me." He laughed, recognizing the standing joke between them. "I'll do my best to get your letter to someone who can slip it across the enemy lines. That's the best I can promise."

She heaved a breath. "*Merci*. I appreciate it, Tobias. I am keeping a promise. That is all." She knew better than to tell Tobias about Matthew being in her house. Reaching back into her pocket, she withdrew the letter and handed it to him, suddenly wishing she had never made this promise to Matthew.

Her friend placed the missive under the cabinet. "For safekeeping."

"Thank you, Tobias. I knew I could count on you." She looked around the shelves. "If you have any potatoes and rice, I would like a small bag of each."

"'Course! We're friends." He gave her a long look before stepping from behind the counter and rounding up the goods. Gathering up an armload of potatoes from a barrel near the door, he came back to the counter and placed them on a scale. "Two pounds," he said, before bagging them. "These just came in. They ought to be tasty." He reached down and handed Dandie a small piece of dried beef. The small dog accepted the beef, and pushed it to the side of her mouth, letting it hang from her lips.

They both looked at the dog and laughed. "That's an unusual dog you got there, Beth. Most dogs would eat it immediately, but she carries her treats around, first."

"*She does!*" she laughed. "And she buries them in the furniture, too. Anywhere she can hide them until she's ready for them. I do not think it's hunger that drives her." She reached for the bags of rice and potatoes.

"No. Let me," Tobias said, picking them up and nodding toward the open door. "I'll help you get this in the boat. Has your grandmother returned, yet?"

The question took her by surprise. "She should be home any day, now." She stepped into the boat and Dandie followed, still holding the piece of meat. Reaching up, she accepted the bags. "*Merci*, Tobias . . . for everything."

"You're welcome, Beth. I'll do my best to get the letter posted."

She nodded and pushed away from the dock with her paddle. Dandie assumed her post at the front of the boat, still holding her treat.

THE MAN STOOD close to the wall and observed another boat pull up as soon as the woman and her dog left the dock. He kept to the side of the building, hidden behind a mulberry bush, and watched the man that had just pulled up, a trapper, wrap that boat's rope around the vacated cleat. The trapper stacked a high pile of pelts on the dock before picking them up and disappearing into the Trading Post.

Through a small, dirty window on the side of the building, he had seen her pass a letter to the proprietor and saw it placed under the counter. He had heard her ask if it could be mailed to England. *As much as he hated to steal something, he needed that letter.*

He watched the owner come out of the building and speak with the trapper. The two men lifted out two more stacks of pelts and carried them into the trading post. Peering through the window, he saw them remove to the back, finally giving the opportunity he needed. Quickly, he slipped in and walked to the counter. With an eye on the trapper and proprietor engaged in conversation in the back—neither seemed to have noticed him—he reached behind the counter and withdrew the sealed missive. Stuffing it in his pocket, he left as silently as he had come.

Chapter Eight

Bethany tied the small boat under the side of the house in the small compartment her grandfather had fashioned near the hidden entrance to the house. She needed it accessible so she could load provisions for their trip. Even though the trip would be short, she felt unsure how long she would be gone. A strange sensation shuddered through her and she looked about the small area, unsure of what it meant. The weather had been overcast, but a little rain could not hurt anyone. Unless became a torrential downpour, they would be fine. For good measure, she looked over and tossed in the small canvas tent her grandparents had fashioned as a covering for the boat. Canvas and perfectly measured sticks are attached to make a small tent over the center of the boat. It allowed some coverage for the hot, blistering days and when it rained.

She looked at Dandie, who enjoyed riding at the helm. The small dog gave her a knowing grin. Dandie liked it for the hot days. This would not be one of those. But the way it had been sleeting intermittently, she might change her mind. She smiled. Dandie made her smile a lot. The dog seemed almost human at times in her ability to communicate.

Bethany opened the hidden door to the cabin and allowed Dandie to go in first. When she closed it, she found Matthew sitting in a chair that faced the door.

He woke with a start. "Who is there? Is that you, Bethany?" Dandie gave a short bark in answer.

"I woke up and no one was here, so I thought I should make myself more aware of my surroundings. It is a different world when your eyes do not see," he acknowledged.

"I had hoped to be back before you awoke. I have brought some goods—potatoes and rice—from the Trading Post. I can make you a hot pot of potatoes and I believe Grandmère has a small side of pork in the pantry."

"That sounds delicious." He gave a nod in Dandie's direction. "Dandie, if you hear a growl, fear not. 'Tis my stomach howling at the thought of a hot meal." He gave a shy smile. "Not to say that the porridge, teas, and soups have not nourished me. They have. And I have enjoyed them. But potatoes!"

"My friend runs the Trading Post. I saw he had a barrel of red potatoes and thought a small portion for our meal this morning would be delicious. I, too, have thought of little else on the way back here," Bethany returned.

"Ruff!"

They both laughed. "Of course, you, too! I could not eat in front of you, my dear little girl. You will have some potatoes. I shall cull some to the side before I add the spices, pepper, and onions," she added. "I think I have some cold fish from yesterday I can add to them." The small dog stood up on her hind legs and turned about at the last comment, causing Bethany to laugh. She landed with a small thud on her front paws, clearly pleased with herself.

"I wish I could see what she just did. She has quite the personality, I know," Matthew said wistfully. "There is something I should share."

"Me too. We should spend a few minutes in here. It would give you a change of . . . space." She started to say the scenery and caught herself, aware of how that could be perceived. She cared that he could not see and wished his sight would return soon. Otherwise, he seemed to heal up nicely. The thought of it sent an unexpected pang to her heart. She would hate to see him go but having him here would put her and her grandmother in danger. When you put a face to your enemy, it made it harder to think of them as the enemy. They were people.

"My friend thought he could get your letter on a boat for England," she blurted.

"The one you wrote to my father?" He was silent for a moment. "I confess I had not given thought to the danger that would put you in. Are you sure he is one to be trusted?"

"I have known Tobias almost all my life. I had no qualms about leaving it with him. It was the only option I could think of. I cannot imagine how else I could get word to your family, and I would not want your father to be thinking you dead. That seems almost cruel."

"Thank you. When we left the coast and started the trek across the land, my unit took some difficult hits, and it became more difficult to get word back home. I imagine they do not even know where I have been fighting, although my father would do his best to find out. I think it has been several months since they would have received a letter from me," he explained.

"I cannot imagine being in a foreign country with an ocean between me and my family and no way to see them," she agreed.

"That is the hard thing about war," he confessed. "I miss my family. It has been so long since I have seen my sister and baby brother . . . and my mother."

"I never even understood all the reasons for the war," Bethany allowed.

"It has always seemed to me to be a struggle for a mother to accept the independence of her child—if you can follow the allegory. The mother would be England, and I understand our country's feelings toward that. At the same time, most in my country only know America to be what they hear and, to them, it is a bunch of ungrateful rebels. But when you are here and you see the country—what it has become, well—there is such majesty in the land." A sadness washed over his face. "It's war, but it seems senseless to me."

"Do not tell me that you see the American's point of view," she teased.

"Yes and no. I am an Englishman. My heart is with England. All I am saying is that the loss of life is sad."

Bethany noticed him sway a little and paid closer attention. He seemed to be healing, even though she had heard him cry out in his sleep. She had assumed it was a bad dream, however, it had seemed too personal to ask about. When she had come closer to the door to listen, she had heard only mumbled words before he went back to sleep. "I mentioned going to see my grandmother, but never bothered to see how you felt about that." She gave a nervous laugh. "You agreed to go, even though you may not understand my reasons."

"I realize you are frightened to stay here. What you have done for me—saving my life—has placed your life in danger. And, blind, I cannot be of much help." He gave a wary laugh. "If I were able to help, I would have been healthy enough to leave, eliminating some of the danger. Although, there are other dangers. A young lady should not be here, alone."

"Dandie goes with me," she said, suddenly vexed. "And I can handle a gun."

His eyes widened. "Whoa!" he said, throwing up his hands. "I seemed to have stepped in hot water. I apologize for the perceived insult. I had no intention of hurting your feelings." He stood and walked to her, holding out his right hand.

She took his hand, and he pulled her to a standing position, softly pulling her into an embrace. "Your arm. You must be careful," she said, backing up. She noticed him lean slightly, unsteady. His right arm kept the pressure, and she acquiesced into the hold.

"You must tell me when you leave. I worried for your safety, knowing there was naught I could do." He lowered his lips to hers and kissed her. "I know we both promised we would not do this, yet I cannot seem to stop myself."

Bethany wanted this so much. How could she even think about his leaving? But she must. Grandmère would see to it, she felt sure. She would find an Indian guide to help him to a port and onto a boat. Something. Her grandmother was resourceful. She would miss his kisses... his touch. She tried to turn this one away, but she wanted the kiss too much. Strange things happened to her body when he touched her. It felt like her butterflies would fly up her arms and down her neck to her toes. She rather liked the feeling. She felt herself pull him closer, craving the warmth that his mouth and arms offered after the cold trip in the boat.

They planned to leave before dawn for her aunt's house, and she would have this to remember. Her hands gently ran through his hair, slowly rubbing the side of his head behind his ears. Pulling back, she gazed up at him. "Do you feel well enough to make the trip in the morning? It's cold and it could be raining. I have a tarp for the boat, but that will hardly keep out the cold."

"I am amazed at how much better I feel. The pain has not left. However, it is not incapacitating, as before," he said, squeezing her hand. "I still tire easily."

"You have complained of a headache. There's a slight indention behind your ear I had never noticed. Would you mind if I take another look?"

He leaned down and veered a little to the right. He stilled before feeling for the chair behind him and sitting down. "This dizzy feeling comes and goes."

"You had not mentioned being dizzy, but you have been asleep or sitting most of the time. It looks like you got hit on the head. A head injury could cause blindness." Bethany cared about this man. She was worried. *I hope it will not be permanent.* "My aunt has been working with herbal medicine longer than anyone in my family. My Grandmère describes her as gifted. I am not sure I told you, but she is blind. However, what she misses with her sight, she gained with her nose. She can detect the differences in many herbs by smell and locates them that way, as well."

"This is the first I am hearing of your aunt's blindness." His voice was soft and reflective.

"It was a childhood illness. They called it the fever."

"Is it scarlet fever?" he responded, sympathetic.

"She lost her sight at eight, just before the fever left her body, according to Grandmère," Bethany explained.

"A tragedy, to be sure, for a small child to lose their sight. Many in our country lose their lives to the fever. We know not much about it."

"Grandmère said that it nearly took her life," Bethany added.

"How tragic. I appreciate how terrifying that must have been for a child. That she has found peace with her blindness astounds me. Even though I find my other senses—like smell—are much better. I notice scents I had never noticed before. Had I been without sight all my life, my appreciation and peace with this would be more palpable. However, I cannot deny the loss I feel." Matthew looked in the direction of the heat.

His tone had become melancholy and detached, and she worried. "Do you truly feel well enough to travel in the morning?" she said, needing to be sure. He was no longer running a fever, but the spot behind his ear and the dizziness worried her. She wondered how she had missed that when examining his head. Guilt began a slow crawl into her consciousness. How had she missed something so obvious? Had she seen it, could she have prevented blindness?

No, she chided herself. She had done the best she knew to do.

"I believe I will be. If I get to rest this afternoon and evening, I feel sure I can travel."

He sniffed the room with a teasing grin. "I do not smell potatoes. Did you say we would have them?"

She laughed and swatted his arm. "Of course. You must be getting better or else you would not risk being tossed out," she mocked. "I will get the meal going if you will keep Dandie company."

"Sure. That should be easy." He gave a quick whistle and the little dog looked up. "Come sit with me, Dandie."

At his words, the little terrier got up from her place in front of the fireplace and jumped into the chair with him.

Bethany fastened her apron and turned around in time to see her dog giving Matthew licks on his face. *Traitor*, she thought with a wry smile. What was it about this man that made both females in this house accept him so willingly? She filled the teakettle and hung it in the fireplace. Wiping her hands on her apron, she walked to the wicker basket on the work counter and pulled potatoes from the small bag. Selecting three large ones, she began to peel them. Bethany withdrew a small amount of lard from the jar and placed it in the iron pot over the fire. She salted and peppered a bowl of diced potatoes and added them to the hot grease. Immediately, the smell of cooking potatoes wafted in the air, eliciting a growl from her stomach. She had not realized how hungry she had been. When the potatoes were almost ready, she moved them to the side and inserted a handful of small pieces of pork.

"My stomach has awakened with a growl," Matthew said, leaning toward the scrumptious aroma.

She giggled. "Mine as well! I do not recall when I last made potatoes like this. My Grandmère usually made them when Grandpapa was alive. Her favorite morning meal is pain perdu, bread dipped in a cinnamon mixture with eggs."

"That sounds delicious, as well."

"Yes. It does. I should make some bread before we leave. It would be good to have on the trip and should not take too long," she mused to herself.

When the food was nearly ready, she cleared the small table she had been using to prepare the herbs for drying. *I love the smell of sage, basil, and rosemary,* she thought, adding a last-minute pinch of dried rosemary to the pot. Wiping the table clean, she laid out two straw placemats, two porcelain plates, and pewter utensils. Using her tea strainer, she filled two teacups with hot water and made black tea for the two of them. Last, she took a small bowl from the cabinet for Dandie's meal. The small dog had been patiently waiting for her food.

"Here you go, little one," she said, placing the first serving in her companion's bowl. "We should let it cool a few minutes and then, you can have it." She fanned the bowl with another plate.

"You treat your dog well," Matthew observed. "She is probably the best-behaved dog I have ever observed."

"She is all I have left of my mother, and she takes good care of me," Bethany replied, fanning the small bowl. "You are a good girl, aren't you, little one?" Her statement was more of an observation than a question.

The dog yipped as if affirming she understood.

Matthew laughed. "You will convince me she is a small yippy person before my sight returns."

"I hope it will return, Colonel. And I feel bad that we had not noticed that spot behind your ear before now. I was focused on the bullet wound and stopping the fever and bleeding."

"You accomplished both. Had I been lucky enough to have had the doctor's care, I do not believe I would have fared as well. You gave me attention that they would not have spared with so many injured and dead."

She could hear some of his vivacity in his tone. Bethany admired the man. He had undergone such horrible trauma, yet his manners were impeccable, and his mood was more upbeat than she would have imagined. She had not understood what to expect and had refused to let fear guide her. She was glad she had rescued him, she thought, stealing a look at him beneath her long lashes. Warmth flooded her as she remembered his kisses. Admittedly, she wanted more of those, making her feel somewhat wanton.

"Here you go, Dandie. I believe this is cool enough for you. And the rosemary will keep those pesky fleas off you," she said, placing the bowl on the floor next to the bowl of water.

"Seriously? A spice rids the dog of pesky fleas," he drawled, sounding impressed.

"Grandmère told me about it, shortly after Dandie came to

stay. I am glad that I enjoy the flavor of it. We use it a lot, as much for the benefit of staving off the fleas as flavoring our dishes," she chuckled, ladling a portion of the hot potatoes and pork onto his plate. She placed her dishtowel on the hook and picked up both plates, taking them to the table.

He waited for her to sit down before taking a forkful of food. "I confess to wanting this more than any meal in recent memory," he said, taking in the mouthful. "This is good. My compliments, Bethany."

"My mother used to make this for us," she murmured, swallowing her mouthful. "It was my favorite morning dish."

"It may become mine," he allowed.

She chuckled. "We have plenty of the cured pork, which I will pack for our trip. We can eat it in the boat. I will pack some cheese and bread, as well. You might want to rest. The trip is short enough, but you could find it taxing."

A noise sounded from the direction of the small boat garage, and she turned to look. "It sounds like it's coming from the boat garage."

Dandie left her dish and stood at the small door, barking.

"Let me look. I cannot imagine it's anything more than a wave knocking the boat . . ." She tried to convince herself of that as she grabbed her gun and cocked it. Walking slowly to the door, she opened it and gasped.

A dark-haired man, covered in filth and mud and holding a large knife, looked up from the boat.

CHAPTER NINE

MATTHEW STOOD, TILTING the table, and then, righting it. *What the Hell was going on?* He grabbed the cane sitting next to the table. He heard Bethany gasp and followed the sound, pushing the cane behind him, determined to appear sighted. After all, with light, he could make out shapes. Perhaps it would work. His sight had been patchy, showing signs only this morning that he might regain it.

Unsure, he had kept quiet, hating to disappoint both Bethany and himself. Somehow, if he discussed it, it made it more real, and therefore, more of a loss if it failed to return.

"What is happening?" he asked, trying hard to disguise his British accent.

"Stop what you are doing and put your hands in the air," she ordered.

Matthew saw her move her arms, nudging a sticklike object in the direction of the door. Good Heavens! She had a gun. She had told him she could shoot, but he thought it was something said to prove a point. Dandie spread her legs in a defensive posture and began to growl.

"Stop untying that knot right now and leave the boat. *Slowly.*"

Matthew noticed Bethany's voice had changed to one that brooked little nonsense. The sweet voice of the woman taking care of him had become rigid and edged with anger.

"Back up, Dandie," she commanded.

To his amazement, the dog complied, giving the person space to leave the hidden boat locker. The stranger's clothing looked shabby. He strained to see. It looked like his arms and face were dark, as if caked in mud, making him appear as a large blob. Matthew thought he could make out eyes and a mouth, although he could not be sure because of the lack of light.

"I don't want to hurt you. But I need your boat," the man said. "They are after me." He leaned his face down to his right arm and wiped a sizeable amount of soot and mud from it onto his still-damp shirt.

Bethany's head jerked back in surprise. "You look familiar. Do I know you?" she asked. She tried not to stare at the dark-eyed, wiry-thin man, but worried how he would perceive her turning her head. He smelled like he had not bathed in some time, and his mustache looked as greasy as the stringy brown hair that hung to his shoulders.

He nodded. "Yes ma'am. Your grandmother saved my pappy . . . years ago."

She found she had been holding her breath and put her hand casually over her nostrils to take a small gulp of air without insulting him. "Caleb Smoot. Right?"

The man shrugged.

"What in tarnation are you doing trying to steal my boat? Does your pappy know you are stealing boats from women?"

A long moment passed before anyone spoke.

"Please do not take this the wrong way, but you will not take my boat, and you will demand nothing of us," she admonished. "I will shoot you. I would never turn you into any authorities, as long as we gain an understanding."

Matthew noticed Bethany turn her head and look at him. Unsure of what she was communicating, he nodded, hoping that affirmation gave what she needed and feeling like a cad for not telling her about the changes to his sight. She had helped him so much. *How could I repay her kindness with dishonesty?* He did his best to resist speaking, unsure he would not slip and reveal his true accent.

"Your family has been coming to see Grandmère for years. She helped heal your younger sister from a fever shortly before the battle started," Bethany murmured. She gave a hard look at the man. "How *is* your sister?"

There was history here. Bethany knew this man and his family, and she seemed determined to keep the man talking. Smart woman. And not missish like the women he had known back home.

A look of recognition passed over the man's face, followed by a look of shame. "She's healed. Thanks to your grandmother," he replied, obviously chastened by the question.

"And your son? I recall your ma brought him with your sister. How is he? If I recollect properly, he had some of the same symptoms—but had not succumbed to the fever."

"You ask too many questions." The man shook with anger. "Jackson shamed us to sign up to fight. Said he would arrest us if we didn't. I was fine with it. But my son . . . he was just a boy. He could not be talked out of it and signed up." His voice cracked. "I lost my son in that battle." He swiped at his face. "Anyway, I got my belly full and left. Fer a time, I was hiding and resting in the weeds and brush. I saw you and your dog coming back from the Trading Post. I thought I should, 'specially when I saw a man run and get his boat and trail you."

"This morning?" She glanced at Matthew with eyes full of concern. "I failed to notice anyone."

A shiver washed over Matthew as he realized the danger in which she had put herself to mail his correspondence. While he could not see her facial features, he heard her breath and voice remain even. Most women would have swooned to find a stranger following them, much less one in their home being threatened with a large knife. He admired her resolve.

He poked his knife in the pot's direction. "No one will get hurt if you'd just follow orders, woman." He turned to Matthew.

"Why won't he say anything? Cat got his tongue?" He gave a crude laugh before turning angrier and making a threatening show of the knife.

"Put that knife down," she ordered.

"No," he said, lunging for her.

Bethany shot at his leg, wounding him. "That was foolish of you. Now, not only will your leg need tending, but you have drawn attention to my home."

"You shot me!" The man screamed and his knife flew out of his hand as he writhed on the ground. It landed a few feet away and Dandie moved over it, guarding it.

"You saw the gun in my hand. Did you think I did not know how to use it?" she replied softly. Her voice shook slightly. "Consider that your warning shot. You will not take my boat."

He moved and Dandie lunged, darting at his head until she bit down on something near his head and pulled.

Matthew felt what must have been blood splatter his arms.

"Ye-ow! Your damn dog bit me." Smoot felt his head where the dog had attacked. "Jesus! He took part of my ear off."

"Dandie, sit." Bethany calmly looked in the direction of her dog. "Leave it," she ordered, and the dog released a sizeable piece of what Matthew imagined to be the man's ear on the floor." She turned to the man. "Now look what you have done!"

"Me?" he yelled back. "Your damn dog bit me, not the other way around."

"You did not take heed of my warning. I may have forgotten to mention she would bite," Bethany answered him coolly.

"Sit," she motioned to the man, pointing to what would have been a chair next to him. Smoot immediately sat.

Matthew approached from behind the man in the chair and motioned for the gun. He imagined her eyes round with surprise as she slowly stepped toward him, possibly trying to decide before handing the gun to him. He gripped the gun and heard her breathe a quiet sigh of relief.

"I will tie his feet and hands," she said. "He's a deserter. Shoot him if he moves."

Bethany reached inside the boat garage and grabbed what he surmised to be a coiled rope from the wall just inside the door. Taking it, she wrapped it around the man's arms, fastening them behind him, and securing the rope to the chair. Using the rest of the rope, she secured his feet, giving the final knot a hard tug before standing up.

Matthew had tried to signal that he would hold the gun. Pleased he could finally see shapes, he prayed his vision would continue to improve. He should have enlightened Bethany about the abrupt progression of his sight and wondered what her reaction would be when she spoke about it. That would be later, he hoped. Without being able to see detail, he could determine little about this person and even with the name Smoot, had little clue who they were dealing with. However, the talents of this woman impressed him, and he rationalized he should remain quiet.

"There are lots of boats around. Why were you trying to steal mine?" Her tone sounded angry.

Hearing her words, the man whipped his head in Bethany's direction. "Like I said. I need it. And the others are mostly gone," he said, his voice livid.

Perceiving an advantage, the man continued. "I seen the man hang back. I recognized him, though. He's been hanging around the area since the fight. He's a stranger in these parts. Like that'n there," he said, giving an exaggerated nod toward Matthew.

"Ah . . . yes," stammered Bethany. "This is Matthew. And I had not planned to do anything but try to convince you to leave. However, I am afraid you have drawn undue attention to all of us."

Matthew spoke up. "I believe we need to determine where this person is that followed Miss Phillips and her dog, Dandie."

Smoot's response was no surprise. "He's English!" he sneered.

She smiled. "Yes. That . . . was . . . *our* secret. Matthew was gravely injured, and this is the first time he has been able to be out of bed. He's been unconscious almost since arriving here."

"You've been living with a man," he accused with a sneer, apparently focused on Matthew.

"I am Lord Matthew Romney in the King's army," Matthew said, speaking up. "I was critically injured in the same battle that took your son, and probably headed for burial." A shudder swept his body. As he had begun to sort through memories following the battle, he recalled thinking he was not going to make it. "Miss Phillip's dog found me still breathing under a stack of dead bodies after several men looking for survivors left me for dead. I was indeed dying. They saved me." Matthew was careful not to give away his loss of sight, confident that if he could see the man's expression, after having heard the sneer in his voice, he would want to rearrange his face. He could maintain his bluff with more light, so he stepped to the side to remove himself from the stream of light he felt hitting his back.

He heard the sharp intake of breath and imagined the stranger gaping in shock at the sight of him.

"I am hoping that Grandmère can help the colonel with . . ."

Matthew cleared his throat and Bethany stopped, looking at him.

"I had hoped Grandmère could help with his healing . . . but she seems to have been detained longer than I expected. I have run through all I know," she finished, punctuating the last words, and her head turned in Matthew's direction.

"Grrrrrr! Rrrrrrrr!" The small dog got up from where she had been laying and circled the chair.

"Don't let her bite me again," the man cried, suddenly nervous again.

"She has done that—if she perceives I am in danger," soothed Bethany, reaching down and petting her dog. "Dandie, he can hardly hurt me. He's bound. It would be very unfair for you to nip his fingers or bite his leg," she continued, her voice taunting.

"Tell me about this man you saw following Bethany," Matthew asked, throwing off all attempts to hide his British accent.

"He's looking for soldiers," Caleb said. "I heard him asking others around town."

"So, you've noticed him for a while," Matthew said, not speaking to Caleb. Something seemed off here. "Did you catch a name?"

"No sir, he spoke hushed-like, and I had my hat down when I was around others, hoping not to be seen. But a man's gotta eat. I would filch some food here and there when people weren't looking."

"I am not getting a clear idea of where you have been, filching food," Matthew said, his tone haughtier than he intended. Truthfully, the man was annoying him with the half-answers. He was not used to having to pry so hard to have answers.

Smoot sneezed. "Sorry." He wiped his face on the shoulder of his shirt. "I been filching food from the small campfires where the womenfolk been feeding the troops—I've gone back and forth, and only taking what would feed me when no one was looking. But someone saw me, so I left and ran here before I got put back on the line somewhere."

"The troops are still in the area?" Matthew wondered if his regiment had left or was still around. If he could find them . . . *but how?*

"Some are, best I can determine," Smoot replied. "I heard the English had run, heading down the river."

A sigh escaped Matthew. He started to respond, but bit his tongue. This cowardly deserter's opinion of his countrymen mattered not to him. What mattered was that they might still be here. It sounded like they could still be in the vicinity. A feeling of hope swelled in his chest at the thought his comrades could still be near—perhaps at a distance he *could* navigate. He needed more information. Unclear on what the man meant, Matthew probed. "*Where* down the river?"

He wanted very much to get home—even as unlikely as it seemed. He could not count on being able to see, which made planning to leave absurd. He would need a guide. Perhaps the better plan was to try and regain as much of his health as possible, first.

Feelings of grief threatened to overwhelm him. He needed to stay focused.

"All that matters to me is staying clear of Jackson," Smoot spat. "Word is they are leaving the area. I've been hiding near here, keeping my eyes peeled for a boat. Yours is a nice one. Once the English leave, I can clear out." He gave a crooked grin. "When you came out this morning, I saw the boat, and I wanted it. They will *not* shoot me for deserting something that I didn't want to do." He gave an expression of earnestness. "I wouldn't have stolen not'n else, 'cept for now that I smell your food, I might like whatever you're cooking."

The door to her cabin slammed open, and another man stepped in, appearing to hold a gun.

"Tobias!" Bethany stepped toward Matthew.

"I heard a shot." He replied before turning his gaze to the man tied to and writhing in a chair in front of a snarling terrier. Matthew imagined blood was dripping from both of their faces. "Smoot, what the Hell have you done?"

"Tobias, help me! She shot me. And that devil dog of hers bit my ear off," he screamed.

CHAPTER TEN

TOBIAS REGARDED THE sight in front of him, suddenly unsure of what he had walked in on. He surveyed the room, taking notice of the blood on the floor. He was certain a gunshot came from here. Who was that man in front of him—*standing next to Bethany*—and what in tarnation was Caleb Smoot doing bleeding and bound to a chair? "It seems I chose a bad time to stop in, Bethany."

"Tobias! We have had an unpleasant morning, I am afraid," she responded, taking a towel from the tabletop, and wiping her dog's face. She stopped and looked up. "What are you doing here? Who's watching the Post?"

"That seems to be an understatement, Beth." Tobias stared at the man he did not recognize, standing protectively next to Beth. "I secured it and left a note. And I am here because I needed to speak with you." His gaze locked with hers. "What have you stepped into this time, Beth?" As far as he could tell, the woman had a knack for attracting trouble. He had hoped she would take his pursuit more seriously, but she had insisted they were friends and would always be. That was not what he wanted.

"Tobias! Free me from these damn ropes," Smoot yelled from the chair.

"What are you doing here?" Tobias said, folding his arms across his chest and making no move in Smoot's direction. "Let me guess! They caught you stealing."

"He was trying to steal my boat," Bethany replied, anger lacing her voice. "You know this man?" She had a look of disbelief on her face.

"Yes," he said simply, focused on the stranger next to Bethany. "Are you going to introduce us, Bethany?" Tobias tried to swallow back his irritation.

"I can speak for myself," Matthew inserted.

"I found Matthew on the battlefield, left behind and dying," Bethany added.

Tobias stiffened. An Englishman! This was who the letter was about this morning. The letter that disappeared. As much as he wanted to dismiss it, Bethany was his friend. "I need to speak with you, Bethany. Can you step out here on the porch with me?"

"Sure." She looked in the direction of Matthew. His head dipped, perhaps in acknowledgment. "Keep the gun trained on him."

"You shot Smoot, didn't you?" It was more of a statement than a question. "And you shot the man in his knee, meaning you didn't want to hurt him more than you had to. So what happened to his head?"

"Dandie bit his ear off. He was threatening me, and she bit him."

Tobias felt pale. "He won't be forgetting that. There's only so much I can do to help there."

"I know. I've made an enemy. Forget that he was trying to steal from me," she finished, frustration evident in her voice. "What did you need to tell me?" She looked up at him.

"I am now realizing how important this probably is, considering the ... patient you have." He swallowed. "I went to grab your letter and take it to my contact, who could have gotten it to the British before they left. But it was gone."

"Gone? What do you mean, *gone?*" Her eyes grew wide.

"I went to take it from behind my desk, and it was gone," Tobias replied softly. "I am sorry. I cannot figure out what happened."

"Caleb Smoot just told us he saw a man hiding at the side of the Trading Post."

Tobias angrily bit down on his bottom lip, his face furrowed in fury. "He saw something and didn't come in to tell me—and after all I've done for him?" Tobias fumed.

"You act like you are the injured party, here. The snake planned to steal *my* boat. He followed Dandie and me home," she declared angrily.

He tugged on her arm. "Let's find out what he knows." They turned and returned inside.

MATTHEW SIGNALED FOR her to join him on the other side of the room. As he watched Tobias' shape move closer to Smoot, still out of hearing distance, he whispered, "I wanted to tell you I am starting to see shapes. I don't think he needs to know I cannot see."

"I agree he should not know." Bethany repressed her irritation at not having known that. It might have made things easier. "At least you wouldn't have been shooting blind," she murmured, unable to disguise her amusement at her joke. "How long have your eyes been working?"

"They are not working, *exactly*. I can see vague shapes. But that is all. And it seems to come and go," he replied. "However, I am sorry we did not have this discussion earlier."

"That is at least something. I pray it all comes back. Let me feed him. Can you keep an eye on him?" As soon as the words were out of her mouth, she grew quiet. "I am sorry. I had not given thought before to how much we verbalize about our senses." A lump formed in her throat at the realization Matthew would leave soon—once he regained sight. She would miss him.

"It is fine. I understand and I do not take offense." He grinned at her.

"What I meant is that you will . . ." she faltered, "be guarded and not let him know your sight is not perfect. It will take a measure of acting, I suspect. However, I noticed you did quite well back there," she added, referring to the conversation they had just had.

"I needed light, so I stepped out of the ray that was filtering through the curtains."

"It bothers me that someone is trailing me. I'll bet it's that Sinclair person," she said, almost to herself. "How would I have missed him at Tobias' place? There was no one else there. At least I thought we were alone." She suddenly grew nervous. He must have seen her give the envelope to Tobias. What was his motive? Was he trying to get her in trouble? Surely Tobias would never share the envelope or its existence with anyone. She trusted him.

"What are you thinking?" he asked, "I am more than a little nervous with this man. And he has not convinced me with his story. My only concern is for you. I do not want you to suffer because of your kindnesses toward me." He touched her arm.

A pulse of attraction thrummed up Bethany's arm at his touch. It warmed her heart that he cared so much for her. Yet, as he was British, she knew he would leave as soon as he was well enough. And, on top of what seemed a burgeoning desire to have him near her, she was also committing what General Jackson would probably term *treason* by housing him here. And she was sure many of her community would see it that way.

She whooshed out a slow breath, trying to rein in her tension, lest she came off as weak to Smoot. He had shown himself to be a thief and a coward. He already had less to lose, which made him more dangerous. "We must be careful with Smoot. Should he go free, he may talk—but what options do we have?"

"I will sit down and hold the gun. I won't train it on him. But I will make it clear that it is loaded. Do you still have my gun and my sword?"

"I had forgotten that I picked those up. They were next to

you. At least, I assumed they were yours. I will retrieve them. I had already hidden your uniform in the boat. Another reason we cannot lose our boat. I thought you would want to keep it close."

He nodded, his face mirroring his appreciation. He walked to where he had hidden the gun, still behind Smoot, and took a seat away from the table. Without stumbling, he propped the gun in his hands and kept it trained in the right direction.

Bethany placed the potatoes and pork in a bowl. "Tobias, have you eaten? We have some potatoes and pork we can share."

"I said I wanted some of that," grumbled Smoot.

"I have no idea of how we can feed you—or if I even want to. I am certainly not willing to untie you," Bethany said. She looked in Tobias's direction.

"Shut up, Smoot," Tobias said, cuffing him. "You have caused enough trouble for three people."

"Ow! Leave me be Smith! Ye got no cause to cuff me like that. Ye hit my damn head where that dog bit me."

Matthew felt the wall of tension in the room.

"You threatened Beth. Her dog won't tolerate that any more than I do." Tobias looked at Bethany and gave her a meaningful look before turning back to Smoot. "Tell me what you saw at my store. Give me the truth—all of it." Tobias jerked the chair out next to Smoot, turned it around, and sat in it, two feet from the injured man.

"You can trust me, Smith. I was just resting on the boat. I haven't had much to eat and no place to sleep."

"You could've talked to me. You never held back when you needed money for a drink. After all her grandmère has done for yer family—yer a coward and a deserter. You got nothing to bargain with—certainly not trust." He edged closer and looked down at the man. "Tell me about the other man," Tobias ordered, his voice terse.

"I got a redback to barter with."

Tobias shot him a quelling look. "You got *nothing* to bargain with," he said in a voice that brooked no argument. "Yer hide is a bigger bargaining chip." He glared at Smoot. "Now, if you hope to escape General Jackson, you best start talking. The general's got men all over the river looking for deserters. All I have to say is I shot me one."

Smoot opened his mouth and then closed it. He pulled up his shoulders and faced Tobias as tall as he could make himself. "Fine! I'll give ye what ye want. I seen the man before. He been hanging 'round these parts. He was hiding on the side of your building. When you and that trapper went inside, he followed you in and came right back out and left. That's all I know." He gave a plaintive look to Bethany. "Can I have some food, now?"

MATTHEW DID NOT trust this man, Smoot, much less his story. It was, as his father would sometimes say, *too pat*. He had become tired after eating but would not leave Bethany in the room with other men. He strained to see what Bethany was doing. It looked like she had just fed Dandie her meal before ladling the last of the potatoes and pork for Tobias and Smoot. That she made both men wait until the dog had a meal told him a lot about the woman. He liked the small dog and would not see her starve, especially since she saved his life. That dog meant more to her than either of these men and if they had been paying attention, both would have realized that.

Damn his vision! It kept going between shadows and darkness, which made his post with the gun a little tougher to carry out. Bethany and Tobias had loosened one arm of Smoots and allowed him to eat. When he felt his sight fading, he would harden his face and do his best to keep his eyes in one spot, unmoving, in case either of the men looked up.

When Tobias finished eating, he pushed back a little from the table and tied Smoot's free hand back behind him before looking in Matthew's direction.

Matthew could see heads turn, but could not see faces. Everything looked amorphous with a halo around it. If things were not already as stressed as they were, he might have felt the need to panic. As it was, he could not allow himself. Having stared so hard, his eyes felt tired. Coupled with a full belly, he fought not to close his eyes. He wished he could see faces more clearly. Seeing shadows helped, he supposed, but it was not the best of options.

He stifled a yawn and walked to Bethany, nodding toward the men. They needed resolution to this. Funny, he looked forward to getting away from this situation, even if it meant visiting a leper colony. "Any ideas on how to get rid of these men? At least long enough for us to escape to your aunt's."

"I am thinking. Tobias wants to help, I believe. We have been friends for a long time."

He grunted in disagreement, drawing her interest. An abrupt noise outside drew their attention. Bethany pulled back the curtain and looked from the corner.

"It's an osprey! She must have eggs in a nearby tree." She glanced around. "I do not see anyone." She drew back from the window as her shoulders slumped. "I am sorry. I had thought to complete my errand this morning and be back here with little fanfare. How could I have missed the man following me?"

He heard the tension in her voice. This was not something that she was used to doing. Of course, she would not have noticed a man watching her.

"If someone doesn't want to be seen, he generally won't be seen," Matthew responded, not wanting her to blame herself.

"That's true," Tobias added, coming up from behind them. "There is no way you could have known, Beth."

Tobias's use of Bethany's name with a sense of familiarity irked Matthew. He had a growing sense of unease and fought back the urge to say something. He wished they would both leave but held his tongue.

"I'm going to take Smoot with me. I am not sure what I will do with him, but I'll figure something out." Tobias lowered his voice and looked at Matthew. "Are you able to see well enough to help Bethany navigate?"

"You know?" Bethany murmured.

"I do." His voice took on a sympathetic tone. "You've done an admirable job, but no need to deny it. I recognize the signs—my uncle was almost blind." He moved closer and glared at Matthew. "Take good care of Beth. If something happens to her, I will make it my life's work to find you and make you pay. We've always been friends, and . . ." He looked at Bethany. "I guess that is all we will ever be. Beth, please stay alert and be careful. These are dangerous times."

Matthew recognized the deep emotion in the man's voice. "I will do my best," he acknowledged, with his respect for this man growing in that moment.

"Thank you, Tobias," Bethany replied in a half-whisper. "However, I think I should try and fix his ear before he goes. He carries on as if he lost the ear, when all Dandie did was bite it."

"Ouch!" her friend said mockingly. "She bit the bottom of his earlobe off. He will never forget your dog."

"Yes . . . well, I shall stitch his ear and watch my dog carefully, just in case Dandie gets sick from the bite!"

Chapter Eleven

Bethany exhaled a long, whooshing breath when the door closed, relieved Tobias had taken Smoot with him. Finally! Smoot had screamed the entire time she stitched his ear—at least until Tobias punched him and knocked him out. That had been unexpected, but at that point, welcomed. She was afraid that they would have to endure his nasty personality into the night.

War and fear do odd things to men, she considered. Never had she imagined Smoot to be a coward—although he had always been a bully. Her papa had always said that cowardice was the motivation of bullies. He was right.

Caleb Smoot was both, and she hoped to never see the man again.

Bethany walked to a window and cracked it open, craving fresh air. She still needed to pack, get food on the table, and tidy up the cabin. Morning would be here too soon.

Tobias' inferences of a future together had worn thin, and as the afternoon wore on, she had become edgy in his presence. He meant well, and she realized he favored a union between the two of them, but she had grown weary of explaining and apologizing to him. There was no attraction—and her heart wanted the fairytale. Her mother had told her stories of princes that rescued their princess. She wanted that, of course, *without* aspirations of royalty. A giggle escaped her, and she glanced in Matthew's direction. He sat on the bed petting Dandie. Her dog loved Matthew but had never liked Tobias. Tobias was her friend, and she cherished that. But she had been telling him for the last six months that she was not interested in anything more than continuing the friendship they had had since childhood.

She shook her head, determined to ready them for the trip. Quickly, she cleaned the kitchen area before packing for their trip. She was uncertain how long she would be gone. Her boat was small, so she planned to pack light. She checked the hidden storage compartment under one of the seats, relieved Matthew's uniform was still there.

Walking into her room, she lifted the false bottom on her linen chest and grabbed his sword, gun, and boots. Quickly, she took them to the boat, stashing them in the compartment with his uniform, mentally checking the items off a list in her head. Luckily, Matthew's feet were the same size as Papa's had been, so his military-issue boots could stay hidden. For good measure, she packed a rolled-up blanket, thinking it could come in handy if they needed to camouflage the sword. She took her papa's knife and her gun. Tobias' warning had not fallen on deaf ears. Bethany well knew the danger. If there had been any doubt, the sporadic musket fire along the river served as an excellent reminder that all had not calmed down. Smoot's frightening visit attested to that as well.

There was still the man that had stolen the letter containing damning information that could get her hanged, if it found its way to the American general. If he was on the side of the British, as he had told her, perhaps the letter would find its way to England, even though he had been searching for a different man. At least she hoped that would be what happened to it.

"Bethany." Matthew's voice sounded urgent.

"I am sorry. I was lost in my musings." She walked back into the house to the work counter, preparing to pack some food for the trip. "It certainly has been a day of excitement I was not prepared for. As Grandmère would say, *I wonder when the next shoe will fall.*"

"That's a curious saying," he laughed.

"It always conjured the image of raining shoes. A painful vision, to be sure!"

"I agree. Speaking of shoes . . . I need some boots for our river trip in case we find us in a tight spot with the need for a push."

Bethany suddenly saw him in her mind's eye, bare-waisted and muscles bulging, and gulped. "I hope the water is as high in the tributaries as it looks here. You should not have to worry too much about that. However, Grandmère kept some of Papa's boots in the bottom right of the armoire. I hope we do not need your military boots—as they scream British to anyone seeing us. The Americans are used to the frontier and use whatever they have."

"I see your point," he agreed.

"I have them packed in the hidden storage compartment of the boat—under the seat. Your saber and gun are also there."

"What can I help you with? I confess to feeling useless and I hear you buzzing around. Surely there is something?"

"I was amused watching you with Dandie," she confessed. "I have never known my dog to take a fancy to any man before. She has always snarled and warned them away."

"Even Tobias?"

Was that jealousy? She could not help feeling a twinge of hope, even if there could be no future for them. "Yes," she acknowledged. "For some reason, *especially* Tobias."

"That is curious," he mused out loud. "He has feelings for you. That was clear to me."

"You noticed." Bethany gave a terse laugh before biting her bottom lip, wondering how much she should say. "He made it known he was interested in a future. However, I am not. I told him I valued his friendship but was not interested in making it more. He has an annoying habit of selective hearing."

Matthew turned his gaze toward the fireplace, as if in thought, before returning his gaze to her direction. "I doubt he has accepted your answer if body language is an indicator. He seemed possessive."

"We have been friends for most of our lives. It was hard to rebuff him. I tried not to hurt him," she lamented. "Grandmère told me he would get over it, but in these parts, men seem to think they can crook their finger and the woman acquiesces. I was not raised to *acquiesce* to a man. I was raised to think for myself. To make my own decisions about what is right and wrong, and what I want for my life. I want a man that is comfortable with that."

She stopped, realizing she had gone too far in her explanation, and suddenly worrying about what Matthew would think. *I want a man like you.*

He stood up and walked to her, reaching out and taking her hand, rubbing slow circles on the back with his thumb.

Dandie trotted over and sat behind him, staring at her mistress and wearing her black-lipped grin.

"I do not know what there is between us, yet I recognize the attraction that we have for each other. Perhaps it was evident to your friend, as well," he said before pausing. "I cannot see but milky shadows with my eyes, but my heart sees your heart, your compassion, and your courage. I have never known a woman like you."

Her heart pounded in her chest so loud, she was sure he could hear. "I . . . I find you very appealing," she confessed in a soft voice. "Yet, I know that once you are completely healed, you will return to your homeland."

"You could come with me," he said with an unexpected drawl.

"What are you saying?" she asked. "And is that another attempt at the dialect here?"

"It was," he laughed. "Better?"

She nodded.

He moved closer. "I have feelings for you, and I confess they are new to me," he answered.

"Of gratitude," she responded. "I pulled you from a battlefield and stitched your wounds."

"You have saved my life. And it is *not* gratitude."

Her heart thudded. "I cannot go to a new world because you are grateful. I did what I would do for anyone, 'tis all," she said, feeling a lump in her throat and a tug at her heart.

Matthew leaned in and kissed her lips lightly, but offered no further explanation before walking back into the bedroom. She heard the springs groan as he sat down on the bed. Her dog followed. She heard Dandie jump up on the bed and nestle herself on the pillow, a place she could only dream of being, herself. The dog would get off the bed before too long and come and sleep on the pallet next to her, as she had done every night he had been here.

She walked to the doorway of her bedroom and looked at the two of them. He sat there, staring at the floor. "I am packed. I wrapped dried pork, bread, the unpeeled potatoes, and cheese into the food sack. That should give us adequate nourishment for the short journey."

He looked up in her direction. "Thank you, Bethany. You need to rest, now."

Bethany realized with sudden clarity that she needed to get Matthew well as soon as she could before she lost her heart to this man. She noticed the window she had cracked open earlier and closed it. Grabbing her rolled pallet from the corner of the room, she opened it and placed it in front of the fireplace, realizing she had not taken Grandmère's bed because she wanted to be near him. She could not think anymore. Today had been too stressful. She needed her sleep.

They needed to leave before dawn.

MATTHEW FELT AN ache in his heart that he had never experienced before. Sure, there had been women in his life, but never one that had so captivated his interest. He had not believed he would find such a woman. This one—Bethany—made him want to smile in the face of all he had experienced, despite the danger he still faced being here in enemy territory, and notwithstanding the fear he faced over his sight. He lifted his feet and laid them on top of the still-made bed, thinking.

What in the world was I thinking, asking her to come back to England with me? As soon as the words had spilled from his lips, his mind had whirled. All he knew was the desire to be in her company. He needed her near him—not from gratitude. It was from something deeper... deeper than an attraction. He squeezed his useless eyes shut and felt hot tears escape, wishing they could release his fears and frustration. And he missed his family and friends.

In a few hours, they would be on the river. It was one more step in her quest to heal him. He would be more of a burden than a help with his lack of sight. Bethany's words came back to him. *Swimming is instinctual.* He knew that was true, yet that did nothing to abate his fears. He knew what lurked in these waters—deadly snakes and alligators. His naiveté with alligators had ended when his men had arrived at the plantation. That was when they had discovered that if there was water in Louisiana, it most likely had alligators. Luckily, except for a few bites, there had been no grievous injuries—even from snakes. And in a few hours, he would be in a small boat... *practically blind.* It was not fear of what he could not see. It was more a fear of what he could not do. He could not protect her.

Bethany was not afraid. The woman never ceased to surprise him with her ability to remain calm under stress. Never had he met anyone like her. The little terrier stirred above his head, as if to remind him of her presence. "Are you reading my mind, Dandie?"

The dog stretched her legs and gave a soft *yip*, making him smile.

He thought back over the day, recalling the letter Bethany had written to his family was now in the hands of a man looking for a soldier—but not him. It would have been easier for Bethany and Dandie if the man had been searching for him. But then, he would have never known her. The way she had taken care of him had been nothing short of amazing. She was the most competent woman he had ever known—his mother and sister excepted, of course.

At the thought of her, he smiled, closed his eyes, and unclenched his fists. Gradually, he felt his body relax.

CHAPTER TWELVE

Bethany woke to Dandie's licks. She furiously kissed her mistress's face and nudged her chin with her nose. The last embers of the fire should have been out, but were burning warm, heating her face. Opening her eyes, she saw Matthew fully dressed and leaning into the fireplace, poking through the logs.

"I thought you might like a little heat as you stirred. It seemed Dandie had other ideas. She thought a face bath was more what you would want," he laughed.

A snort escaped her. "I confess, I was having a dream that we had already arrived at my aunt's," she said, sitting straight up. "To wake and find that the trip is still ahead is a little defeating. I have never taken off in the darkness, before. But it seems necessary this time."

"Yes. It seems we cannot stay here. I am more concerned about Smoot and the trouble he could cause than the man that got the letter." His words were pensive.

"I hope you could sleep. I feel quite rested, although it is always hard to pull myself out from under the warm coverlets." She stood, having slept somewhat dressed. With Matthew unable to see, she had not worried, as she normally would have about her state of dress. "Thank you for stoking the fire. It is probably smarter to go about things with that lower light than lighting the candles. I will bank it just before we leave." She finished folding the blankets and stacked them on her bed, noticing Matthew had straightened the bedding.

Going back into the living area, she reached for a long leather tether that hung next to the fireplace. "I will put this restraint on Dandie in case she sees something in the water. I don't want her going after it." The dog whimpered at the sight of the leather lead.

"She is unused to that, I take it," Matthew offered.

"Yes. However, sometimes, merely having it attached keeps her in check. She hardly ever leaves my side. However, I do not want to look for her, just in case she sees something in the water." She trembled at the thought of the cold, murky water.

Bethany walked over to the window and peered out. "We have a full moon and fog—a lucky combination for our travel, I hope. The fog will burn off soon enough with the sun rising but will provide adequate cover. Let me put the food supplies in the boat. Then, I'll pull it around and we can leave."

Once Matthew and Dandie were in the boat, Bethany gave a last check to her windows and door, carefully securing the small items such that they would alert her if they were breached, before climbing into the boat herself. Quietly, she pushed away from the dock and began the trek down the canal.

The boat moved quietly through the water as she carefully kept toward the middle. Birds had begun to chatter along the tree line, while frogs and crickets still chirped their existence as they all searched for bugs and other sustenance for their breakfast. Her boat cut through the river, making quiet ripples. Dandie sat next to her, the tether attached but not taut.

No one spoke for about a half-hour, until they had moved beyond the first bend.

"How many miles did you say we would travel?" Matthew whispered.

"It's about ten. It should not take us too long. It usually takes about two to three hours, depending on the current. At least we don't have the strong current of the river to deal with. These are fairly mild and allow us to go both ways pretty easily." She was relieved that the weather was cooperating. The full moon provided enough light for her to see around her boat.

"Don't be alarmed if you hear splashes. The inhabitants of the canal are just going about for food," she explained. "We are safe in the boat. We should keep our voices down, though, as they carry over water."

"I *was* just wondering about those splashes," Matthew admitted quietly.

"Yes, I heard them too. I think it was a gator. They do not bother people. Only small animals, fish, birds, and other smaller prey. That is one reason I put Dandie on a tether. She knows better and minds, but she is untested during the darker hours, so I am being cautious."

"That is wise. She is a very inquisitive dog. I am probably here today because of that part of her nature," he mused aloud.

Bethany giggled softly. "Yes, my grandmère calls us quite the pair. I was just thinking about what her reaction to you will be."

"Does she hate the British? You mentioned she came from Canada as a child. If I recall my history, it was not always pleasant in the Canadian territory. She may not be pleased with my presence."

"I never recall Grandmère disliking anyone. She seeks the goodness in others, as she will do so with you. She will want to help you. I am sure of that."

"Your Grandmère sounds like a lovely person, very generous of spirit," Matthew whispered in return.

Bethany remained quiet, listening to the surrounding sounds. She had decided to use one paddle, moving it on the left and right of the boat slowly so as not to make too much noise. Pulling it up for a moment, she listened. It sounded like the familiar small splash of a paddle was still hitting the water behind her. Turning slightly, she scanned the area, searching but seeing nothing. It would be light soon, and she could confirm her suspicions.

She stayed quiet for a few more minutes before whispering to

Matthew, "The sun will rise soon." Her tone was more hushed.

"Is something wrong? I noticed we slowed down," he replied quietly.

"I think we are being followed," she returned, keeping her voice as quiet as she could. "I am not sure, though. It's just a suspicion. But I could hear what sounded like my paddle hitting the water, twice."

"I have my pistol and my knife near my feet, just in case we need them," she added.

God, she hoped they would not need them. She wanted so much for this trip to move quickly and without incident. She went over what she knew in her head over and over. Smoot was probably still tied up with Tobias. He had given his word—even if he had not, she knew he wanted her safe. She hated the jealousy that had sparked from him toward Matthew, but there was nothing for it.

The last thing Bethany ever wanted was to hurt him. He was dear to her, even if he could find her last nerve and jump on it! With those two unlikely, who could be following them? Her imagination was going wild. *Stop it,* she willed. *It's probably someone like us, hoping to get started early on a trip.* In her heart, though, she knew better. Someone was out there, and this did not bode well.

"Matthew, do you feel like you can paddle?"

"I can. I will be glad to do that. And I think I can balance my strokes easily with yours. I never told you, but my friends and I used to row in school. It will feel good to do it again."

"Perfect!" she said, pausing to hand him the extra paddle. "You paddle on the right, and I will paddle on the left. I think we can do this. The canal runs straight for a while, so there are no bends to navigate."

"I could be mistaken, but it seems like it's starting to get lighter out," he said softly.

"It is. We got at least an hour on sunrise with our early start, but the moon is starting to fade."

"I've been enjoying the sounds of the wildlife. I have never noticed that they seem to answer each other—the frogs and the crickets," he supposed.

"I had never noticed that. But you are right," she answered, her voice lighter. It was good to have him helping her and the two of them talking some. It took her mind off her fear. Grandmère always told her that fear should be respected. It was your mind keeping you aware and safe. She fully believed that. It was what allowed her to live on her own when Grandmère left. That had not happened often.

But when her father left home, and her Papa was gone, it meant she and Grandmère only had each other. With Aunt Theodosia blind, Grandmère felt obligated to check on her sister frequently, so Bethany had become more and more used to maintaining things while her grandmother was away.

"We haven't discussed much regarding the battle, but my troops came in through these canals. The men constructed redoubts along the way. I can't help but wonder if we shall run into any of those. Should we run into the British, I believe I can help."

"I will be happy to let you," she said. Why did her stomach just knot up at his words? It would make things easier for both if they ran into the British. He would have a ship to take him home. She would no longer have a British soldier in her care and would no longer have to worry about being arrested for helping a very injured man. *I care about him.* Her thoughts drifted back to his words last evening.

You could come with me.

The offer sounded as fresh in her mind as when he said them. She opened her mouth to say something but closed it.

"I know we should not talk too much on the water, and all, but there is something that I would like, no need, to explain," Matthew said, interrupting the silence.

"If we keep our voices low, I suppose talking is fine. I enjoy conversations with you," she responded, feeling a sudden lump in her throat. He was going to tell her he did not mean what he had said last evening. She had expected this. He was a member of British nobility, and she was . . . a Creole woman from the land that his country was fighting.

"I offered that you could come with me last evening." His voice was low, but steady.

"And then you got up and went to bed. I understood. We got caught up in our . . . friendship," she said, suddenly finding herself holding back tears. Dandie nudged her side and she looked down into the concerned face of her very perceptive dog. Impulsively, she leaned down and kissed Dandie's head, needing that affection.

"I was not caught up in our friendship," he bit out softly. His tone was clipped. "What we have between us is special. I have never experienced it with another woman. I find myself wanting to be in your presence," he explained. "I have never felt that way. I went to bed because I cannot see, metaphorically of course," he gave a light, sarcastic laugh, "how I will even get home, much less bring someone with me."

"You feel like you will never see your home? I cling to the hope that your sight is returning," she said, hopefully.

"You are an optimist. I thought I used to be one, as well. And truthfully, I have not been miserable. Being here with you has been better than I would have ever imagined, considering how it unfolded."

"I appreciate your situation, Matthew," she whispered. "I only want what is best for you." She considered her next words carefully. "I have no expectations. Perhaps we should continue this conversation when we can be assured of our privacy."

The sun had begun to creep over the dark clouds. She saw him slump at her words and felt miserable. There was so much she wanted to ask, to hear. She craved his soft kisses, although she knew that by going to her aunt's home, there would be little opportunity for that to happen. It was just as well.

Surely Aunt Theodosia would know what was going on with Matthew. She prayed it would be so.

A noise behind them drew her attention and she lifted her paddle from the water. The fog was lifting, and visibility was improving. Turning, she could see the stream of water for miles, but there was no sign of a boat. She let out a long breath of relief, only now realizing how tense she had been.

Dandie had curled at her feet and was snoozing away. She trusted Dandie's instincts. If there had been someone, the little dog would have nudged her or worse, barked.

"I can feel the sun stronger. The shapes are lighter. It seems a little better than yesterday," Matthew offered quietly.

"That's wonderful news," she said, her heart gladdened. She needed to cast her selfish desires aside. He needed to get home to his family and friends, she thought, feeling buoyed not to see anyone behind them. "Tell me about the rowing you and your friends did in school."

"You would like to hear my tales?" he sniggered. "It was a boys' school, Eton. And we were quite the trio, having become fast friends as soon as we arrived."

"How old were you when you left for school?" She had heard that the rich people in Europe went to fancy boarding schools—boys and girls, each to learn different studies. Her grandparents had made sure she learned math, her native language, English, and the history of her people. Of course, she had learned to read and write. Grandmère felt an education for her granddaughter was most important, especially considering the dangers that ignorance would have.

She heard a heavy splash from next to the bank and shuddered, involuntarily. It was probably a gator. She hated them, although their meat was fairly tasty. Bethany tried to ignore the sound as Dandie crawled closer to her feet.

"I started at Eton when I was twelve. We have been friends for years. Truthfully, memories of my friends kept me alive in my darker moments over here. 'Tis like I can hear them speaking to me at times, cheering me on," he said.

Dandie slowly climbed to the back seat, giving a low throaty growl.

"Shhh, Dandie. We must be quiet," Bethany said, instinctively tugging the leash shorter. She eased paddle into the boat and picked up her knife. Slowly, she turned. An alligator was following them closely, his eyes barely out of the water. He had spotted her dog.

"Matthew, there is an alligator ahead of us. Keep paddling on both sides if you can. I have to hold Dandie. I am afraid she will try to defend me."

"Both of you come off the seat and sit down on the floor of the boat," he returned. His voice brooked no discussion.

She wanted to be anywhere but here right now, fearing she might lose her small dog if she did the wrong thing. Alligators were known to lurch from the water at their prey. She pushed her knife in front of her and, holding her dog tightly, moved to the center of the boat, closer to Matthew.

"Curse my eyes!" Matthew hissed. "I am of little use."

"We will have to risk being seen. Can you hold on to Dandie, tightly?" her voice trembled.

"Yes," he said, taking the small animal and pulling it close to him. He tucked her into his jacket, limiting her mobility.

Bethany dreaded having to use her gun, but she was at a loss as to what weapon would best serve her needs. The gun would have a loud report, but she knew her strength was no match for the gator. She laid the knife down and cocked the small pistol.

Dandie whimpered at the sound of the gun.

"Hold her tight. I don't want her to get out of the boat and the gun will scare her," she whispered, her eyes never leaving the alligator, who seemed to be slowing. She raised her gun, prepared to fire, when the creature suddenly turned and dove down into the water.

"He . . . he's gone. He dove under the water." Fear quaked her voice.

A sudden splash broke on the side of the boat as the creature lurched itself onto the side.

Bethany fired and the animal immediately fell backward.

The force of the shot knocked Bethany off balance, and she stumbled back into the water.

Chapter Thirteen

It happened quickly. The gun discharged and the shadow of what looked to be a large gator fell backward, hitting the water with a loud thud. And Bethany catapulted off the other side of the boat. Matthew quickly tethered the barking dog and readied himself to dive into the water after her. Surely, he could feel her body.

"Matthew, help me!" the words gurgled forth in a rush.

He eyed the water on the other side of the boat trying to determine where she had fallen. It would be of no help to dive in the wrong direction.

Seeing what he thought looked like her, he dove into the water, aiming a little away from where he had heard her voice, unsure of what he would find. *I have to save her.*

"Matthew, I'm here. My foot . . . it's caught on something. It feels like a rope and I cannot get free."

He could hear her cries of frustration. Swimming toward her voice, he found her. Neither mentioned the alligator that had only moments before threatened them. He felt her shoulder, trying to pull her, but could not get her closer to the boat. She was right. Her foot was caught on something. "Can you tread water?"

"Yes," she gurgled, spitting the brackish water. "My knife. It's in the boat."

"Try to tread water slowly," he cautioned, instinctively knowing she would draw attention to herself from another gator. He wasn't sure the first one was gone.

"Hurry . . ." she choked.

Grabbing the side of the boat, he felt along the edge until he found the back where she had been sitting, and thrust himself over the side. He looked at the now barking dog, trying to calm her with his words. "Shhh! Dandie. Quiet. I will get her. I promise," he said, grabbing the knife and sliding back into the water.

This was the largest knife he could remember holding. Carefully, he felt the blade side, making sure he knew where it was, as he reached Bethany. He pressed her arm gently before diving, following her leg. At her foot, he felt a coarse rope covered with squishy stuff. He cut it, freeing Bethany, who immediately started kicking toward the boat, her dress flowing next to his arm. He returned to the surface and helped hoist her into the boat.

"Hurry," she cried. "There is another gator. He's close."

Seizing the side of the boat, he tossed in the knife and hoisted himself after it, rolling to the floor in a tuck position, just as he heard a loud snap—a snap that would have claimed his leg had he been a half-second slower.

"I am safe," he said out loud, as much for her sake as his own. The three of them were safe, thankfully.

Clutching her squirming dog close, Bethany stood and, with her other hand, seized Matthew's paddle and slammed it against the snoot of the gator. "Oh my God! He went back into the water," she squealed.

"Paddle," he yelled, hoping to cut through the tension. They needed to gain distance.

"I saw a gator floating. I must have killed it. I hated to do it, but it was intent on getting my dog," she whispered hoarsely in a shaking voice.

For her part, Dandie had become still and had curled up in the bottom of the center of the boat, perhaps aware that she had just missed being an alligator's meal. He could not be sure, but was grateful for the quiet.

"Do you see anyone about?" he asked when his breathing slowed.

"No... well, yes. There is a boat behind us, but it's pretty far," Bethany replied, still paddling.

Adrenaline seemed to have taken possession of both of them. They were silent as they paddled like the hounds of Hell were upon them.

It seemed like an eternity before anyone spoke.

"Thank goodness the sun is up. We might have never seen that gator," Bethany ruminated aloud. "And thank you for saving me, Matthew." Her voice was soft.

"Bethany, my heart stopped when you fell into the water. I would not have stopped until I found you."

"You were so brave, even without your sight, you saved us both—Dandie and me. If you had not tied her down, she would have followed. I might have lost her," Bethany choked out.

"I think your little companion was very brave, too," he said, smiling. "She did not try to follow us, but did her best to warn us without making matters worse." He patted her head. "I do not know where your mother found this dog, but she is the best dog I have ever known."

"I only know of Dandie," Bethany replied, her voice laced with laughter.

It relieved him to hear her voice much more relaxed. As much as he wanted to hold and kiss her, he dared not, lest they be seen or become fodder for another gator! "She is a unique dog, to be sure," he said, instead.

"I think we should be almost there. I recognize that tree. There should be two tributaries coming up. We must take the first one. It's narrow, but the center runs deep. A mile or so down that is where the camp is located."

"You can recognize one tree among the many that blur before me," he guffawed.

"Only because it was toppled by a storm and looks like it was chewed in half by a massive animal," she giggled.

"Oh, please tell me there is no monster that can chew trees!" he teased. He tried to keep his voice light. But Matthew felt tired. His side burned and his eyes alternatively ached and itched. He was afraid of losing what brief vision he had gained, so he kept his hands away from them.

The war notwithstanding, he had experienced nothing that rivaled what they had just been through, and felt exhausted from his exertions. He recognized the need for more recovery time, no longer worrying that he was staying near a leper colony. He craved two things—Bethany's touch and sleep, both of which seemed out of reach. His only thought was of having a soft bed where no alligator could reach it.

BETHANY SAW THE juncture where the small stream veered off the channel. Her emotions warred with her. She felt apprehension, excitement, and overwhelming sadness. But it was the sadness that was hard to reconcile. Dandie seemed to sense something. The small dog came over and crawled next to her in the seat. "I feel the same way, Dandie."

The dog whimpered and laid her head down on Bethany's lap.

It was as if the little dog was more able to express her emotions than Bethany. "I will miss him when he goes home. He wants to go home. He has a family wondering about his whereabouts, I feel sure." She hoped her letter to his family made it to his father. Yet, she had her doubts. It seemed that her life had pivoted in a different direction since finding him on that battlefield. Yet, she did not wish for it differently. Instead, she wished for possibilities, knowing that the only possibility was that she would be waving goodbye to him . . . and hating it.

"Bethany, how are you feeling?" Matthew's voice broke her from her reverie.

"I feel much better, now that I'm drying off. Thank you for remembering about the blanket—I just feel bad that you refused to use it."

"You were in much longer than I was. My friends and I used to jump into the cold creek in chillier weather. I finally discovered how to make my mind transport me to a warmer clime and ignore the frigidness. The one that could stay in the longest was declared the winner. It was probably a stupid game; however, I pulled on that memory today. When I see my friends next, I shall thank them for the training." He chuckled. "They will see the lark in it."

"I have heard of doing things like that—jumping into an icy pond to 'revive' you. I always thought it a bit of mischief, but hearing your explanation, it sounds like there is some real value to it." She shivered at the thought. "I am afraid I am too used to the warmer weather and spared myself any such adventure until today," she laughed. Her grandmother would not find it at all amusing if she found herself sick from this experience. "You saved both of us—Dandie and me. Thank you for rescuing me."

"Last night I will admit to some apprehension to being on the water and unable to see clearly. It's been frustrating. Yet, you told me that I would still know how to swim, and your words came back to me today – after we were away from danger. You were right," he said, softly.

"It was something that my papa told me. He compared swimming to walking and thought that once you learned things like this, your body remembered it."

"Your papa was a smart man." His voice sounded reflective. "I would have like to have met him."

"He was the greatest of men. I miss him immensely. It amazes me how well Grandmère does without him. She is a very kind person, yet strong and perceptive." She smiled at the thought of seeing her Grandmère, realizing how much she had missed her presence. "I am grateful for all she has taught me."

The small stream was much more scenic than the main canal had been. Cypress trees leaned over the water and lined the edges, and with tall cattails and other marsh-like plants, they dominated the landscape. The brackish water looked dark, but you could see it was deep enough for the boat to pass easily through. She leaned over and gazed at the fish darting between the small plants under the water.

"Have you ever had crabmeat?" she asked.

"I believe I have, but it has been a long time. My parents would occasionally have seafood dinners."

"Grandmère and Aunt Theodosia love to cook things like trout and crab boils. I will ask them if we can have something like that," she offered, finding herself salivating at the thought of eating more of the salted meats of late. "I wrapped up a small basket of herbs that I had gathered from the Villeré Plantation that morning and brought them for my aunt. I am sure she will make use of them in some special dishes. She loves to cook."

"You said your aunt is blind. I have discerned that there must be many degrees of being blind, having gone from darkness to this . . . this shadowed sight that I have now."

"I cannot shake the feeling . . . the hope . . . that yours is related to the battle. However, I do not know how to change it. I continue to pray that it gets better," Bethany explained.

"I do too," he acknowledged. "However, I am not allowing myself to dwell on it if I can help it."

"Matthew, your positivity is contagious," she said. "I do not know many people that would not be wallowing in misery much more than you allow yourself to do," she added. "I believe I would feel quite lost and miserable."

You are someone I wish could be with me all my life.

"I feel sorry for myself. I try to give myself limits, having seen a much darker outcome for so many others. So many of my friends and comrades met a much harsher fate. They lost limbs and much more." His tone was somber.

He was probably thinking of his batman, Bart, she thought. They must have been very close. "I think we are close to the colony," she said, purposely changing the subject.

"I thought we must be. You said we were two-to-three miles from the colony when we turned."

"Yes. We have another bend up here and the place we will dock the boat should come into view."

They were quiet for a few minutes.

"Bethany, I have tried to say something for a while, now. I still feel that I owe you an explanation for our conversation last evening." He put down his paddle and carefully found his way over to where she was sitting. Sitting down on the seat across from her, he reached over and touched her face. Then he lifted his other hand so that he gently held her face between both of his hands. "I have feelings I cannot explain. I have never known any woman like you and have never felt this way."

Matthew leaned toward her and kissed her softly, before pulling her closer and kissing more intensely. She loved his kisses—craved them. She pulled in her paddle and allowed herself to meld with his kiss, feeling her body warm beneath his touch. His kisses were like nothing she had ever imagined. As a girl, she wondered about what a kiss felt like. Now her mind screamed it was glad she had waited to find out . . . *waited for him*. She decided that she would live in the minute . . . and enjoy every second with him.

I will not waste my time with him wondering about life after he goes. It tarnishes the time I have with him, she determined.

She took her tongue and met his, boldly swirling it against his teeth, their breath mingled as she curled her arms about his head, with her fingers swirling the curling hair at the nape of his neck. Remembering where they were, she gently pushed them apart.

"We might be seen by someone once we turn on the bend," she said in a whisper, more to herself than to him. "I could lose my mind in those kisses," she quipped.

"Yes . . . I tend to lose my head with you," he returned.

I am losing my heart to this man, she realized.

"There will be a bend in a few minutes. We will turn, and then, we will put in at a small dock that is off to the right. I will put some brush over the boat, once we get our things out." She wondered about the sword and the guns. "I think we should bring the guns and sword with us—in case the boat gets stolen. I hate to always say that, but it happens, as you now must realize."

He sniggered. "I guess it is a commodity around here. I see that, now."

"I had forgotten the food I brought as a light meal. I packed a canteen of water and some bread and cheese."

"I think we almost became a meal!" he joked. "I would like some water. And I would bet Dandie would enjoy some."

A small yip at the mention of her name got them both laughing. It was nice that they could laugh about everything. She still felt terrified when she remembered the face of that gator. And hated that she had to kill it. It was a waste—and he was only doing what he needed to survive. She just was not giving up her dog to his belly.

The cypress trees seemed to push further into the right side of the stream, signaling that the turn was upon them. "Matthew, if you will pull up your paddle, I will guide us into the turn," she offered. He had not stopped helping her paddle, which had made it easier. It would be wonderful to see her aunt and her grandmother.

Ruefully, she thought another kiss would have been nice, too. But they had both been mindful of appearance in the open canal. The small boat that had been following seemed to have disappeared. Shaking the thought off, she studied the small stream.

Nothing seemed to have changed. Tall pine and cypress trees surrounded the sides of the water. The cypress trees had large boughs of moss hanging from their limbs, giving them a silvery shimmer in the bright sunshine. After taking the sharp bend in the stream, it opened into a wider area where the fenced-in colony was in full view off to the right. They had arrived.

THE MAN IN the culled-out pirogue hung back until he was sure to have dropped from their view. He maintained a steady pace, determined to keep up with his quarry, but out of their sight. He had heard the shot go off and raced to help them, only to see that they had survived what had looked like an alligator attack. Evidence of the short battle floated by his own boat, but by this time, it had become prey to another gator who was dragging the bloodied gator toward the edge of the canal, intent on removing it to the shore where it could eat.

Having read the note he had stolen, he was more determined to follow these two, and promised himself he would not let them escape a second time.

No one saw the small canoe move into the turn and hug the left side of the stream, camouflaged by hanging moss and low-hanging branches of the trees. If he had not seen the way the boat had been hidden before, he would not have known to look for it under the heavy drape of cypress and pine. He watched the two of them, along with their dog, enter a cabin.

He would need to know more about this place before he could act. *Where exactly was he?*

Chapter Fourteen

"I smell something cooking—perhaps we are timing this arrival well," she said. "It smells like fish."

"I think you are right, he said, turning his head toward the smell. My stomach is signaling a need to eat."

She guided the boat into the small cover off to the right and tied it up. Dandie leaped out and stood waiting, still dragging the leather leash.

"Girl, you need to keep the leash on for a little longer," she coaxed, reaching over and patting her small dog. Dandie sat and watched them, her tongue hanging out the side of her mouth in a swirl-like fashion—her usual.

"Let me help you out, Matthew," she said, reaching her arm into the boat. He laid the paddle down and picked up his stick tucked alongside the interior of the small boat. Clasping her hand, he stood and stepped out of the boat.

"I can carry things, so do not be afraid to load me down."

"Thank you. I will," she said with an appreciative smile.

Once they had the basket of food and the blanket with the weapons rolled up and tied within it, they left the small dock area.

Her aunt's home was ahead. Bethany gave a quick look to her right as they stepped up to the door, smiling at Matthew, even though he could not see it. It felt right to have him with her. Once they met him, she knew her grandmother and aunt would feel that way, too.

Before she could knock, her grandmother opened the door. "*Bonjour!* Bethany, what are you doing here?" The small woman stepped out onto the step and looked up into the smiling eyes of Matthew. "Who is this young man?" she asked softly.

"Matthew, let me introduce you to Grandmère," Bethany returned. "Grandmère, Dandie and I rescued Matthew from the Villeré Plantation. We found him near death and have managed to . . ."

"Heal him nicely," her grandmother finished on a murmur. She gave an appreciative smile at Matthew, looking between the two of them with an unfamiliar glint in her eyes.

"Your granddaughter has been my salvation. I have not fully recovered, but she is the only reason that I am not dead," he offered.

The older woman shook her head as if clearing it. "Where are my manners, Bethany? Come in, all of you. I will want to hear all the details but let me bring out my sister. She was in the kitchen." Reaching down, she petted the small dog on the head. "You kept them safe, *non?*" Said soothingly in hushed tones. It was more of a statement than a question to her grand dog.

"No need," another feminine voice sounded from behind her grandmother. Her aunt's lithe form stepped forward, tapping a thick, weathered stick in front of her. "I heard the voices and came to welcome my niece. We welcome any friend of Bethany's to stay," she said.

Bethany noticed Matthew's shoulders relax, and she slowly whooshed out the breath she realized she had been holding.

"Thank you, I am glad to meet both of you," he said. "My name is Colonel Matthew Romney of the King's army."

Bethany held her breath, but nothing happened. Instead, Grandmère reached behind Matthew and ushered him into the house.

"Welcome. May we call you Matthew?" her grandmother asked. As they walked, Grandmère glanced back at Bethany, her eyes questioning.

"Let me get us some tea," offered Aunt Theodosia, tapping her cane into the kitchen.

"I'll help," offered Bethany, realizing that her aunt would probably make two trips—one carrying in the hot kettle. She could make that much easier.

"I hoped you would follow me, *mon petit*," her aunt whispered. "Your man has something wrong. From the careful way he walked into our home, I think it must be his eyes."

"He is not my man, Aunt Theodosia," replied Bethany. *I wish he were, but he is not*, she thought. "Matthew has something wrong with his vision. I had hoped you might know how to help him—you and Grandmère. He could not see since he was wounded. I feel like the explosions on the battlefield must have had something to do with it, although I could see no injury to his face—*none*. He struggles with blindness. At first, he said there was blackness, but it has gradually gotten better. He says he can make out shapes, and with enough light, he says he can make out what things are."

"*Pas-bon*. That is not good," her aunt responded. "Here, take the tray of cups and I will bring the kettle."

Bethany accepted the tray and followed her aunt into the room. The two of them set everything down on a large round table in the dining area. Her grandmother and Matthew joined them at the table. Matthew used his stick to navigate the area, tapping much as he had learned while living in Bethany's cabin.

"Your man does good," whispered her aunt for her ears alone.

Bethany turned to say something, but it was too late. Everyone was at the table.

"I suppose we should start with the morning that Dandie and I found Matthew. But first, I wonder if I might unwrap the sustenance I brought with us today. We had quite an adventure finding our way here and forgot to eat anything."

"Oh, goodness. My manners!" her grandmother rose.

"Grandmère, we have plenty. I will get it. I am sure Matthew is hungry." She looked down at Dandie, who had cocked her head to the right with her tongue in its funny hanging spiral. "I think Dandie is, as well."

"Give your pup some of the stew. There are no onions or anything that can sicken her. It's a small amount leftover from yesterday's meal. She would enjoy it."

"She has earned it," Bethany said, agreeing with the choice. "Dandie, come here and get this." The small dog followed her. Bethany placed a bowl with the cold stew on the floor in front of her pet. The dog needed no second invitation and began to attack the meal immediately. "She loves it. Thank you, Grandmère."

Smiling, Bethany returned to the table with the basket of bread, dried pork, and cheese that she had packed for the trip. "We forgot to eat it until we got here and realized how hungry we had become," she said, laughing and placing the two halves of the fresh baguette in the center of the table and unwrapping the cheese and meat.

Matthew nodded and waited, as was his custom, until everyone else was served before taking some for himself.

Her grandmother noticed this and smiled in Bethany's direction. "Tell me, children. As much as I want to hear about today's adventure, I'm curious to hear everything from the beginning."

"I thought you might. I can start," said Bethany, glad her grandmother and aunt were as welcoming as she had hoped. "It started the morning of the enormous battle. Dandie and I had gotten up early to pick the last herbs and winter vegetables, hoping to return before anything happened."

"You went to the battlefield for vegetables?" her aunt's voice sounded incredulous.

"It was not a battlefield, yet. It was the plantation, and you know Monsieur Villeré had always encouraged us to get as much from his gardens as we wanted. I feared the British would destroy the garden and had hoped to clear it before anything happened. We went before daylight, hoping not to be seen. We did not expect a battle."

Her grandmother's eyes rounded. "*Mon petit*. They could have killed you."

Bethany realized how lucky she had been, but relating the story gave her a renewed awareness of how stupid her actions had been that morning, and it was not a good realization. "We were safe, thanks to knowing the plantation and where we could hide. Dandie and I had gotten the vegetables and herbs and had already put them in the boat when the fighting began. We hid inside until we could leave, not daring to attract attention to our little boat. But you are right. My choices were probably not the wisest that day." She gave a sidelong glance to Matthew, who sat silently listening to her recount the day. "When the battle stopped, they took the injured away. Before we could leave, more men came, and we stayed hidden, watching them steal from the soldiers before taking their uniforms. When they left, Dandie heard cries of help and shot out across the field before I could restrain her. She found the colonel under a stack of dead bodies. They had left him for dead, but he was alive. I had to help him. We could not leave him."

"Oh, *mon Dieu!*" her aunt exclaimed, fanning herself. "Even though I cannot see, what I picture in my mind seems too dangerous for words."

She noticed her grandmother's silence. Occasionally, she glanced from Matthew to her. She continued relating the story, telling about Matthew's injuries and his slow recovery. "He is still recovering," she finished. "But he was well enough to save me, today." She looked over at Matthew, who now was looking in her direction with a look of concern on his face.

"I had not realized all that you witnessed, Bethany. We have not spoken of the battle," he interjected.

"No. We were well enough. There was no need," she replied softly, drifting her hand a few inches on the table in his direction. She stopped before touching him, but it was too late. Her grandmother appeared to have already noticed.

"That was as terrible a day as anyone could have imagined," Grandmère inserted. "I never imagined my granddaughter to be in danger. Angels surely protected you that day, *mon petit*."

"Tell us about your trip here. You said it was an adventure," her aunt said.

"Perhaps Matthew can relate it better than I can. He saved our lives," she said, unable to control the involuntary shudder at its mention.

"Please," her grandmother said in Matthew's direction. "Tell us, Matthew." Her voice was gentle and encouraging.

Matthew silently scratched at an itch on his arm that had been bothering him for the last few hours. He nodded and told them what had happened. He related how the alligator had followed the boat and had tried to grab Dandie, and how Bethany had killed it. Somehow, he told it matter-of-factly, as if he were reporting to a commanding officer. Bethany laughed as he was finishing the story.

"Had Matthew not jumped into the water, I might have become a meal. My foot had become caught in some old rope or something."

"*Mon Dieu*. It must have been those old crab nets. They are dangerous and left behind by fishermen," Grandmère said. "I did not know all of this had taken place in my brief absence. What made you come here? I had planned to return this week."

Bethany quickly related the story of Caleb Smoot and explained about the letter. "So, I felt we needed to leave. I worried about staying longer."

Chapter Fifteen

Hearing Bethany relate the day of the battle sent chills down Matthew's spine. They were not for him, but for her—for the danger she had endured. They could have killed her. As the days had passed at the cabin, he had not given thought to how her day had unfolded, realizing now how critical she had been in saving his life. Had she not been there, it could have been hours before they found him—if they discovered him at all. He could have died.

"I do want to add something," he said, placing his teacup in its saucer. "Bethany has been very good to me. She saved my life and has not thought of herself. If you are wondering if anything improper has taken place, let me assure you it has not. I would not intentionally injure her reputation. I have a sister about her age. However, I realize that staying with her, as I have done, has probably damaged her reputation and will take her as my wife." Oddly, he felt no reticence.

Silence ensued for several long minutes before Grandmère spoke up.

"Son, you are an honorable man. Bethany is a good girl, and I have faith in her. While this story makes me quake with fear in its telling, I am thankful that you have both arrived here safe. Marriage is a decision that is left to my granddaughter. Our lives differ somewhat from that in the more formal society where you live. While we have similar social customs, I would never insist on marriage. That would be Bethany's decision entirely. However, I had always hoped she would marry for love, as has been the tradition in our family for generations. Without friendship and love, a marriage loses much of its heart."

Aunt Theodosia smiled and nodded in agreement, but said nothing.

"Matthew, I... appreciate what you have said. But I cannot marry you, not without love. I want to marry someone I love, who also loves me," Bethany replied, placing her hand on his. "What I did for you, I would do again. You needed someone to help you. This is a time of war. People will understand if need be."

He realized his mistake the minute he looked into their faces. Matthew had repeated a blunder his friends often accused him of making. He had made the grand gesture and done the noble thing—offering for her yet forgotten to include his own feelings. He *always* did the noble thing and *always* kept his feelings in check, separate. He was not in England, and this was no compromised debutante. *Here*, they did not arrange marriages. *Here*, in this wilderness of America, matches could be made based on feelings, not fear and not riches. *How did I misjudge this so badly?*

He wanted to talk to Bethany, alone. *I need to tell her how I feel, but I am not ready to share that conversation with her grandmother and aunt. But how and when? I already feel like a cad.*

"Matthew, would you be able to go with me to walk Dandie? I want to keep her on the leash and get her used to the area, and I thought you might enjoy the fresh air," she said, reaching down and attaching the leather leash to the dog's collar.

Dandie came up from behind him and licked his hand.

"Yes. I would very much like to do that. I still need to stretch my legs after our trip." He gave what he thought was a sincere smile toward his hostesses. Light spilled in the door when Bethany opened it, and he took his cane and followed her.

When they had walked a little way from the front of the small house, he reached down and felt for Bethany's hand, grasping it into his own. It was the first time he could recall holding her hand, and a sense of intimacy hit him. "Bethany, I did not mean to blunder that . . . proposal," he stammered, "but I am not just offering out of a sense of duty. There was more to it than that."

"I confess, I am confused," she said, slowing to a stop and carefully pulling her hands back. "What are you saying?"

"I am not sure," he said. "However, I have known many women and have never felt a connection to them as I do to you. Perhaps saving my life had a little to do with it in the beginning, but now it feels like more. 'Tis like a need, I have to be where you are. I am not accustomed to feeling this way. I know you wish for more, yet I would wish that you reconsider my offer. Take your time . . . please."

She stood there listening to him and had not moved while he spoke. He wished he could see her face and discern her expressions. But she was a shadow with a light behind her. He became more frustrated with his lack of ability to see, realizing that it could be permanent and that he might not be able to cope with that reality. What would he do if he remained blind? His career would be over. What could life possibly hold for him?

"Whenever I am feeling sorry for myself, your nearness makes me smile," he said slowly. *Surely this friendship between them counted for something.*

"I have feelings for you, Matthew, but I cannot bring myself to marry someone without love," she responded. "It is a promise I made to my mother."

Did that mean she loved him? Matthew had never been in love before. He could not say he loved her.

Dandie foraged along the path which led them behind the house. Tall trees formed what resembled a wall behind the house, as the color of their bark blended into a larger shadow.

"What made you ask me to marry you? Was it all for duty?" Her voice was low and sounded vulnerable.

He thought about his answer, suddenly wondering to himself what had prompted the proposal. He never imagined he would offer for a woman and have it turned down. Had he been in England, his friends would never have let him forget the spurn. While here, he understood her need. "I listened to all I had put you through—what we had been through. While I referenced your reputation, it felt different than just being honorable." *I care about her.* "I offered because I care very much about you." He reached out and touched her arm, feeling his way down to her hands and clasping them. "Promise you will think about it."

She squeezed his hand. "I will."

Dandie started barking and pulling on the leash. Frustrated, he could hear the small dog growling and chewing. "Can you tell what she is upset about?"

"I am uncertain. She is darting back and forth, wanting to run toward the edge of the property."

"Has she ever been here before?" Matthew asked.

"She has. And she has been good about not going near the water's edge," she said. "Although we had no problems before with the gators, I am now even more cautious." A nervous laugh escaped her.

"Perhaps you should walk her in the direction she is trying to pull. There must be something."

"I agree. She is usually sensitive to things and doesn't make a fuss unless there is something."

They walked up to the gate at the property's edge closest to the water. "Thank goodness we have tall, thick fencing here. The fence keeps the alligators out of the yard," Bethany described. "But there is a hole . . ." she said. "Let me look and see if I can see anything." He could see her form leaning into the fence.

A minute later, she leaned back. "There seems to be a pirogue out there under some bushes. I cannot get a good look at it. No one lives there, so there may be someone around that Dandie is responding to."

"Is there usually hunting around this area?" he asked, calmly assessing.

"I cannot be sure. Of course, gator hunters come and go, but they picked this area for its remote position. It is a small tributary and once the leper colony was placed here, others seem to avoid it." She pointed to the property next to them. "That's an old plantation house. The colony uses every bit—gardens . . . all of it. The matriarch of the family that used to live there died about five years ago, and they donated the property. A family member had died of the disease years ago, and it was a way to support others. The family was very involved in seafood and game hunting. So, until then, there were hunters. Now, since the colony occupies the manor house, it's quiet."

"Understandable. Please do not take that as a judgment on the occupants."

Bethany picked up his hands and held them. He felt his body react immediately to her warm touch.

She was about to say something when a noise outside the fence alerted her. Dropping his hands, he saw her go back to the opening in the fence and look. "The boat is moving. I cannot see the face of the man in it. But it looks like one person. It was hard to make out much."

That someone was outside the compound disturbed Matthew. He wanted to investigate. But with his limitations, could not do much more than absorb the information she offered.

"Watch him and see what he does. Does he look in this direction or somewhere else?" he asked.

"He appears to be watching this property fairly intensely, but his face is too distant to make out other than it having dark features."

"We should alert the others to his presence. It was probably someone looking for a quarry. Hopefully, they did not find any and left," he asserted. He hoped that was the case, but he did not think so. His instincts told him that something was amiss here. Not only could he not see, but he could feel a headache coming on. At least he was here with healers, he thought, wincing with a wave of pain in his head.

"You do not look well, Matthew. Perhaps we should sit down. There is a small bench closer to the house. Come." She placed her hand in his and guided him to the bench.

For a winter day, it seemed the weather had turned rather mild of late, reminding him of the up and down temperatures experienced in London. The consistency of the climate was another reason he preferred his country estate to London.

"You look a little pale, of a sudden, Matthew."

"I was fine until this headache started coming on. It feels like waves of pain and is coming from my eyes," he said. Even to himself, his voice sounded strained.

"It could be from the excitement of all of this. Let's go in and see if a cup of tea helps," she urged.

"You are probably right." This felt like the stress headaches his father would describe. He had never had one, but it had to be stress. The stress of knowing someone was watching them. The stress of knowing that if she was caught with him, she could be in trouble. The stress of being blind in a land full of danger.

EDWARD SINCLAIR HAD been watching the compound, trying to determine who owned the old plantation house that sat on a fenced property. The well-constructed stone and brick fence was considerably shorter than the adjoining property, where Matthew had entered. It was in an unfamiliar area, and he sensed he needed much more information about the area before he could make any move to help Matthew. One thing he had discerned was that Lord Longueville was blind. He saw him walking into the house using a long walking stick in a fashion used by unsighted people. That complicated things considerably. He tugged at the unfamiliar beard that covered his face. It had been two weeks since he had shaved. Hopefully, it would keep him from being recognized until he was ready to make a move.

Judging from the way she catered to him, the woman, Bethany Phillips, obviously cared for Lord Longueville. Edward was not sure how that would help or hurt a rescue. The letter had been most revealing—not to mention it confirmed that she had Lord Romney's son. He had suspected as much.

Why had she told him otherwise? She seemed to have believed what she told him. As soon as the thought rolled through his head, the answer dawned on him. Matthew had probably used his military address and not his title. She would not have recognized the name he gave for the lost man. Had he given thought to that, much of this chase could have ended sooner.

But Sinclair owed his friend, the former Earl of Romney, and he would see the man's son back home. Sinclair did not care what it took to get this young man home. With what he had discovered so far, he thought wryly, that was a good thing since transportation had become more difficult with this latest battle.

With the loss of the battle, the British had not needed to stay beyond the time necessary to put their affairs in order with the casualties of the battle. They had pulled up stakes and were leaving and that complicated things. Most of their ships had already left the New Orleans area. He had hoped to use them for transportation back to England. Now he would have to think of a different route—with a war going on, that was no simple task.

Sinclair had lived in the country long enough that he easily blended in and could speak with an American dialect, as if he had been born to it. That gave him a slight advantage, and he needed any benefit he could gain. He had been in New Orleans long enough to get to know many of the locals.

Sinclair studied the fencing from across the water, observing through the long, low-hanging cypress branches. There appeared to be two compounds. A smaller one, surrounded by taller brick fencing—probably a deterrent to the alligator population—and a larger one next to it. The fencing on the larger property was not as high, and he could easily see into the enclosure. Besides the old plantation house, it had several gardens and small buildings and the land behind appeared more wooded. It seemed to be a self-supporting colony of some sort. But he saw none of the inhabitants.

For a late January day, it was warm. He noticed small pockets of mosquitoes that swarmed along the edge of the water, trapped behind fallen logs. He was not a fan of the unpredictable weather here and missed the northeast, where the seasons were more defined. Here it could be cold and hot within days.

His stomach reminded him of the need to eat. He had done all he could, it seemed, and he still wanted to check the British strongholds a little further up the river before calling it a day. He was certain he would find the last of the British already gone, but needed to be certain.

Sinclair needed more information. He would lie low for now.

CHAPTER SIXTEEN

There was a man in that canoe. Bethany was certain of it. However, without having seen him definitively, she knew better than to speak about it. She should not raise unnecessary alarms. But when she gave thought to it all... the canoe was very similar to the one she had seen in a distance on their way here. Yet neither occasion had allowed her to recognize the occupant, and she could not swear they were the same person.

For now, she was content to be safe. Who could have imagined the near catastrophe they had encountered today? She had planned everything down to the bread and cheese, never expecting a gator would see Dandie as its food. And she never expected being saved by Matthew. She shuttered her eyes and remembered the feel of his muscular arms holding her up. She couldn't relish the feel at the moment. However, the trauma had emblazoned the sensations on her brain, and she would re-live them often, she was certain.

Her poor dog! Dandie had been as quiet as a church mouse for the rest of the trip, which was a marvel considering Dandie never restrained herself from barking. The stress of Matthew's blindness had relaxed a little when she realized he could still do things. Clasping her hands, she repeated the silent prayer for his sight that had become part of her daily ritual. She hoped with all her heart he would regain his vision. She could no longer deny her feelings for him, recognizing the pang in her heart every time she thought of his leaving.

She knew he would leave one day. She had done what she could to make things easier for his departure, despite the ache it gave her heart. Matthew's clothes were safely hidden with his saber and gun from any prying eyes.

They needed to make their way to the house. Her stomach was empty and there was much more to discuss with her aunt and her grandmother. After the day they had already had, she and Matthew both needed to rest.

She thought about what he had tried to say earlier and tried not to read too much into his words. She understood it had been awkward for him and could not help chuckling to herself. At least she was not the only one who was uncertain of what was happening between them. *He has feelings. He said so.* Bethany was sure she was falling for him and would have to contend with a broken heart when she sent him on his way. For now, while she hoped only good things for him, she hoped she could gain some sense of when he would leave—how much time they still had together.

"Bethany, your aunt and I have rearranged things a little," her grandmother said, coming from the kitchen area and wiping her hands on her apron. "I will bunk in your aunt's rooms on this side of the house, and you can take my bedroom. The colonel will take the guest room at the end of the hall. We have plenty of blankets, so he should be comfortable should the nights get chilly."

Bethany looked around and noticed Matthew had stepped out the backdoor for a few minutes. "Grandmère, he has been having night terrors. I just want to warn you in case you hear him yelling."

The door opened, and Matthew walked into the room using his walking stick.

"I was just telling Bethany that my sister and I will sleep in the rooms on the left side. We are placing the three of you in the rooms to the right."

"I am happy to sleep where you put me. I took Bethany's bed for weeks. She and Dandie slept on the bedroll. I appreciate the hospitality."

Her grandmother arched a brow and looked in her direction.

"It was a suitable arrangement for him, and I was not sure when you would return home, Grandmère." Bethany explained yet another action. How could she say that she had wanted to be closer to him? *What if he had taken a turn for the worst?* "By the way, Grandmère, I brought a bag full of herbs that I picked from the garden. I thought you might need more."

"Thank you, sweeting. That was very thoughtful," the older woman said, hugging Bethany. "I had noticed the bag and wondered what it contained," she said with a wink.

"I expected that you might have run out of a few items, and I wasn't sure you could find them on this side of the canal," Bethany said.

"I confess, I am not as comfortable stepping around the marshes with the snakes and other critters. I'm getting older and don't want to find myself the victim of another moccasin bite."

Her aunt agreed. "There are many snakes. I imagine you may be unused to it, Colonel. But it'd serve you well to stay on well-traveled paths, away from the edges. Snakes like the shade. Not all are poisonous, but the moccasins are mean'uns, and they can kill a body."

"Surely, most are hibernating, Aunt Theodosia," Bethany inserted.

"Yes and no," her aunt returned. "This winter has inconsistent temperatures, and they sometimes take an early peek. People are snake-bitten plenty in the winter months."

"I am not used to having many snakes to contend with, back in England," Matthew added, a wrinkle on his brow.

"I believe that based on your experience getting here, you have seen the worst the bayou offers. Just stay vigilant," Grandmère laughed.

"I should say so!" he agreed, in only a half-jesting tone.

Bethany thought she saw the tall man shudder and giggled softly. "I have stayed safe most of my life—that is until Dandie attracted a hungry alligator's attention. I do not recall her barking. She may have growled." Now that she thought about it, she could recall nothing her pet did to attract the alligator. Perhaps it was after her. The thought chilled her to the bone, although she knew alligator attacks on people were rare.

"Let's change the topic," she begged, suddenly clasping at her arms unconsciously.

"I agree. The thought of diving back into that frigid water was a wake-up call. I was safer on the battlefield."

All four of them laughed. Bethany was glad to see Matthew accepted by her aunt and grandmother.

"Matthew, was there any injury to the eye or your head?" her aunt inquired softly, bringing a change to the conversation.

"I would not be the one to ask for certainty, but I recall that there were bits of shrapnel being fired from cannons everywhere. I could have had a glancing blow. I recall being shot, but the bullet went into my chest." He looked in Bethany's direction. "I would not be here today, I am convinced, had Bethany not found me. I had grown too weak to summon the men to help."

"Dandie heard you, though," Bethany interjected. "She frantically tried to reach you. I held onto her collar and begged her to stay still while they were still there. As soon as they left, she shot across the field to the pile of men. You were under several men they had stacked there." She closed her eyes and could see the chilling sight of smoke clearing and leaving fallen bodies and bloodied limbs in its wake.

"My child, it shakes me to the core to know you were there. I thank the Lord above that you and Dandie came to no harm," Grandmère said in a trembling voice. "I did not know when I left, things would worsen so quickly."

"I had sent word that I needed her. I had felt poorly and could not help myself enough to get past it," Aunt Theodosia said. "It horrified me to find out all you have been through in my sister's absence."

"I know where you are going, Aunt. Please do not. I am eighteen years old, and Papa and Grandmère trained me to be accomplished. I went about my life. It was simply bad luck that I was at the plantation that morning, picking herbs. I knew the British had camped there and had hoped to come and go unseen. I almost accomplished it." She grew quiet. "Now that I think on it, I recall nothing more than a slight cut in your hairline. It was not such that I needed to stitch it. I do not think you can even see it now, Matthew."

Matthew guffawed. "I think we have digressed, and it was my fault. We did indeed go from the alligator chase to the battlefield." He felt to his head. "Aunt Theodosia, what I recall is flashes of fire and light. And I may have hit something on my way down. I remember being shot. That is all."

It was so nice to hear his warm laugh—a laugh that came from his belly. She watched his face as he talked, noticing how his lips moved. It had been too long since he had kissed her, and she craved his touch. Looking around the table, she noticed that Matthew and her aunt were now talking, but her grandmother was watching her, a slight grin on her face.

"Grandmère," she said softly. "Can I help you with dinner? It's been a long day, but my stomach is, once again, hungry. I brought a sack of dried pork and cheese."

"I thought we might enjoy some crab," Grandmère responded softly, also letting her sister and Matthew talk.

"I hope that Matthew's eyes fully regain sight," Bethany said, glancing back at her aunt. "I had hoped Aunt Theodosia could help him."

"She may know what he needs. This is not an area that I am overly familiar with. Come, let us ready your beds while they finish talking."

Bethany nodded, and she and her grandmother slipped down the hall to the linens. They took clean linens and blankets into the rooms. Her grandmother's bed was fairly clean, so she left things as they were. Her aunt inherited the furnishings with the house. Each bed had wooden frames with mosquito netting surrounding them.

In the room Matthew would occupy, they took off the dust cover for the bed, carefully folding it, keeping the dust contained. After making the bed, her grandmother sat on the edge.

"Come here, *mon petit*," she coaxed, patting the edge of the bed.

Bethany sat next to her and leaned her head onto her grandmother's shoulder. "I missed you, Grandmère."

"I missed you, as well. Papa's and my little angel has grown up." She looked at Bethany. "You did a good thing, Bethany. I am proud of you."

"Thank you, Grandmère."

"I am concerned for you, though. I see that your heart is engaged with this one," Grandmère said, putting her arm around Bethany and tugging her close. "Hearts can be fickle things. They can make everything soar and make you feel immune to any pain. But when the heart breaks . . . everything appears bleak, and the physical ache can hurt worse than you would think."

"We were good, Grandmère," Bethany said. "He kissed me. And I do like him, very much. He asked me to go back with him," she admitted.

"What did you say?" Grandmère probed.

"I said no. His family could not accept my type. I am not cultured, do not know of their society . . ."

"Pish, *chérie*. You are every bit the woman the ladies in England are. He should be lucky to win you. Promise to follow your heart."

"Grandmère, I would only marry for love, and his offer mentioned nothing of his own heart. It felt like gratitude. I don't want gratitude. I want what you and Papa had," she admitted, pushing back a rogue tear.

"That is what I want for you, too, *mon petit*. I want you to have a life—wherever that may be—that makes you happy."

"Thank you, Grandmère." Bethany looked around the room. "I suppose we should get back to the others."

Grandmère nodded.

The two women stood and walked back into the main room where her aunt and Matthew were still deeply involved in a conversation. She laughed to herself. Had they even noticed they had disappeared?

"Sister, we still have that delicious crab soup we made yesterday. I would be in favor of having it tonight if it would suit you," Grandmère said.

"Yes. I think that would be marvelous. Let me help you in the kitchen." Her aunt started to stand, but Bethany put her hand on her aunt's shoulder, stopping her.

"No, Aunt Theo, you and Matthew stay here and let me help Grandmère."

A short time later, the smell of bread wafted through the small house. Bethany walked into the room carrying a tray with a basket of the delicious baked good and set it on the table. She took a smaller dish and set it on the floor. "Dandie, I hate to pull you away from the fireplace, but if you are hungry, your supper is ready." She watched her pet shake off her sleep and walk to the bowl, apparently gaining enthusiasm as she neared it. She bent over to eat, wagging her tail—which propelled her back end to move back and forth as she settled into the meal. It was always entertaining to watch.

Satisfied Dandie was happy, she turned to the others. "Grandmère has the soup heating. It should be ready in a minute. Matthew, would you be able to grab a couple of logs from behind the house for the fireplace? They are just outside the door." She held her breath, realizing that she was asking a blind man to get wood.

"Certainly." He stood with his cane and walked to the door.

She smiled, thinking about how easily he did that and noticing that he seemed different, somehow.

"It's ready, *mon petit*." Her grandmother walked in with the soup bowls. "The soup is in a tureen. I will return with that in a moment."

Before Bethany could utter a word, her Grandmère returned to the kitchen for the soup. She was returning at the same time Matthew opened the door, carrying a couple of logs.

"Can I help you, Matthew?" she said.

"No. I think I have this. I can feel the direction of the heat," he returned, tapping toward the fireplace. Once he placed the logs, he returned to where Bethany stood next to the table.

Leaning in for her to hear, he whispered. "I must make myself learn to get around. I can do this. I am still capable—but I must make myself do things I found easier before. I cannot be a burden to those around me." He kissed her lightly on the cheek and moved to the seat next to hers.

Grandmère walked into the room with the soup and placed it in the middle of the table.

Bethany watched Matthew take his cane and follow the chairs around the table. At Grandmère's chair, he pulled it out, waiting for her to sit. He repeated the same for her and, skipping the chair next to her, he helped her aunt into her chair. Her heart tugged as she watched the gentleman she had rescued from a broken battlefield settle into his chair.

CHAPTER SEVENTEEN

MATTHEW'S CONVERSATION WITH Aunt Theodosia had been uplifting for him. He admired the woman whose sight had been gone most of her life. She was happy and content here, helping people.

He recalled his feelings when he had dove into the water after Bethany. It was a little heady. Matthew felt alive and able to contribute for the first time in weeks. Her voice had led him to her. He saved her. He had not allowed himself to think about it before, but as he reflected, he realized he was capable. Nevertheless, it could be some time before he felt ready to leave. Aunt Theodosia had offered to teach him the things she had learned which might help him, if he could spare a few weeks to stay here and learn.

He had not immediately responded, but as he thought about it, it seemed right. He felt better about things.

"Bethany," he spoke up. "Your aunt has invited me to stay here for a little while. She wishes to help me learn more ways to overcome my . . . loss of sight." It was still difficult to say. He reached for her hand next to him. "I would like to take her up on that."

"She will be delighted," Bethany returned, her voice animated.

The time together would give him more time to examine his

feelings. He had grown attached to Bethany, but was it gratitude or something more? He would not break her heart—not on purpose. However, he could not deny the attraction that he felt toward her.

"What a marvelous idea!" Grandmère added, scooping soup into their bowls. "I hope you don't mind my serving the soup. Much of the crab has settled to the bottom of the tureen and I want everyone to enjoy it. So, I ladle from the bottom as I fill the bowls."

Matthew nodded, smiling. For the first time since the battle, he felt positive about his future. "I think I would make a mess of that," he snickered, causing the rest of the table to laugh as well.

"Perhaps we can take the boat out later in the week and check the crab traps," Bethany offered cheerfully. "It makes a delightful meal. I had hoped we could have a crab boil on one of the warmer days. Matthew would enjoy that."

"Are those the cages with the rope? And what is a crab boil?" Matthew recalled the rope that he had cut in the main channel.

She laughed. "Yes. The same. They should not be hanging in the center of the channel. And most people have a floater on the water, signaling where they are. Perhaps my foot got caught on one that had been abandoned," Bethany replied, a tremor to her voice.

"It will be awhile before I forget about that moment, too," he said. "I am happy that we are here . . . now."

She cleared her throat and continued. "A crab boil is an enormous pot full of crabs boiling with spices. The meat is delicious."

"I am intrigued about the crab boil," he responded.

Aunt Theodosia offered a quick blessing. He wished he could see how she ate soup without making a mess of herself. No matter. He would take his time. Certainly, he knew where to find his lips. He grinned at the thought.

Leaning over the heated bowl of soup, he took his spoon and began. With each mouthful of soup, he felt the urge to smile, but resisted, determined not to make a total fool of himself.

"I was curious," he said, looking up at no one in particular. "This seems to be an old plantation. What is the history of it?"

"Ah. You are very observant," Aunt Theodosia replied with a smile in her voice. "The Bellovere family, a powerful family, once lived here. The source of their money was trading—some believed it had origins in slave trading, although they did not continue the horrid practice. It is rumored they originated from France."

"I believe I have heard the name. Perhaps it is through my association with the earlier Napoleonic wars," Matthew replied.

"They also traded goods. When I was a young girl, there were rumors associating the family with pirates, although that was largely speculation. No one ever proved anything. It was the fever that depleted the family, however. They had a series of unfortunate illnesses that wiped out much of the family until only a few survived. The mistress of the household was very charitable and left the plantation to people that had no other place—those stricken with leprosy. She had been a friend of mine growing up, and that is how I ended up with this house. It had been a small house that was used for the widows of the masters over the years when their children married."

"Ah . . . a dowager cottage," he said.

"Yes. My friend lived here before she died. I took care of her. As you know, my sister and I are fortunate to know herbal medicine, a knowledge passed down through our family," she said on a note of sadness. "Bethany has learned much of it. Her mother was excellent."

He hesitated to ask about the neighbors but ventured, anyway. "And the people . . . next door." He cleared his throat, unsure about how to ask this without insulting his hostess. "I have barely heard of leprosy. How are you able to help them without catching it?"

"I have always fashioned a cloth cover over my nose and mouth, if need be," she responded. "It has long been my belief the air transports small particles of sickness—bad humors—to our bodies. I have no way to know for sure, of course. However, by wearing my covering, I have never caught the disease."

"Ahh," he answered, thinking back to school. There were many examples in history where masks were believed helpful. "That makes sense. I was thinking of what I had learned of the plague. Masks were used if I recall my history. Several whacks on my knuckles in school secured my attention to the lesson," he laughed.

The four of them laughed. The sound relaxed him.

"You were in trouble a lot?" Aunt Theo asked, curious.

"I was always involved in... activities," he responded smoothly. "And I have always had a special ability to conjure up a good time. My friends call me the Viscount of Excess; I take trouble to new heights." His tone was somber as he thought about his friends. They were as close as brothers. He missed them.

"You are a lord?" Grandmère asked.

"It is a title. But yes. My father is an earl," he said matter-of-factly, wishing he had not mentioned his title.

"Grandmère, if there is more, I should enjoy another small bowl. Some meals are worth repeating," Bethany laughed.

"My! I am truly flattered. You eat like a bird. It's rare that you ever get additional helpings of anything," Grandmère replied with a chuckle. The older woman ladled another healthy serving of the soup.

"I confess, I missed your cooking," Bethany said. "This is very good!"

"It is, indeed. Meals with the military are bad. The food has been a positive for me," Matthew quipped jovially. "That, of course, includes Miss Phillips' meals."

"I am honored, then. It's always good for the cook's food to be so appreciated," her grandmother replied.

Matthew got up from the table and made his way to his room. He felt more than tired and welcomed the rest.

Bethany watched Matthew leave the table. He looked a little like he did when he was recovering from the fevers—washed out. Probably a good night's rest would restore him to his usual self. She had been famished and thoroughly enjoyed the crab soup. It had been a while since Grandmère had made it. Before she left the table, she wanted to make her aunt and Grandmère aware of the boat and man she had seen earlier. It had plagued her mind the rest of the evening. The whole thing just seemed so unsettling.

"Grandmère, when I was walking the grounds with Matthew this afternoon, I saw a man in a pirogue, parked across the water, hidden beneath the branches of a cypress tree. Is that usual? I do not want to be difficult. It's just that I have had an unpleasant visitor or so in the past month and I have become guarded."

"I cannot believe that Mr. Smoot was one of those. That disheartens me, greatly," Grandmère said. "As to this man you describe, I have never noticed him. I wonder what business he could have here. It is alarming. We are off the beaten path. The old Bellovere Plantation houses the colony, and there is very little traffic here. When there is, it is usually strangers."

"That is as I thought," Bethany replied, feeling uneasy. "There was a man that visited me ahead of Mr. Smoot. Of course, he did not steal my boat. But he visited the day after the battle, looking for a soldier. He said they had seen me on the battlefield. I have played it over in my head many times, fearful that I made some sort of mistake."

"This man," her aunt interjected. "Who did he say he was searching for? Did he give a name?"

"He did. A Lord Longueville. I did not know a lord," Bethany answered.

"Matthew is a lord. How well do you know the colonel?" asked her aunt.

"We have gotten to know each other very well," replied Bethany, feeling the heat rising in her neck. *Where was this leading?* "I assure you, nothing improper has occurred between us if you are thinking along those lines."

"*Non, cher.* Not at all," Grandmère said. "Aunt Theodosia is only asking questions to parse this into making some sense." The older woman patted Bethany's hand. "Was the man looking for an American soldier or an English one?"

"He never told me. However, my thought at the time was he was searching for a British soldier. And certainly, I asked the name. Yet, the name he gave was not who I knew the man in the bed to be." Bethany noticed her grandmère's back stiffen a little.

"This man . . . could he have been the one in the canoe that you saw?"

Bethany felt a chill hit her stomach. It was a feeling that she usually equated with feeling ill. Was she . . . going to be ill? "I do not know, Grandmère."

"I can see you growing pale, dear. I am not asking these questions to make you feel bad. Our point in asking them is because Matthew could be who the man may be looking for. It makes sense if you realize that often lords have several titles—a surname, as well as a title. Did you mention who the man was looking for to Matthew?"

Bethany felt that chill spread throughout her body. She had not shared the name with Matthew. She had only heard him say a name she was unfamiliar with, and she responded curtly and sent the man packing. It had been most inhospitable of her, although she was not in the habit of entertaining men, much less housing one in her home, alone. "No, I did not," she said in a meek tone. "Oh Grandmère, what have I done?" She placed her head in her hands.

She felt her aunt's warm hand on her shoulder. "Shush, child, *mon petit.* You could not have known. We have never discussed such a thing. The important thing is to watch to see if the man comes back. If he does, we must ask him more questions."

"I should also talk to Matthew. He may be furious with me. I believe the British have departed the area, and with them his chances to leave with his people," she said in a shaky voice.

"Pish! If this man is looking for Matthew, we shall endeavor to help him get Matthew home. However, I have a feeling he will know what to do on his own. Did you not say he was an ... investigator?" Grandmère's voice was soothing.

"Bethany, you followed your instincts. You must always trust them. If it is meant for Matthew to leave with this man, I believe he will show himself again. However, we should like to know more about him. Did he give a name?"

"His name was Mr. Sinclair. I told Matthew about him, giving him the man's name, and he had no recognition of it." Bethany felt a little better as she recalled that tidbit. "There was no way Matthew could have traveled, Grandmère. He was fevered for days and slept off and on for almost a week after I extracted the bullet and debrided the wound. He appeared close to death when I found him."

"Hmm," her grandmother said, smiling. "He looks very much alive now."

Bethany blushed. She recognized her grandmother's astuteness, a trait she showed when she was musing over pieces to an interesting situation. "What are you saying, Grandmère?"

Her Grandmère laughed. "Only that he seems very interested in you. I dare say that if this man is someone that is searching for Matthew, Matthew will not feel bad that you did not realize it. He seems most taken with you, *mon petit*."

Bethany thought of Matthew's passionate kisses and her responses to them, and the blush deepened. "I cannot be sure what you mean," she responded, trying to look nonchalantly toward the hall. "I suppose I should rest as well." She rose from the table and noticed her aunt touch her grandmother's arm, knowingly. "If you hear a man's screams, it is probably Matthew. He has been having nightmares almost every night. He talks a lot but does it in such a rush, I cannot understand his words. Sometimes he laughs and I think he is with friends in his dreams." She caught her Grandmère's look and realized too late she had said enough.

"I should go to bed," she said, gathering hers and Matthew's bowls and utensils and taking them to the kitchen. "I will do the dishes in the morning if that is acceptable," she added meekly. She was now full of worry she had turned away a man that could have helped Matthew get home, and the concern did not sit well with her. She had never meant to do anything but help and protect him. *He may not forgive her if he were to find out.*

"Nonsense. You go to bed. However, take Dandie out, first," Grandmère said.

How could she have completely forgotten about Dandie? She searched the room for her before she remembered Matthew had gone to bed early. "I will bet she is with Matthew. The little pup has been spending time with both of us."

"How unusual," her grandmother said, amusement clear.

"Yes. I find it very unusual considering she greeted every man she met until Matthew with growling and barking. She does not approve of them . . . until he came along. Now I share her." She did not feel bad. After all, Dandie had proven an astute judge of character.

"Go to bed, Bethany. Tomorrow is another day. I think we should sort this out with Matthew, however. If you did not share the name of the man the investigator was looking for before, perhaps doing so will help Matthew know that his family is looking for him."

Grandmère's advice was sound. And she hated it. Feeling gut-punched by her own actions, Bethany retreated to her grandmother's bedroom. She found Dandie waiting on the bed. The little dog raised its head as if to say, *what took you so long?* before dropping her head back to the mattress and falling asleep. A few minutes later, she felt the dog get up and move to her pillow, wrapping her lithe little body around the top edge of Bethany's pillow. Bethany liked this. It felt comforting and helped her sleep. Her last thought before she fell asleep was of the feel of Matthew's hands around her waist as he hoisted her onto the boat, and it brought a smile to her lips.

CHAPTER EIGHTEEN

Matthew woke the next morning feeling only somewhat better. *What in the world was the matter with him?* Soup had never left him sick. His stomach was usually cast iron, yet today, nausea hit him. His dreams had been vivid, and he recalled much of them. In one, he had dreamed of Bethany. His mind's eye had conjured Bethany from the touch and feel of her. She was beautiful with rich, brown hair.

In another, he dreamed of a rogue alligator. Of course, he knew what a gator looked like, but in the dream, this one had hurled itself from the water into a small boat. *Their boat.* He tried to protect Bethany, yet no matter what he did, he failed. When she fell into the water full of hungry gators, he feared he had lost her. She was gone, save for her voice, which he heard in a distance. *But where?* He stripped off his shirt and dove blindly into the dark, brackish water, opening his eyes and realizing the water was clear. He could see her just beyond him . . . so close, only no matter what he did, he could not reach her.

Whether it was the frustration of his dreams or the uncomfortable heat from the sunlight in his room, he opened his eyes and noticed the shapes of shadows and objects around the room. They had left the curtains open, allowing the first rays of sunshine to stream into the room and wake him. Matthew had seen them open when he came to bed, but had felt too tired to close them.

It felt similar to what he normally experienced at home, although the way it was done had always irritated him. Rather than simply waking him, Bart irritatingly always pulled the drapes and ushered in the sunlight when it was time to wake. The man would say it was the most effective way to rouse him—and did it wherever they were. *If there was one thing he would change,* he thought, squeezing his eyes tightly closed... then he remembered that his valet... who had also been his batman... was no longer with him. Inexplicable sadness swept over him. The battle... everything... had happened so quickly. And the one before it.

The Americans had proven to be crafty foes, using this untamed wilderness as their partner in crime. No one thought the Americans would win the last battle. Yet they had. So many on both sides had died for this war. The reasons still seemed vague and insufficient for President Madison to declare war. Except for the defense of the Canadian territory, the rest of it made little sense. Taking their men and making them serve the British Navy angered the fledgling new country. They went to war with Britain even though the French did the same thing—unbelievably, America allied with the French! It was a war few understood or took seriously. *Except it was serious.* Men had died beside him. He might have died, if not for Bethany and Dandie.

He felt a small headache emerging and cast it off as the result of bright sunlight in his eyes. Shaking off the sleep, he pulled himself up and swung his legs over the edge of his bed, before leaning over. His stomach felt a little like it did when he and his friends returned from a night of carousing. He leaned over and then back, trying to stretch his body.

A knock at the door roused him from his musings. "Who is it?"

"It is Grandmère. I was just letting you know breakfast will be ready in about ten minutes."

"Thank you. I will dress quickly," he said. He pulled up his pants and tucked in his white shirt. Frustrated, he strained to see his boots, before remembering he had been wearing Bethany's grandfather's shoes. "Ahh. There they are." He felt around the floor and found the corner of one sticking out from under the bed.

He wiped his eyes with the heels of his hands, a habit he always had when he woke up to clear the sleep. It made no difference when he could not see, he realized. His face felt warm, and he swiped at it, feeling the growth of his beard and wondering if he could get someone to shave him. He had never been fond of the scruffy look and wanted to rid his face of the beard. Seeing the hazy image of what appeared to be a wash bin, he took his walking stick and made his way to it. It had fresh water and a bar of soap. Quickly, he wet his face and washed it, before wiping off the residual soap and drying it. *At least a clean face feels much better,* he thought. Instinctively, he knew Grandmère had left the soap. He would thank her and perhaps ask her if there was a razor to be had. Cutting the beard might make him feel much better—maybe not as warm as he was feeling.

He wondered how Bethany had slept as he opened the door. He did not have to wonder long. She was in the dining room when he arrived.

"Good morning, Bethany," he grinned.

"How do you always know it's me?" she asked cheerfully.

"You smell like honeysuckle. I think it must be your soap. I rather like it," he answered quietly, leaning over her shoulder. He hoped to keep his answer between the two of them.

"Ah! We make our soap, and honeysuckle is plentiful in the spring and summer. I had forgotten how keen your nose has become," she giggled. "Aunt Theo's ham, grits, and biscuits are all I can smell." She touched his hand as he slid it from her shoulder, stopping him. "Perhaps we can take another walk around the property this morning if you are interested in stretching your legs."

He started to answer when he heard the footsteps approaching. Instead, he squeezed her hand and moved to stand behind the seat next to her.

"Good morning, you two," Grandmère said as she walked into the room. "My stomach is crying out to break my fast, this morning."

The subtle sound of a tapping cane signaled that Aunt Theo was with her sister. He waited for both ladies to sit before seating himself.

Once the two ladies sat down, they passed the bowls of food around.

"Thank you for bringing the ham, Bethany. I had just mentioned to your grandmother before you arrived that pork would be a pleasant change of pace," Aunt Theo said, taking a bite from her plate. "What are your plans for today?"

"I was hoping someone could shave this beard that is taking up permanent residence on my face," Matthew joked.

"I always enjoyed shaving my husband's face and would be happy to do that for you, if you have no objection," Grandmère offered. She turned to her sister. "Theo, do you have a razor?"

"I have not held a razor in years, but perhaps in the top drawer of the dresser in your room, there could be one. I stored Ned's things there when you lost him to the fever. There could be one," her sister replied quietly.

"I had forgotten about that box of Ned's belongings. Thank you, Sister. And it will honor me to use it to trim that beard off you, Matthew," Grandmère said.

"Perhaps afterward, we could be a little lazy and take a walk. I also thought we might cast a line for some fish, for dinner," Bethany added between sips of her morning coffee.

"That sounds wonderful. I am going to dry some of the herbs you brought so I can make soap. Matthew may want something besides our floral-scented ones. You could walk some of the rest of the herbs to Mr. Duplantis, next door," Grandmère added. "They will appreciate the winter herbs."

"I would be glad to do that, Grandmère," Bethany said. "But I did not think to bring any face scarves."

"I have them and I've already soaked them in herbs, so they will handle the foul humors. They are hanging on the back of the pantry door. I will retrieve two for you," Grandmère offered. Before they could say a word, she stood, left, and returned with two white muslin scarves. "After you use them, just leave them in the empty pail next to the door. I have some washing to do before we leave and can clean them with the other things. You can even leave the herbs on the porch if you are uncomfortable."

"Thank you, Grandmère."

"You have explained to the colonel about our neighbors, I am assuming," Grandmère continued. "Matthew, no one knows what causes leprosy, but we are very careful in our associations. It is minimal and usually is just talking over the fence. However, when we meet, we cover our noses and mouths with herbal scented scarves and do not touch them. It is sad, but we have learned to co-exist this way. It is a small group of people—a family."

"Bethany explained that to me. It makes sense, although I fear your thinking is more progressive than most," he responded.

"Using the scarves to cover our mouth and nose? That is not new, Son," Grandmère explained. "As you mentioned earlier, it was used as far back as the days of the plague by the doctors treating victims. The masks were heavy and made with a pronounced nose. They stuffed herbs and spices in the beak as a barrier to the miasmas carried by air. De Vinci used covers over his face while painting to keep the smells of the chemicals in his paints from affecting him.

"It seems to be effective, but one never knows except through trial and error. The affliction seems to be hereditary, as people in this colony are all related. We help them with herbal medicines and things they need and occasionally visit to help if someone is sick. They are respectful and do not wish to spread their disease, so they maintain distance."

"Remarkable," he murmured.

"Yes, and sadly or fortunately, depending on your perspective, it keeps people away from our neck of the woods," her grandmother replied. "You are very concerned about something, Bethany. What is it?"

"Nothing. I wanted to fish and thought Johnny might like to join us. Have you seen him lately?" Bethany asked.

"He was here the day before you arrived and fished off the dock. I think his father was with him. His father, Dom, brought the crab we ate in the soup last evening." Aunt Theo added.

"Perhaps we should not visit Aunt Theo, but will instead, leave the herbs and speak from the porch. It will keep the visit shorter, and I would love to relax and catch some fish."

"That sounds like a good idea," agreed Grandmère.

Bethany could feel her grandmother's scrutiny over Matthew's condition, and that worried her. "Grandmère, we should be back soon, and you can shave Matthew's beard."

"Thank you, Bethany," Grandmère responded and turned to Matthew. "It will be good for the two of you to relax after that harrowing trip, here. You look peaked. The exertion from yesterday seems to have taken a toll on you. I had hoped a good night's sleep would be enough, but you appear to need a bit more."

He still felt fatigued and did not know what to make of it. It concerned him he looked ill. Normally, he felt quite energetic. He would take a walk with Bethany and take the herbs to the neighbors. "Perhaps you are right," he admitted. "I do still feel a little tired."

Thirty minutes later, he and Bethany were on their way next door. Bethany showed him where the gate was that opened onto the old plantation grounds. He could see the shapes of the buildings and, with the sun, make out a little more detail. *Was his sight still changing? He hoped so. He prayed for it.*

BETHANY WAS WORRIED. At first, she wondered if Matthew had

gotten sick from the soup served last evening. It had been delicious from her perspective. Bad seafood could make you very sick. Yet, crabs never lasted long enough to go bad, and her grandmother always threw out shrimp if they were not eaten. Usually, they ate them fairly quickly. When he had not complained of queasiness, she decided it had not been the soup. Yet, he was pale again today. She monitored Matthew, almost willing him to feel better.

Bethany had hoped he would feel better because there was so much she hoped to tell him about—realizing he still could not see—in the area. She had not been here in some time and wanted to look in on Johnny, who lived with his family in a small cabin on the plantation next door. The family had an arrangement—food for a place to live. They provided fresh fish and vegetables for the family next door, and in exchange, they lived in a small cabin away from the main house for free.

Johnny was eight or nine years old. Often, he kept Aunt Theo busy, helping her around her house. The child always smiled. He never seemed to feel sorry for himself that he had no other companions around. It made him that much more magnetic. Dandie enjoyed playing with him. Hide and seek was his favorite game, and fishing was his favorite pastime. She hoped he could throw in a line with her and Matthew.

As they approached the steps, she felt Matthew's hand clasp hers and squeeze it. They walked up the steps and she knocked on the door, then stepped back toward the edge of the porch, giving Mr. Duplantis room to step out without being close. Even though they had the scarves to protect them from the bad miasmas, they only made her think about the disease more.

Perhaps she should not have brought Matthew here. But if she had not, she would have risked being arrested and his being taken a prisoner. In his condition, she was not sure the outcome would have been good.

The door opened and Mr. Duplantis, a tall, greying man with his head and hands wrapped in cotton cloths, stepped out. Only his hair, eyes, and mouth were exposed. His clothes were loose-fitting cotton garments, and he wore sandals on his feet. While the clothing may have been comfortable, Bethany always thought the strips of cotton around his hands and face had to have been uncomfortable in the Louisiana heat. Mr. Duplantis' blue eyes filled with mirth and, as always, the man had a pleasant word for everyone.

"Miss Bethany! It's mighty good to see you." He looked at Matthew. "And who is this young man?"

"Mr. Duplantis, this is my friend, Colonel Matthew Romney," Bethany replied. "We arrived yesterday." She held out the herbs. "I picked these herbs from the Villeré Plantation's garden and thought you might enjoy them."

"Goodness! A man from the other side. There has to be a good accounting with that, Miss Bethany," he said lightly. "We could hear the fighting all the way here a few weeks back. With your Grandmère here, I worried for your safety," Mr. Duplantis said.

Her neighbor was a man who never minced words. She chuckled. "Yes! I can honestly say that in retrospect, I should have worried more about my safety. It's a long story, but all seems well, for now. Colonel Romney was most gravely injured and left for dead. Dandie found him and we helped him back to the house where he has mostly recovered," she explained, knowing the man would be empathetic toward Matthew's plight.

The older man gave a nod of his head. "So many good people on both sides of this nasty conflict. Makes me very thankful for our small spot on this planet and the goodness that surrounds us. Colonel Romney, it is good to meet you."

Matthew gave a brief bow. "Thank you, sir. I realize that this may be awkward. But Miss Phillips has been most kind in her efforts to aid my plight. I would ask that you not share that I am with her, to minimize any retribution brought to her," Matthew said.

"Certainly. I understand. There is much to recommend Miss

Phillips' generosity, and I would not wish her harm by anyone's hand. Your secret is safe. I appreciate the trust that she and her family have in me and my family. We would never place them in any danger."

He turned to Bethany. "*Merci*, Miss Bethany. Your generosity is always appreciated. Do not worry about your young man. With you and your Grandmère to help him, I expect he will make as full a recovery as anyone has a chance of making."

"Thank you, Mr. Duplantis. Would you mind if we fish off the dock in front of your home? We thought it would be an excellent way to relax with the warmer weather we seem to have."

"Certainly, you may. I would join you, but I am eager to finish drying these herbs. I am sure that my missus will want to use them in the kitchen with her soap-making." He picked up the bag of herbs and started to leave, before turning back. "A man was hanging around here yesterday. Just over there," he said, pointing to the overhanging cypress branches in a pirogue. "I noticed him around the mid-afternoon. Dark-headed man. He's new around here."

"Thank you for the warning. I do not know who he could be," Bethany replied, feeling icy fear in the pit of her stomach. *Did someone follow them here?* She swallowed hard. "Have you seen little Johnny? We were hoping to fish today, and I wanted him to play with Dandie."

"Ah, your cute little dog. He seems to enjoy the puppy. He is usually down here every day, but I did not see him yesterday. Perhaps, he will join you today."

"*Merci*, Mr. Duplantis. Let us know if you require anything else, or if your wife needs more of the herbs. My grandmother may spare more," she grinned.

She watched her aunt's neighbor go back into his house, and she and Matthew walked back toward her aunt's. "I wonder who he spoke of," she murmured.

"I am not sure," Matthew said, maneuvering his walking stick to his right hand and clasping Bethany's right hand with his left. "I do not want anyone in trouble because of me."

"No," Bethany replied. "Of course, you do not. No one is going to get in trouble. We are safe, here."

She realized they were alone, and in a place that could be private for a moment. They had walked back into her aunt's yard but were still out of sight of the windows and behind the brick wall, near a cast iron garden bench. "What is it, Matthew? You seem anxious about something."

"I am. I do not know what is happening with my sight, but it seems to improve, steadily, which makes me happy. Things are still very blurry, though. And I have missed holding and kissing you." He set his cane against the bench and leaned down, tilting her head up and gently brushing her lips with his own. His kisses took on urgency as he pulled her closer, his tongue gently gaining entry into her mouth and swirling softly against the sides.

She wanted time to stand still—this time with her in his arms and his lips on hers. She could think of no more perfect moment. Needing to be closer still, her tongue met his and played artfully in his mouth, as he had shown her with his kisses. As she did, a feeling of alarm hit her. His mouth seemed much hotter than usual and his hands, still holding her face, were very warm. Despite a growing need to stay in this delicious moment, Bethany pulled back, panting. "Matthew, I do not want to stop kissing, but your skin... you are too warm." She looked up at the sickly pallor of his face and grew more alarmed. "You are sick. I fear you have a fever."

"I confess I do not feel well, of a sudden," he said.

"Here, let's sit on the bench and see if you feel better." She backed him up slowly, and the two of them sat on the bench. She studied his face and noticed that his color was returning. "When you are feeling better, we should make it into the house."

"I am not sure what is going on. I was feeling great until last evening. I feel better at this moment. Perhaps you are right. We should go into the house," he agreed.

The two of them made their way onto the porch and then into the house. "Grandmère, please come quick. Matthew is not feeling well."

Aunt Theo and Grandmère met them at the same time in the front room of the house. "I heard you come in and heard my name," Grandmère said, wiping her hands on her apron. "I was just preparing to make soup with the wonderful herbs. I made some liquid soap to use for your shave," she said, before noticing how pale the man in front of her had become.

"He is hot to the touch, Grandmère," Bethany added. "Aunt Theo, do you still have that willow bark? I feel we should make some tea with it." A slight chuckle escaped. "He does not like it but tolerates it."

He heard her and gave a weak laugh. "I fear that was my first actual memory when I gathered my faculties—Bethany feeding me this horrid tea. But it made me feel better."

"Yes, let's get you to your room, Matthew," Aunt Theo agreed. "I will brew you some of that favored tea."

He laughed again but took his cane and made his way to the back bedroom that he had used the night before. "I feel like I have been a tremendous burden," he muttered. "I do not know if I will ever be able to repay the kindness you continue to show me."

"Nonsense, young man. You are our guest and Bethany's friend. This is the very thing that we enjoy doing... helping others," Grandmère replied.

Matthew sat on the edge of the bed, and Bethany helped with his shoes and helped him move his legs back onto the bed. His eyes closed nearly immediately, and his shoulders relaxed. She had dragged him out to the neighbors when he was sick. Bethany felt terrible.

Grandmère smiled and gently touched Bethany's shoulder, showing her approval when she noticed the shoes Matthew had been wearing.

"Perhaps we should get this willow bark into him before he gets to sleep," Aunt Theodosia said, tapping her cane into the room, holding a mug of tea in her free hand.

"That's a good idea," Bethany said. "Leave it with me, and I will get it into him."

"Oh, and I have this for him." Her aunt dug into her pocket and withdrew a small pot of aloe. "Put a little of this over his eyes. Perhaps it will help. Not using his eyes, they could be dry."

"You don't need any help, then?"

"No, just find Dandie. She wandered out with us, and I did not see her when we came into the house."

"I'll get her," volunteered Grandmère. "You take care of Matthew."

Bethany tugged on his shoulder. "Matthew, drink this before you doze off."

At her urging, Matthew opened his eyes and accepted the cup of tea. He sipped it, looked at her in between tastes. "Thank you, Bethany. Please tell your grandmother and aunt how sorry I am for this." His voice was thick and slow. She could tell he struggled to focus.

"Nonsense. Drink up and let us hope you feel better after a nap." Bethany wondered what he would think of her when he could finally see her—if that ever happened. That he could see at all seemed a miracle. She would not worry about what he thought of her, she decided, taking the empty cup from him. She watched his eyes shutter as he fell asleep and leaned in and kissed his forehead. "Sleep well, Matthew."

Chapter Nineteen

"How is the colonel feeling, child?" her aunt asked her when she returned the cup to the kitchen.

"He fell asleep after he drank the willow bark tea and so far, does not appear better. He seems worse than when he went to bed last evening. I'm worried," she replied.

"I agree," Aunt Theo said.

"Your grandmother plans to trim his beard when he wakes up from his nap. It could make him feel better, less hot." Aunt Theo turned to her. "We need to determine his symptoms and make him more comfortable, even if we don't know what is wrong, just yet." She reached out and touched Bethany's hand. "Your colonel probably has something that will pass quickly. Just keep an eye on him."

"He isn't *my colonel*," protested Bethany, suppressing a smile.

Aunt Theo chuckled. "If you say so, *mon petit*. I cannot see, but I can hear. And I hear his heart in his voice when he talks of you, a softening."

Bethany felt the heat rise on her neck. She knew her aunt stopped short of commenting on Bethany's obvious feelings. "I just want for him to feel better. I had hoped we could fish today. That reminds me. Grandmère must still be in the yard looking for Dandie. I will join her. Excuse me, Aunt." With that, Bethany shot out the door, her heart in her throat. There were untold dangers out here for her little dog. It had been very careless of her to forget that Dandie was behind her. As she thought about it, the little dog had not gone over to the Duplantis' place, either. Panicked, she ran around the house calling the dog.

"Dandie, where are you?" It was February, but snakes never sleep in the Bayou. "Dandie! Where are you?" Panicking, she felt bile rising in her throat.

At the sound of Dandie's familiar bark, Bethany rounded the back of the house and saw her grandmère reaching down and patting the little dog. Johnny stood next to the two of them. She relaxed and let out a sigh when she saw her dog was safe and unharmed. "Dandie, you worried me. You know better than to take off like that."

"She was with me, Miss Bethany," the little boy cheerfully piped up. "I came through the back gate and she spotted me, she did."

Her grandmother gave a slight nod and walked back into the house.

"*Bonjour* Johnny! I'm so glad to see you. I asked Mr. Duplantis if he had seen you. I have a friend I cannot wait to introduce you to, but he became ill, so maybe later," she said excitedly.

"My pa came home yesterday morning. I was helping him in the fields. He's leaving to go back to New Orleans soon." He slapped at his left arm before reaching down to pet Dandie. "Darn skeeters."

"It's nice that you've gotten to spend time with your pa." She had not realized Mr. Roeux had been spending time apart from the family. "How are you and your little sister, Amy, doing?"

"Pa brought her a doll from the city. She is happy, happy. He brung me some new hooks for my fishing pole!"

"That's wonderful," Bethany responded, smiling down at the boy. "So, your father works in the city, now?"

Johnny shrugged. "He says there are opportunities, right now. He comes home mostly ever' weekend to help Ma with the crops. I help her, too. Pa says I'm the man of the house when he's gone."

Bethany smiled as he straightened his shoulders and stood up taller.

"Pa says he likes where we live, it being quiet and all." Johnny squinted in the distance for a moment, as if looking for something. "Pa says he likes the pay better in New Orleans, he does," he added, "but he likes living here in the sticks."

How *curious*, she thought, but gave it no more consideration as she turned to her dog who was holding a small ball in her mouth. "Dandie, when I call you, come." The fright had made her irritated. "Give Johnny back his ball." Her spunky little white dog shot her an innocent look, hanging her tongue out the side of her mouth while she wagged the entire backend of her body. "Drop it." She commanded, softly. The dog complied, and Bethany picked up the ball and handed it to the boy.

"Reckon we might fish tomorrow?" the boy asked, thoughtfully. His gaze was still on the river, and Bethany turned to look at what he was seeing.

"What is it, Johnny?" she asked, seeing ripples in the water. "An alligator?" The thought gave her shivers.

"Nah. It's a man. I saw him here a day or so before," he replied, nonchalantly.

The alligator would have vexed her less. "Do you know him?" She felt a familiar fear in the pit of her stomach. *Had someone followed them?*

"Johnny, can you describe this man?" she said, worrying her bottom lip.

"He had long hair and was dirty looking," Johnny said, screwing up his face. "He was in an old canoe and pulled up to the dock. Asked if I knew you. I said no," he said, visibly worried.

"Did he say anything else?" she pressed.

"No. No, he pushed off and left the way he had come," the little boy said emphatically.

"That is odd. I cannot think." Her voice fell off. *Caleb Smoot!* How could he have known where her aunt lived?

"Johnny, if you see him again, please come and find me," she said in measured tones, still worried about how he found her aunt. She needed to ask her Grandmère if she had said something when she treated his father. "I should take Dandie back inside. I'd like to feed her a little early."

She started to invite the young man to dinner but wasn't sure what was wrong with Matthew and thought better of it. "I might want to cast a line tomorrow," she said instead. "You are my favorite fishing partner . . . I thought I would see what your plans might be." She grinned.

"That'd sure be nice, Miss Bethany. We'd pass a good time and I'll bring home dinner, jest like Pa does."

She hugged the child and mussed up his hair, affectionately. "Thank you for playing with Dandie, Johnny. I will see you tomorrow." With Dandie in tow, she returned to the house. When the screened door closed behind her, Bethany turned and watched the whistling little boy open the back gate and head toward home.

Entering the house, Bethany found her aunt and grandmother at the kitchen table, their heads bent down in a discussion. Grandmère looked up and motioned for her to join them.

"What's wrong, Grandmère?" Bethany sighed inwardly. Could this day get any worse?

"Your colonel seems very sick. His fever is fairly high," she said. "Has he complained of anything?"

Bethany ignored the playful jab. Instead, she thought about what Grandmère asked. "He did not complain. Besides appearing so pale, he has only acknowledged feeling fevered. I noticed he was flushed and touched his skin earlier, just before we came inside. He was very hot. I felt so bad that I had taken him to meet Mr. Duplantis."

"Child, you had nothing to do with this. And you did not make it worse. You know that. We should keep the willow bark going and see if we can bring down the fever. Poor fella." Her aunt pushed a cup of hot willow bark tea toward Bethany.

"Would you like to give it to him?"

"Sure. Has he awakened?"

"No, but I think he should have the tea at regular intervals to fight the fever," her grandmother responded.

"Thank you, Grandmère." Bethany picked up the tea and then set it down. "I should tell you what I just learned."

"You look worried sick, Bethany. What is it?" Grandmère asked.

"Please, tell us what is wrong, child," her aunt added.

"It's Caleb Smoot. I think he followed us. Johnny described a man that has been hanging around outside—and it sounds like Caleb. Not only did he break into our house, but he was stealing my boat when I found him. Did I tell you that Dandie attacked him and bit a piece of his ear? Matthew held him at gunpoint, while I tied him up. Luckily, Tobias Smith arrived and took him with him. He promised to take care of the situation. Something must be wrong. I cannot imagine Tobias knows Smoot is here," she finished.

"The man is blind, and he saves you from drowning and being bitten by a gator. And now I find out he helped hold off Smoot?" The older woman leaned back and hooted. "That colonel of yours is some catch, granddaughter. We need to get him well!"

Her aunt joined her in her mirth. Frustrated, Bethany picked up the cup and started down the hall to Matthew's room. They ignored what she had tried to tell them about Caleb Smoot. Grandmère never commented on it. Bethany wondered if she had gotten it wrong. Maybe it wasn't him. But inside, she knew it was. She recalled his nastiness when he heard Matthew's accent. He hated the British, but he was not alone in that. Many of her countrymen had not found favor with the English.

Why was Caleb Smoot hanging around the plantation?

Dandie jumped off the couch and followed Bethany. They stopped in front of Matthew's room. Bethany could hear him talking inside. She recognized the voice he used when he spoke in his sleep. It was fast, and he mumbled. She knocked on the door, hoping to draw his attention. No answer. She lifted her fist to knock again when the door opened. "Bethany. Is everything all right?"

"How did you know it was me, Matthew," she asked in a light-hearted manner.

Matthew looked pale, and his cheeks were hot. "As I have said, you smell like honeysuckle, Bethany. I am thinking it's becoming my favorite flower." He grinned.

"I brought you some tea. We need to control the fever."

Dandie licked his hand.

He nodded. "Will you sit with me? I feel dizzy and my head hurts. I hate to complain, but things feel like they are getting worse, and I don't know what's wrong."

His voice sounded strained and weak. "Let me get this chair, Matthew. You should sit."

"That sounds like a good idea," he replied feebly.

As he drew closer to the chair, he lost his footing and hit the floor.

"Matthew!" Bethany shoved the cup of tea onto the small dresser and moved down by his side, cradling his head. "Grandmère, Aunt Theo, please come quickly," she yelled in a trembling voice.

"What happened?" Grandmère asked.

"He got dizzy and fell—I could not catch him. Help me get him on the bed, please." Bethany struggled with her grandmother to get him on the bed.

"Colonel! Let me help you." Grandmère knelt on one side of Matthew. "He's hit his head . . . badly. A bump is already rising on his right temple."

Bethany grabbed him under one arm, and her grandmother grabbed him under the other arm. "Lift," she said, as the two women lifted him onto his bed.

"How did you ever handle him after the battle, *mon petit?*" Grandmère asked, standing back and panting from the exertion.

Bethany swiped at her brow. "He could help, a little. I think he was a little in shock. I've never seen him so weak. What's wrong with him?"

"I am not sure," Grandmère said.

"Argh." Matthew heaved over the edge of the bed and vomited black fluid.

She looked at her grandmother. "*Mon Dieu!* It's the fever. Matthew has *yellow jack.*"

Someone knocked loudly on the front door, and she jumped.

"You answer the door, *cher*. Do not let anyone in the house. We need to isolate. I will clean the floor. I have gloves." Her grandmother quickly brushed past her towards the kitchen.

"Grrrrr . . ." Dandie barked, darting toward the door and backing up, repeatedly.

Dazed, Bethany approached the door and looked out the window. It was the man, Sinclair.

Determined not to repeat her earlier rudeness with the man, she opened the door, stepped outside and closed it behind her. "Yes?"

The dark-headed man backed up a few steps. "Miss Phillips. I know you have Lord Longueville."

THE WOMAN IN front of him stared at him with a pained expression. *What is going on?* Edward Sinclair had found Matthew. The British ships were gone, and he wasn't sure how he would get him home, but by God, he had found him!

"Miss Phillips . . . is there something amiss?" he persisted. "Is Lord Longueville here?"

"You stopped at my home almost a month ago," she intoned.

"Yes, I did." He studied her for a moment. "I asked you then if you had seen the man. You told me you did not know the man. Yet, he is here, is he not?" he said, arching a brow. Sinclair realized his tone had been harsh and gentled it immediately. "Miss Phillips, I apologize. I fear I have put my worst foot forward in this." He was growing more concerned by the moment. Had something happened to Longueville? "I am a family friend, engaged by his father to find him. He lost contact with him shortly before his regiment came to Louisiana. His family is anxious about him. They feared him dead. This is an enormous country. I finally tracked him to New Orleans yet found no sign of him—*dead or alive*—on the battlefield." He blew out a long sigh of exhaustion. "You said you had not seen him."

"Yes. I did," she said.

"Yet, I am in receipt of the letter you wrote to his family, Miss Phillips. And you have Lord Longueville."

"You stole my letter?" She exhaled slowly and studied him.

Did he detect relief in her tone? He watched her curiously as she squared her shoulders and took a deep breath. A different woman stood before him.

"I did not know he was the same man. I rescued Colonel Matthew Romney from the battlefield," she said, looking him in the eye.

Suddenly, it dawned on him. She had told him the truth, as she knew it. He felt like a cad.

"Please accept my humblest apology. I realize *now* that you would not have known his titled name," he said, contritely.

"I owe you an apology as well. I had not understood." Her face contorted with pain. "Perhaps it would have been . . . *better* for him, had I known. He is blind and now, it seems, he has yellow fever." She felt the hot tears roll from her eyes and swiped at them. "He is very sick. I had hoped he could finish recovering."

"Lord Longueville has yellow fever?" Sinclair felt terrible for the young man. He recalled getting yellow jack and miraculously surviving it. It was the sickest he could recall being in his entire life. "How can I help?"

"No, you cannot help. You can catch . . ." Bethany began.

"No. I have had it already, and hope to never have it again," he interrupted and then lamented his rudeness.

"Yes." She backed up and allowed him to come into the house, leading him into the front parlor. "Please wait here."

Miss Phillips exited the room, leaving her dog behind. As if given silent instructions, the dog jumped into the chair opposite him and sat, watching.

A few moments later, an older woman with a thick grey braid wrapped around her head in a crown-like hairstyle followed the young woman back into the room. She was wiping her hands on her apron.

"My granddaughter tells me you are the gentleman that visited shortly after she and Dandie rescued the colonel. I tell you in all sincerity, my Bethany did not know the man you were looking for is the same man who lays gravely ill in the bed in the back. However, we are grateful that you have returned. Bethany tells me you have already had the fever. That is good."

"Why do you say that?" he pushed.

"The young man is very sick, and he had just recovered from the bad wounds received on the battlefield. His body is still weak. We are doing our best to help him," Grandmère said in soothing tones.

"Do you have some experience helping with illness?" he asked. "Is there a doctor near that I can summon?" An alarming sense of panic clawed at him. How would he tell Romney that he had found his son, only to lose him? The grief could overwhelm the man. He knew Matthew to be adored by the older Romney.

"I am an herbal healer, as is my granddaughter. Your colonel could not have been luckier than to have been found by her. However, we will need to pray hard, for he is very sick. And with his recent illness, it could take him some time to recover—if he can recover." Her voice was solemn.

He swallowed hard. "May I see him?" He wanted desperately to lay his eyes on the boy. He had tracked his units down the east coast, only to lose him on the battlefield.

"You may. Please wear this to keep the miasmas away."

Grandmère handed him a clean scarf. He noticed the women had donned them, as well.

Sinclair tied the scarf around his face and followed the ladies to the back bedroom. He paused at the door when he saw Romney laying on the bed sleeping. He walked to the side of the bed and gripped the young man's hand. "Romney, I did not track you down only to lose you. We will get you feeling better. I promise."

Matthew's eyes fluttered and opened.

Sinclair noticed he seemed to look past him, rather than at him. He was blind.

"Sinclair, is that you?" Romney asked weakly. "What are you doing here?"

"Your father sent me to find you. Your family is worried."

Chapter Twenty

"Sinclair, what are you doing here?" Matthew said, his voice dry and strained.

"Your father became worried when he stopped hearing from you before the New Orleans battle," Sinclair replied.

"He checked often and feared for your safety. When I heard what had happened at Villeré, I had to find you. Word had gotten out there were dead British soldiers everywhere for at least a quarter of a mile."

A lump formed in Matthew's throat. He remembered the general going down. He had seen two other high-ranking officers fall before he was injured. Laying there, the world had gone dark for him. "I wrote to him, but we could not frank our letters. Bart handled it," he said, turning away. The last he had communicated with his family was following the Battle of Plattsburgh in September 1814. The letter must never have been posted.

"Bart is your batman," Sinclair nodded.

"*Was*," Matthew corrected softly, keeping his head turned. Bart had lost his life in the most brutal of ways. Little remained of his friend.

"Oh." Sinclair was silent for a moment. "I gather your dad had been depending on those dispatches, and when they stopped, he scrambled to get a word from Horse Guards—but it was probably hard, being a continent away, and with the Napoleonic wars. This war has been one of the most bizarre affairs I've ever witnessed. The Americans do not fight like the Europeans."

"I know. They fight better, smarter. If we had learned from the first war forty years ago, we would have not lost so many." He probably should not have spoken so, but he meant it, by God! And he felt like crap. The British were powerful, regimented, and respected. The Americans were scrappy, and only somewhat disciplined. However, with their winning display in this last battle, he had to begrudgingly admit they were due some respect."

"I understand the sentiment," Sinclair admitted. "Just do not voice that to many people," he said, giving a wry smile.

"Yes, I hear you." Matthew tried to laugh before coughing and choking.

"Easy. Settle down. This virus is difficult on your lungs and digestive system," Sinclair began.

"You speak as if you know," Matthew said, raggedly.

"I survived it, but it was a long haul. I was sick for longer than the week, many had speculated. It was touch and go. The illness is not known to our country, and I had ignored the headaches and digestive issues until the virus took hold and was well and fully upon me. I nearly lost that battle. But a lovely woman... Lizzy..." He stopped. "I feel terrible, Romney. I was rough on your friend, Miss Phillips. Rude, actually. Of course, I apologized, but until this moment, I had not realized how I would have felt if someone had spoken so to Lizzy... Miss Pritchett—the woman that helped me get through the yellow jack."

At the thought of Bethany, he could feel his body struggle to improve. He wanted to be well, wanted to fish with her—anything, if he could be with her. "Bethany has been very good to me. She risked her life and the life of her small dog to save my life. I believe we came here to keep me out of danger of being discovered. She has endured much to help me. Please try to make amends," he entreated. "She is a good person."

Exhausted, he focused on his body, limb by limb—mentally

willing each one to relax. He could feel himself sinking further into the feather mattress beneath him. It was a trick that Bart had taught him. He had learned it in India, although where, exactly, escaped him at the moment.

"Can you help me get word to Bart's family? I just realized that I never wrote to them. I stopped writing when he died, I think." He reached for the glass of water near the bed, suddenly very thirsty.

"Let me." Sinclair picked up the water glass with his right hand and helped Matthew lean up with his left. "I can try my best. I think I will also frank the letter that your Miss Phillips wrote," Sinclair said.

Matthew pulled back from the water glass and gave a dry, cynical laugh. "*You* were the one that stole it from the Trading Post. You probably saved our lives, as I think of it." He took a deep breath. "The owner of the establishment . . . came to tell Bethany and . . ." Drained, he leaned back against the pillow.

"I think we have talked enough, Romney. You need rest. The women will not let me see you if I exhaust you."

Matthew nodded, understanding. "Bethany . . . can be firm," he rasped.

"Yes. I have seen evidence of her courage and spine," chuckled Sinclair. "I must return to New Orleans to check on arrangements, in the event I can return you to your country and your family. I should not be away too long."

Matthew rubbed his eyes sleepily. "I will be here." He noticed that his vision had improved, but his body felt like a horse had kicked him. He was alternatively hot and cold, sicker to his stomach than he could recall having been in his life, had a headache, and his body hurt . . . ached. But he could see . . . at least better. Things were still fuzzy.

The door opened and a woman with dark hair, lightly greying and worn in braids, spoke from the doorway. "Mr. Sinclair, perhaps the Colonel should rest." He recognized the voice as Aunt Theodosia, amazed that she looked a lot like the image he had conjured in his mind when he could not see much except her silhouette.

"I think you are right," Sinclair said. He turned to Matthew. "I should like to talk to your hosts, and I will leave, but will be back as soon as I can, Romney."

"Thank you, Sinclair," he ground out, hoping he did not sound ungrateful. Right now, all he wanted to think about was sleep . . . and maybe, Bethany. Matthew's eyes closed, and he fell into a deep sleep.

⇶⇷

ROMNEY'S WEAK APPEARANCE worried Sinclair. He had seen him only a day or so before looking much better. The virus had already begun extracting its toll.

"I know you must be worried. We are as well. We can do nothing but treat the symptoms and hope his body is strong enough to carry him through this, Mr. Sinclair," the woman said. "I am Theodosia Rand, Bethany's aunt. Her grandmother, Angelica, is my sister."

"I appreciate the help you have given him. In conversation with Lord Longueville, I reminded myself that I am only here because of the generosity of a woman that helped me. Had I not met her, I would probably not be here, myself."

"My sister mentioned you had survived the saffron fever," she quipped. "It is a nasty punch in the gut. If we only knew for sure how it spread or even what causes it, it would help so much. There are beliefs, of course." She tugged lightly at the scarf around her neck. "We use these to keep the foul air from getting into our bodies. It is all we know to protect us." She turned and tapped her walking stick. "My sister thinks a lot of your . . . Lord Longueville. And certainly, my niece does as well," she chortled.

"I was rude to your niece—not meaning to be. I apologized," he said simply. It was all he could say. All he could do. "I must return to the city if I am to plan his lordship's return home." It was hard to miss this woman's blindness. He wondered briefly if Miss Phillips had had her aunt in mind when she brought Long Longueville here.

"To England? Good luck. The only people that might visit England would be merchants and perhaps, the pirates," she acknowledged softly.

"Yes, you make a good point. We may have to stay a little longer until a ship becomes available."

"Let us focus on getting the colonel well," a woman's voice said behind him. "Aunt Theo, Grandmère wanted to know if you could meet her in the kitchen."

"Certainly. Thank you, *mon petit*." The older woman took her cane and tapped down the hall to the kitchen.

He noticed Miss Phillips waited until she was gone before turning to him. "I do not know what to make of this, Mr. Sinclair, but there could be a danger. A Mr. Caleb Smoot was spotted in the area. I would ask that you stay for a day or so, just in case. The man was in my house before we left. He tried to steal our boat and knows Matthew is English." Her voice trembled.

"Yes. You will need to tell me more, but perhaps, not outside Lord Longueville's room. Are you sure it would not be too much to put me up? I can help with food. I have more questions . . . there are some things I would like to discuss." Sinclair wanted to know more about Matthew's sight. He had noticed the way the young man looked towards the door when Aunt Theodosia had cut their visit short.

"I will speak with Grandmère and Aunt Theo. However, I am sure we can make room for you."

"I plan to go to New Orleans and try to secure passage as close to England as I can manage—if any ships head that way. I expect commerce will pick up now that the war is over."

"Wait. What? The war has ended?" Bethany gasped. "We did not know."

"Yes, both sides signed the Treaty of Ghent in December, but with communication being what it over an ocean, it was just acknowledged within the ranks. The British ships recently cleared out of the area without another battle. There was still tremendous strength within their ranks, including almost sixty ships. Speculation was, an assault on Alabama was aborted when they were informed of the Treaty of Ghent."

Miss Phillips looked stunned. "Where did you get this information?"

"I only heard it when I was in New Orleans. News has been slower to make it to these shores, because of the war," Sinclair explained.

Her eyes glistened. "That's wonderful . . . that the war is over," Bethany exclaimed.

He noticed she did not ask who had won. She had not seemed to care. Her only concern had been that it was over. Matthew Romney was very lucky to have been found by this woman, he mused.

"May I hang this scarf somewhere, for the time being? I am astonished to see the measures being taken in your home, Miss Phillips, to prevent illness."

Bethany gave him a wry look. "You have not met our neighbors. Very good people—and generous—but sadly, afflicted with leprosy. Indeed, it is something we do not want. But we have been able to be friends with them safely for years, which Grandmère attributes to wearing the scarves dipped in an herb mixture."

"To keep away the foul smells in the air emitted from breath . . ." He let the sentence die as he thought back to his studies in school and recalled the leather mask used during the black plague. The practice had enabled physicians to attend to victims. And he knew they still did it in some form, as people would dip bandanas in vinegar to restrain foul odors and smoke from entering their lungs. He smiled. "Lord Longueville has been lucky," he murmured.

"I thought he could heal before finding his way back to England... here. Few people come through this part of the canal because of the colony," she admitted.

"I saw it was relatively quiet but did not know why," he said, with unmistakable awe.

"The lady that owned the plantation died and left it to them. She left this home to my aunt. They had been friends most of their lives," Bethany said.

"I should speak with your grandmother and your aunt," he said as they made their way into the kitchen. The two ladies were at the table, their heads bent in deep discussion.

"Aunt Theo, Grandmère, Mr. Sinclair just advised me the war is over. There was a treaty." Bethany shook her head in disbelief. "I can't believe we are at the end."

"Mr. Sinclair, you will join us for dinner. I pulled up a crab basket this morning early. We will eat good tonight," the grandmother spoke.

He smiled. "I would be delighted. I would like to see how Longueville—Matthew, as you know him—does before I go to New Orleans to secure some sort of transportation back to England. The war might be over, but it could be a while before travel between the two countries resumes. I would like to earn my keep, however."

"We could use a couple of strong hands around here if you are willing," Grandmère spoke up. "I have a couple of places where the fencing needs a little mending. I have the bricks to replace the broken ones with," she added.

"I have seen the work done before and think I can help with that. I would also like to learn more about this man, Caleb Smoot. Miss Phillips told me he tried to steal her canoe, and that they had to secure him. While I cannot profess to understand how she and Lord Long... Matthew... could do that, I am concerned that he knows Matthew is English. Judging from her tension over it, Miss Phillips seems to feel that knowledge could be a liability."

"You are perceptive. I had not admitted that," she breathed.

Her aunt snorted. "If you marveled at their ability to secure Smoot, ask her about the alligator they killed on their way here," her aunt said.

Sinclair turned to Miss Phillips and gaped. He encouraged her story and spent an enjoyable hour with the three women, rehashing the recent exploits of Matthew Romney and Miss Phillips. He could not miss the light in her eyes whenever Miss Phillips spoke of Romney and realized that he may have to look for passage for two.

CHAPTER TWENTY-ONE

BETHANY WOKE WITH an ache in her neck. She had spent the previous night sitting in a chair next to Matthew's bed, cooling his head with a damp rag, giving him fluids, and praying the fever would end. She and Grandmère thought he had gotten past the high fever, but after a couple of days of low-grade fever, it began again, as hot as he had been in the beginning. At least the vomiting had subsided. She was worried. Matthew seemed so weak.

Dandie had followed her everywhere, as if she was guarding Bethany against becoming sick. While she had no memory of having had it as a child, she was immune to the fever, thankfully. Most Louisiana natives were. It was the people that came to visit that usually picked up the fever. And many never lived to leave.

True to his word, Mr. Sinclair had helped around the house. Grandmère and Aunt Theo had jumped on his offer to help. The man had mended the fence, replaced a few weak boards, and painted the porch white. He had proven an outstanding worker. With his investigative talents, he had also helped Aunt Theo find some things she had lost around the house. That made Bethany laugh. Grandmère teased her she was growing sweet on the man, and her aunt took it in stride, laughing and being a good sport.

All the while, Matthew lay in the bed, sick.

They had seen little of young Johnny these past few days—

mostly because she had been helping Matthew. Also, Bethany was unsure if the young lad had already had the fever and was not willing to take the chance. She considered it good luck they had not gone fishing, as she had wanted to do. It would break her heart if anything happened to the lad.

However, she needed to know more about Caleb Smoot. Had he shown up again? If so, he would not have seen her—only her aunt, grandmother, and Mr. Sinclair. Maybe he left and went back home. Maybe he never came back. She prayed that be the case. Mr. Sinclair had a description of him and was keeping watch for him to show back up, although what Smoot could find important about Matthew now eluded her. The war was over. And . . . *he was still a deserter! What was she not seeing?*

"Bethany. I brought you some hot coffee. You should rest," Grandmère said, handing it to her.

"Matthew is still so sick. I am afraid to leave his side." She took the cup and noticed Matthew moving his lips, shaking his head, and smirking. Her grandmother stared at him and chuckled.

"Grandmère, he has been talking to his friend, Chris—I think about old times. They talked about some sort of prank they were planning. They must have been very close. It feels wicked to listen to his dreams, but you will have to pay close attention if you want to hear what he says. His babble has preoccupied me. Perhaps I should stretch." Bethany stood and stretched.

"I'm happy to watch over him for a while," Grandmère said, taking Bethany's seat.

"One more thing. Besides his British accent, the man speaks very fast in his dreams—much faster than when he is awake. I feel a little like I am spying on him. But I cannot help it. He laughs a lot when he is with these friends of his," she said. "It makes me happy to hear him laugh. It's so much better than thinking of him in pain," she added, thoughtfully.

"I will watch your colonel." Grandmère smiled. "Get something decent to eat. Maybe a bath. Your aunt has the copper tub in her bathroom. I am sure she would not mind you using it. She only uses it when I am here to help her."

She had grown used to Grandmère's jabs about Matthew being *her* colonel and ignored them. "Thank you, Grandmère. I will ask her." Bethany left the room with her coffee, glad to stand up and be able to stretch. She stepped into her room and grabbed her bar of honeysuckle soap and headed into her aunt's bathroom, noticing that her grandmother had already filled the tub for her. She would be certain to thank her later.

Stripping off her clothing, Bethany eased herself into the tub. It felt delicious. She dipped her head into the water and emerged, lathering her hair with her soap. Once the water started cooling, she stood, dried, and put on a navy muslin dress. The weather seemed a little warm, and she wanted to be comfortable. She hurried with her stockings, slipped her feet into small leather shoes, and tied her hair back, away from her face. Feeling refreshed, she walked into the kitchen, where she found her aunt and Mr. Sinclair talking and laughing. The man had become a good friend to the family almost overnight.

"Grandmère is relieving me, right now. I can help with dinner," she offered.

"You look lovely, Miss Phillips," Mr. Sinclair said, before clearing his throat. "How is the patient?"

Bethany thought she saw him blush. "Thank you for the compliment. I feel so much better. Unfortunately, Matthew's fever is still high. I hope it breaks soon. However, I am encouraged that he has not become worse."

"I am leaving tomorrow for New Orleans," Sinclair said. "There must be business to attend to, including messages. You have convinced me that Matthew will need more time to recuperate and regain his strength," he added. "It will probably take time to find a ship that can provide passage to London. I would hope to find something from New Orleans. However, I realize we may have to make our way to the Carolinas—perhaps, Charleston."

"What about engaging a privateer?" Aunt Theo asked. "If the

war is over, perhaps some privateers may be interested in securing legitimate 'cargo' for Europe–not just England. I suspect many will transport merchandise."

"I am not sure," Sinclair responded. "There's a trust issue with England and the privateers. They have taken many British boats as prizes." He sighed. "It may be awhile before shipping resumes any sort of normalcy."

"It was *war*." Aunt Theo persisted.

"You do not have to convince me," he chuckled. "But my homeland can be rather rigid where the Americans are concerned."

"You are British?" Aunt Theo asked, obviously startled and taken aback. "You do well with concealing your accent."

"I spend a lot of time in the wilderness of America among the different dialects. I enjoy adopting them and have for these past years. There's a lot to recommend this country. However, at some point, I will return home," Sinclair returned.

"I would never have guessed," Aunt Theo said. "You are very good. You sound like you could be from among us here in Louisiana." She laughed.

"How long will you be gone, Mr. Sinclair?" Bethany asked.

"I'm not sure. If things go well, a week. I could be gone longer," he answered. You still have the address where I get my mail?

"I do." Bethany gave an appreciative smile before turning her attention back to the stove. "Look at all of this catfish! I hope everyone is hungry!" She pulled the last piece from the skillet and put the vegetables in the bowl. She readied Dandie's food. While Dandie would love the fish, Bethany never allowed it. She did not want to risk her dog choking on a bone. Satisfied everything was ready, she excused herself and went to retrieve Grandmère.

Bethany was totally unprepared to see what greeted her when she opened Matthew's door.

Matthew was sitting up in bed, with Grandmère sitting across from him in the chair she vacated hours earlier. They were engrossed in conversation. He glanced at the door and smiled at her.

"I thought you must be beautiful, but *you a*re *truly lovely!*" he said, shamelessly staring open-mouthed at her.

Bethany gulped, unsure of how to respond. Her face and neck colored. *He can see!* She looked from Grandmère to Matthew and saw his eyes twinkle.

"I should have let you know, but he just sat up ten minutes ago. His fever appears to have broken, and he was asking me if I had only teased him about shaving his face." She gave a quick nod of her head towards the patient and whispered loudly. "I'm uncertain, but I think your colonel can see!" Grandmère said.

Bethany cringed. She should have insisted Grandmère and Aunt Theo stop teasing. Her face had to be blood-red. Thankfully, everyone filed into the room and began talking excitedly, almost at once.

"He is not completely out of the woods, but it appears the fever has broken," Grandmère said.

Dandie heard his voice and bounded into the room. She sniffed his face, but backed off and curled up at the corner of the bed. Matthew laughed. "I think she just gave me the cut direct," he said, tugging at his beard. "I smell bad. Even I can smell myself. How long have I been in this bed?"

"Over a week." Sinclair stuck his head in the room and grinned. "Good to see you alive and well, my lord," he said jovially. "When Dandie stopped staring at the fish on the table and shot off down the hall towards your room, we had to follow. Then, we heard your voice down the hall."

"She is as adorable as I imagined," Matthew said, still looking at the dog. "I could feel those bottom teeth and knew she would make me smile if I ever saw her."

"Look who's awake!" Aunt Theo said, tapping her walking stick into the room. "We are glad to have you back, Colonel."

"Can you see, son?" Sinclair inquired.

"Not perfectly, but much better. I can make out faces," he intoned. "Things beyond a few feet are still a little blurry, but the shadows are gone, and everyone doesn't look like a colorful blob." He sobered. "I am hopeful all of my sight will return. I will never take the gift of sight for granted, again."

Sinclair walked to the end of the bed. "You look much improved," he said. "The ladies are right. You need to give yourself plenty of time to get stronger before we attempt a long voyage."

Bethany felt her heart tug. Too soon, he would take a long voyage back to England. His words came back to her and she felt more confused than ever. *Come with me,* he had said. At first, she had dismissed them. It was ridiculous. What would she do? But then, he had never made the offer again.

"Perhaps we should leave you and Mr. Sinclair to talk," she offered, dropping her eyes. "You got little time before."

"No. Everyone stay," Matthew pleaded. "I feel like all I have done since you've found me is rest," he laughed. He looked beseechingly at her grandmother. "Grandmère, please tell me there is nothing else I can catch while I am here."

Her grandmother's face crinkled with mirth. "Young man, you have certainly kept your life full, if not well. Once you clean up and we trim that beard, you might feel more alive. And in the future, I hope you catch nothing more than an occasional fish," she guffawed.

They all laughed.

"I will see about that bath, Grandmère mentioned," Bethany offered. She needed to leave. The walls felt like they were moving in on her. As happy as she was to see him awake, she did not want to see him leave. She nearly sprinted down the hall to her aunt's bathroom, where she closed the door and sucked in huge gulps of air, fighting tears. *What was wrong with her?*

"Bethany, wait. Let me help you," Grandmère said.

Her grandmother's footsteps came up quickly behind her. Bethany tried to clear up the tears from her face, choking down the sobs that begged to come forward.

Grandmère opened the door and pulled her to her, allowing Bethany to sob on her shoulders. "It's fine, Bethany. You can let it out. This has been hard."

Bethany could never hold back. When Grandmère coaxed, she allowed herself to cry. "Grandmère, I do not understand what is wrong with me. It should thrill me he can see better. For an entire week, I've been so worried that I would lose him. He gets better and I cry selfish tears."

"You are not being selfish, girl. You are mourning a loss that you feel is coming. But you need to let him go back to his family. He has responsibilities," Grandmère said gently.

Bethany sniffled and tried to stem the tears. "I understand," she said in between hiccups. "I do. Yet I cannot help these feelings. They feel so . . . physical, so painful."

"Ah. That is the heart, *mon petit*. Your heart is engaged, and it will require some time to adjust."

"You were right. I should have been more forthcoming when Mr. Sinclair first showed up. But I truly did not know the lord he was looking for was the same man I had rescued. Had Matthew left then . . ."

"He might have died on that voyage back. He certainly could not see," her grandmother interrupted her and finished the sentence. "His wounds were serious. He might have had more trauma. And the ship's doctor, they only know to cut and bleed a person. The colonel was much better off with you. Do not second guess yourself. You followed your heart and did what you knew to be right."

She sniffled. "I guess we should at least shave him. He will be too weak to bathe himself in a tub. Perhaps he can wash himself off by sitting on the edge of the bed."

"That is good thinking. Let's get what we need and return," Grandmère whispered.

They stopped by the kitchen and prepared a small basin of water. Bethany carried the basin, and her grandmother carried the towels. When they arrived in the room, Matthew was eating some of the cornbread from dinner, as Dandie eyed every piece. "This bread you call cornbread is delicious," he said, ladling some butter on the top of Grandmère's skillet creation. "It has a grainy consistency and is very enjoyable." He took a swallow of his tea. "We do not have this in England."

"*Cornbread?*" Bethany was astonished with his excitement over something she took for granted. Grandmère served it at least three times a week. As Bethany thought about it, she realized Grandmère had a talent for it as her own efforts usually ended up with a much dryer result. In contrast, her grandmother's cornbread was moist.

"Yes! Your aunt brought me some food while you were away. I am famished, and Dandie acts like she expects a share," he chuckled.

"That is a wonderful sign," agreed Grandmère. "But Dandie is only making sure that you eat it all." She winked.

"Yes," agreed Bethany. "Dandie has been worried. She has rarely left your side all week."

"I have never known an animal to take such an interest in me," Matthew mused. He handed the small dog a little piece of the bread.

"You will spoil her," warned Grandmère, good-naturedly. "I need to return to the kitchen to clean it."

As her grandmother left, Sinclair and her aunt followed, leaving Bethany and Dandie with Matthew.

"I'm glad you are awake, Matthew. I have been anxious. The fever has not been kind to you."

He pushed a hand through his hair. "I feel positively wrung out," he despaired. "And you and Dandie are good for my spirits. Please stay." He patted the bed.

Bethany walked up and sat across from him in the chair.

"Ah," he said, smiling. "I think I get it."

"I will place the water here. There are some towels and soap. Perhaps you want to clean up a little," Bethany returned with a smile and wrinkling her nose. "I think you might like a little privacy. Perhaps I can visit in a half-hour?"

He gestured towards the basin with a smirk. "I must first

make myself more presentable, and then, we have much to catch up on, I think."

As she started to pull the door closed behind her, she heard Dandie jump from the bed to follow her. "Ah . . . we are both going to give you privacy," she chuckled. She looked at his bright eyes and smiling face and fought the impulse to hug him. Instead, she pulled the door closed behind her.

Chapter Twenty-Two

A week later

MATTHEW AWOKE FEELING stronger still. He learned how lucky he was to have survived the fever, especially in his weakened state. Sinclair left for New Orleans the day after he had awakened. The man was superb company and provided much information about the state of the war—which, thank goodness, had ended! That news alone was worth celebrating. They would do it when he returned. Sinclair said it had been over five years since he had been home. He hoped he could convince him to return to England. He and his father had been friends since their school days. It would be grand to surprise his father.

A lump formed in his throat when he thought of his family. His brother, Jason, would be nine and his sister would already be out in Society looking for a husband. She could even be married by now, at twenty years of age. He hoped she would find a kind man—one that could deal with her temper. He laughed at the notion. Charlotte was a beauty with a big heart. Whomever Charlotte married would be a lucky man, indeed. If they weren't good to her... he let the thought drop. Spring was well underway. Matthew needed to return home soon. He sensed a reticence about leaving. Something about *here* also felt like home. He felt torn.

A knock sounded on the door.

"Come in. I am decent," he replied with a slight laugh. Things seemed so informal. He rather liked it. Grandmère put her head in. "I cleaned the razor and mixed up some more soap for you. My husband, Ned, always said the liquid soap was good for shaving. I thought you might like to have some for your ablutions."

"Yes. That's thoughtful. I am trying to look less like a man who has been lost in the woods for months," he chuckled.

The older woman returned his smile. "You have," she said, placing the items on the bureau. "Should I close your door?"

"No. Please let it stay open. Dandie makes herself at home between my room and Bethany's. Also, the open door keeps me from feeling so isolated. After being in bed so long, I find I enjoy the company that much more."

"Bethany mentioned you might go fishing."

"Yes. That is the plan. I hope it is a relaxing adventure and one which does not require me to wrestle any snakes or alligators," Matthew returned with a chuckle.

"I think that might be a good possibility," Grandmère replied. "Break your fast when you are ready."

He stared at his reflection in the looking glass. His eyes were sunken, and he was still pale. He hoped sunshine and fresh air would solve it. He lifted his shirt and noticed the line of stitches Bethany had made on his side. The even line of stitches was still pink and raised, but no longer angry. He could tell they had gone down a lot, and hopefully that meant the healing had progressed considerably beneath them. He no longer ached where the wound had been, and the thread had long since fallen off. His body needed to regain his strength, but that would come with patience.

His stomach growled, and he set down the glass.

Walking out of his door, he met Bethany.

"I was fetching you for breakfast. Johnny stopped by, his cane pole in hand, and asked about you this morning. He is anxious to meet you."

"This is the little boy that lives in one of the small houses on the adjacent property, right?"

"Yes, his father and mother are sharecroppers—well, more than that, really. They provide food for Mr. Duplantis and his family. His father also brings goods back from the city for them."

His stomach growled *again*.

Bethany heard it and laughed. "We need to get you fed! I had some oatmeal earlier. Grandmère made oatmeal and laid out some dried pork and biscuits."

"It's about time you joined us, Colonel," Grandmère teased when they sat at the table. They heard laughter coming from the front parlor and Johnny emerged, tossing a small ball in the air while Dandie jumped up and down, trying to reach it.

"Look!" he exclaimed. "She walks on her hind legs fer the ball."

"She is talented," Bethany agreed, selecting a piece of pork. "Come join us, Johnny." The little boy nodded and stood behind Matthew and waited to get food.

"Johnny, this is Colonel Matthew Romney, the man I wanted you to meet earlier."

"I heard you were sick with the fever. I got it, too, but not near's bad as you," the young boy said.

Matthew glanced at the little boy with amusement. "I am very glad to meet you, Johnny," he said as he filled a bowl with oatmeal and took some pork before sitting down. "Bethany said you brought your cane pole. Are you ready to fish?"

"Yassir!" Johnny said in a serious voice. "Pa left yesterday for New Orleans. It's up to me to catch dinner."

"That's a lot of responsibility," Matthew observed, giving the little boy his full attention.

They dissolved into a discussion about fishing and the best spots, finally deciding the dock in front of the Duplantis' house was the best.

A half-hour later, the three of them left, with Dandie in tow.

THE THREE OF them sat side by side and passed the afternoon quietly on the dock, laughing and fishing. Johnny had forgotten his bucket, so the boy ran back to the house to borrow one of Grandmère's larger ones with a handle. He measured each fish, spreading out his fingers to determine the length. It was obvious the child knew what he was doing. Besides the crabs that continually grabbed their lines, they brought in a dozen fish.

Earlier, Bethany had heard Grandmère mention the need to empty the crab bucket and have a shrimp and crab boil that evening, so she encouraged Johnny to take all the fish he wanted.

"Miss Bethany, it's just me, my Ma and my sister, right now, it is. We can spare you some. If'n Pa was home, we might need all of them, though," he said with a grin.

"If memory serves, your pa loves catfish the best," Bethany said.

"Sure does!" the little boy hooted and pulled his line up to check his bait.

Bethany noticed Matthew was quiet. He appeared to be looking everywhere around—everywhere but where his line was hanging. "You have fished, haven't you, Matthew?"

He turned to her and amusement glinted in his eyes. "I confess I haven't in years. I would only want to fish when I was in the country during the summer. I was sitting here trying to remember the last time, and it was when I was the same age as Johnny, here." He reached over and scratched the boy's head. As he spoke, his eyes stayed fixed on the overhang of cypress tree limbs across the water.

Bethany scanned the area across from them. She noticed light reflecting off something, but nothing out of the ordinary. Trying not to raise suspicion, she leaned closer and squinted her eyes, but still nothing.

Matthew brought his pole out of the water and caught the

line. The bait had gone. While he re-baited the hook, he whispered to her. "I wish I could count on my vision. I would have sworn when the wind blew and the limbs parted, I saw a person on the shore, watching. But I cannot be sure. Things still look blurry, but it looked like a person."

"I've been looking," she said in a whisper, "but I have seen nothing unusual, except the reflection." Bethany looked over at Dandie and noticed she was also studying the area.

Bethany found herself content to fish until she felt a growl in her stomach. "Is anyone else's body alerting them it's time to eat?" She glanced at the almost full pail of fish and motioned with her head to Johnny.

He had already pulled his line up and was hooking it to the bottom of the pole. "I got all I need. I'll leave some fer tomorrow in case you need to eat," he said with a grin.

Dandie barked her approval.

Matthew stood and held out a hand to help Bethany up.

She grabbed his proffered hand and felt a fluttering in her belly that differed completely from her hunger. It felt like more than an attraction to Matthew. Bethany wanted to pull him closer and ask him to never leave. Instead, she placed her hand in his and allowed him to pull her to her feet. Bethany took one last look across the water and would have sworn she saw someone lay on the ground.

"What is it?" Matthew asked, looking concerned.

Flummoxed, she shook her head and pointed across the water. "I keep thinking I see something over there. I've watched all afternoon and something, or someone, keeps moving. It may be the sun playing tricks on me."

He peered across. "I see nothing, but you know my vision." He gave a self-deprecating laugh. "I have an idea. I noticed a brass spyglass on a shelf in the parlor. It might have been your grandfather's. Let us ask Grandmère if we can borrow it."

Her face crinkled in confusion. "I cannot think who would have owned it. I have visited here for years and I have never noticed it."

He gazed down into her eyes. "I cannot help it. I seem to notice everything I can, coming this close to being blind. I do not see as well as I used to; however, my vision is continually improving of late."

Johnny walked to his right with the bucket between them. Matthew picked up her right hand and gently squeezed it as they walked Johnny back toward his house. Her skin quivered from his touch and she thought of words she wanted to say . . . but didn't.

They opened the back gate leading into the plantation's sprawling land and walked several minutes in silence, crossing a small footbridge over a rambling creek. "Ma is hangin out the wash," Johnny said, pointing toward his family's cabin. "If'n you get me as far as the gate, she'll hep me the rest of the way. My ma'll be happy with this catch, she will." He looked down at Dandie. "I'll bring my ball tomorrow."

Smiling, Johnny waved until he got his mother's attention. She finished hanging the sheet and came to help. "That's a mighty fine dinner, Son," she exclaimed, and gave him a kiss on the forehead, causing him to redden.

"Aww Ma. I got an image to keep up."

Undeterred, she mussed his hair. "Johnny, you will never be too big for me to kiss."

Bethany stood with Matthew as they watched the boy and his mother haul the big bucket home. They could hear him talking about catching the fish and laughed.

"He grows on you quickly," Matthew observed on their way back to her aunt's.

"He does," she agreed.

After they crossed the footbridge and were out of sight of Johnny's house, Matthew pulled her close. "I have been wanting to do this since I woke this morning. It gets harder and harder to keep my distance." He tilted her head up and gazed into her eyes as she loosely wrapped her arms about his neck.

"Bethany, you are so beautiful. I knew your inner beauty first and only imagined the outer beauty—which has quite overwhelmed me." Closing his eyes, he brushed his lips against hers before dropping his lips to her neck and then to her décolleté. He kissed along the edge as one hand gently dipped beneath the fabric and touched her breast, and his fingers began to gently circle the tip. The stomach flutter she had felt earlier dove to her nether region, and she clung to him as her breathing sped up.

"Even in my darkest hours, I felt comforted by your presence, like nothing I have ever known. I have had a hard time staying away from you," he said in between kisses.

"Matthew, I never thought to miss anything like I miss your kisses," she breathed in between pants. "I don't know what I will do when you leave . . ." Her worst fear had slipped out.

"What do you mean, when I leave?" He lifted his head until his gaze locked with her own. "Are you not coming with me?" he asked.

Bethany searched his eyes. "I cannot simply tag along to England. What would I do when I arrived? My family is here."

"No, Bethany. You misunderstand. *I* want to be your family. I knew it before I could see you. I have done a terrible job of telling you." He dropped to one knee where they stood. "Bethany Phillips, would you do me the great honor of becoming my wife?"

"You are asking me . . . you want me?"

He smiled and gave a slow, seductive nod. "I want you, Bethany. What do you say?"

Dandie sat back on her haunches and watched the two of them, silent.

Could it be possible? She would live in a strange land among people she did not know. Her Grandmère and Aunt Theo would be here. They had always encouraged her to marry for love. He had not mentioned *love*. He had, however, told her he had feelings for her. Could that be enough? *She loved him. Would it be enough for her to love him?*

He was waiting for her answer.

If she said *no*, he would leave her behind. She would never see him again. If she said "yes," she would be part of his life forever. Thoughts raced through her mind. Taking his face in her hands, she looked into his eyes. "Yes, Matthew. I will be your wife," she said.

Matthew stood up and swept Bethany into his arms, spinning her around. "You have made me the happiest of men." Setting her down, he leaned in and kissed her. She felt giddy with anticipation. This man was like no one she had ever known. He was gentle, witty, warm, and cared about her. *And he would be hers.*

"You mentioned your grandmother planned to check the crab cages. Do you feel up to checking them for her? I do not feel like being indoors, suddenly. I want to be out here, with you, feeling the sunshine on my face, gazing into your beautiful green eyes," Matthew enthused.

She looked up at him, suddenly unsure. "What about Dandie? I would not leave my dog."

He laughed. "Of course, Dandie comes with us. I would never leave her behind."

"Let us check with your grandmother and make sure she has not already emptied the cages."

The two walked hand-in-hand through the gate and towards her aunt's house.

When they reached the house, Dandie sniffed the air with her tail pointed straight behind her.

Bethany touched her pulsing head. A slight headache was coming on. Something felt wrong. She just did not know why.

"It took him long enough to leave," Smoot muttered to himself, as he watched Bethany and Matthew go towards the house. "You might go places, but it ain't home, soldier, and it ain't with her," he sneered. "Soon, you will see what I mean."

CHAPTER TWENTY-THREE

MATTHEW COULD NOT believe his good fortune. Bethany had agreed to be his wife. He had thought she would decline because of her family. His sight had mostly returned, and each day now, it seemed to improve. He wanted to curse the war, damn it to Hell for what it had cost him. It had taken Bart and countless others. He had hated America, or at least, he had until *her*.

Here they sat on a dock in the bayou, pulling up crab baskets and carefully placing the critters in a large bucket.

One crab bolted from the basket before they could usher it into the pail, and began making its way towards Bethany, who nearly catapulted into the water to escape it. "I have it, my dear," he said, suddenly feeling sorry for the crustacean. His hand accidentally, on purpose, knocked it into the water. He looked up and met the gaze of a grinning Bethany.

"I have done it myself, a time or two," she teased. "Their little eyes look up at you with such fright, I cannot help it. If they are so ambitious that they take off, I let them go."

"Now you are making me look at all of them," he admitted, finding his attention drawn to the crowded bucket of clamoring and clacking crabs.

"Don't do it," she warned, laughing. "I know what you are thinking. Aunt Theo is not the forgiving sort if her crabs have absconded." Her voice was light.

"Tell me this does not bother you," he dared, pulling her up into his arms.

"It does. I assure you. If it were up to me, I would only eat fruits and vegetables," she admitted. "But my aunt and grandmother love seafood."

"I will admit, I have never stared down into the face of a crab," he said with a laugh. Another crab escaped, crawling up on the pile beneath it, and he watched it tumble out of the bucket into the water.

Bethany's lips twitched as she threw the lid over the bucket, locking the rest of the crabs in the pail. "Come," she said with her arm outstretched. Let's take the crabs to Grandmère and go for a walk. We have much to discuss, it seems."

"That sounds wonderful. Is there a good place we can walk?" he asked, looking in the colony's direction next door. Honestly, most of what he had seen, seemed threatening in the sense of communing too closely with snakes and such. He whacked at another mosquito that had landed on his arm. "Ouch! These blood-suckers are such a nuisance."

"To answer your question, there is a good place—just over there." Bethany pointed towards the back of the plantation. "The Bellovere family had some beautiful gardens at one time, and they fell into disrepair. However, Mr. Duplantis has restored much."

"When should we tell your family . . . about us?" he ventured.

"I do not know. How would you like to approach it?" she asked quietly.

He heard the note of anguish in her voice. "Are you having second thoughts?" he asked, gently.

"No, not at all," she answered. "I just do not want to hurt my aunt and my grandmother. I am all they have. Well, there is my father, but we haven't heard from him since the beginning of the war."

"We will find a way to mollify their fears, I promise you," he soothed. He could not wait to introduce Bethany to his father. While she was not part of Society, he was certain when his parents met her they would love her.

"I hope so. I cannot suffer to have them hurt, and to cause it would be agonizing," she said.

"'Tis a long voyage, but I could never deny you the opportunity to see your family. We will come here as often as you wish," he offered.

She smiled at that, and he thought his heart would burst. He cared so much for this woman. It was something he had never thought possible. What would his friends say?

He thought about the men who had been as close as brothers before he had accepted this assignment. He had planned to sell his commission and settle down, but the need for officers had been great. Now he was planning to marry a woman he had found in the wilderness of America. Evan would surely give him grief. The man would probably never marry if he had his way. Of course, Clarendon's mother would have something to say about that. He liked Lady Clarendon very much. However, the thought of Evan becoming snared in the parson's trap seemed too fantastical. It would never happen, he thought.

They were about to leave the dock when Dandie jumped up and began barking uncontrollably. She bared her teeth at a small pirogue as it rounded the clump of trees just beyond the edge of their dock. Tobias Smith waved, and Dandie snarled at his approach.

"She really does not approve of him," observed Matthew under his breath to Bethany.

"No, she hates him. I have no reason," replied Bethany with a slight laugh.

The canoe floated up alongside her own boat, which was still covered, and Tobias grabbed a wooden cleat and secured it with rope. "Hello Colonel Romney, Bethany. May I visit?" he asked. He looked upset.

"Certainly," Matthew replied, casting a quick glance at Bethany at the same time he stretched his hand to their visitor. "Is everything all right?" he asked the man.

Either Tobias was uncomfortable with his sudden intrusion, or he had just swallowed something as foul as cod liver oil. Matthew could not decide. But he recognized the look of jealousy. He had sensed it from the man's voice when they were at Bethany's cabin, but standing here, now, he could see it.

The announcement of their impending nuptials would have to wait. Something was wrong.

"I'll get right to it," Smith said. "Jackson is looking for Caleb Smoot. Somehow, he found out the man deserted on the battlefield. And worse . . . his Ma says he has gone to get him a British soldier to trade and clear his name. Says he's sure General Jackson would forget that he ran from the battle, if he turns in a redcoat."

"He plans to capture me and turn me in to General Jackson?" Matthew sounded incredulous. "The war is over!"

"That's madness," exclaimed Bethany. "I cannot fathom that his family can be happy with his behavior of late."

"They aren't happy, at all. Caleb and I have been friends most of our lives. His ma came to me out of desperation. They could not reason with him. He left a day or so ago and took one of my pirogues." He took a resigned breath. "I could only think to come here. Poor woman doesn't know what to do." He looked at Matthew and then at Bethany. "Jackson hangs traitors. Perhaps he should leave—go west until the furor of the battle dies down." He took a deep breath and let out a sigh. "I came to warn you both. We have tried to reason with Caleb, but he is difficult." He looked at Matthew. "I know you secured him once, but that only made him madder. He could be dangerous."

"I believe you. There's no telling what is going on in his head," added Matthew. "He sounds desperate—more desperate than he was when he tried to steal the boat." Matthew was confident that he could fend off Caleb, if challenged—unless he ambushed him, of course. He was not sure, however, how his hosts would feel if Smoot attacked and ended up being badly injured. He had no desire to suffer anymore hurt or illness, himself. An involuntary shudder shook him.

"Why don't you come up and see Grandmère?" Bethany offered, reaching down and shushing Dandie. The dog had continued to growl and looked mutinous at being told to stop growling.

"We should let Grandmère know about this." Bethany turned to Tobias. "Come inside, Tobias, and have some lemonade. Grandmère would be most upset if she missed seeing you."

"I would like to greet your aunt and grandmother. Thank you." He looked at the large, covered basket. "Let me help you get the crabs in the house. It looks like your grandmother may have cleaned out the canal," he joked, picking up one side. Matthew picked up the other.

"No, at least two leaped to safety," Bethany laughed as she spoke.

Grandmère and Aunt Theo's reaction to Smoot's threat surprised Matthew. They were angry the man would dare come after Matthew, hoping to trade one life for another.

"The nerve of Caleb Smoot," Grandmère exclaimed, clearly agitated. "This is a personal affront to my family."

He noticed Smith draw up in surprise. Matthew had been astounded himself. Grandmère had referred to him as *family*. But then, the woman had an uncanny ability to see beyond what they presented to her.

"Tobias, please say you will stay for dinner. It's midafternoon. You are welcome to stay the night," Grandmère offered. "We have plenty of room and we are having a good crab boil for dinner, with greens and cornbread."

"Thank you, Grandmère," Smith said, looking overwhelmed.

His discomfort was obvious to Matthew. Yet, he did not know how to put the man at ease. It appeared they both wanted Bethany. The real problem was the discomfort that Bethany obviously was feeling.

"Grandmère, if you would excuse me, I would like to take a quick walk and let Dandie do her business," Bethany announced.

Matthew started to go with her but wanted to hear the rest of what Smith had to tell them. When she looked at him, he winked at her to assure her he understood her discomfiture.

Wearing a smile, she put on her straw hat, and they left the house.

BETHANY NEEDED FRESH air. The day had started off so wonderfully until Tobias had arrived with the news of Smoot. She shivered despite the warm temperature of the day. The man disgusted her with his greasy hair and nasty attitude. If given the chance, she was sure he would hurt her dog for biting off part of his ear. Try as she might, she felt no empathy for him. It wasn't like he was an upstanding member of their community. It was rumored he could regularly be found drunk propped against the outside wall of the local bar. There had to be more to his connection to Tobias, who seemed more upset over Smoot's disappearance than she had ever seen him. She could not imagine what it could be, thinking her friend the complete opposite of Smoot.

Bethany felt sorry for his ma, though. She was a kind woman who did her best to raise his sister.

Retracing her steps from this morning, she opened the gate and wandered onto the plantation grounds next door. Seeing no one outside tending the gardens, she let Dandie run around, enjoying the sight of her dog chasing a rogue butterfly in the patch of red and yellow tulips. The star magnolia and the flowering cherry trees had bloomed and made a beautiful backdrop for the lovely gardens Mr. Duplantis had recreated. She observed a bench sitting in front of a tall grouping of pink flowering camelias and sat down. Bethany had not noticed it before, but it met her needs for the moment. She needed time to reflect.

She saw Dandie look over at her, a look of alarm on her face, before finally going back to chasing the butterfly. Unconcerned, Bethany relaxed and leaned her head back and closed her eyes. With her eyes closed and lost in her thoughts, she never saw the gag that was shoved into her mouth. A burlap bag was thrown over her head and was secured with a single pull before she could react.

The rag tasted filthy, and the foul smell of body odor gagged and assailed her. Kicking and sending muffled screams, she felt herself hoisted over someone's shoulders. She heard Dandie growling and barking—louder than she had ever barked. She could tell that her dog had her mouth on the person's leg, trying to bite. A loud thud sounded, and her heart dropped to her stomach when she heard her dog's loud whimper and then nothing.

"You deserved that and more," he spat. "I should kill you for what you did to my ear. I'll kill you if you come back," she heard him add, as they went through the hedge of bushes. He had his arms tightly around her waist, holding down her own arms. The only thing she could do was kick—which she did as furiously as she was able. A few minutes later, the man dropped her down on the ground. "I had hoped you wouldn't be this much trouble," he sneered. "Too bad I won't see yer green eyes when I have my way with you." With that, he slammed his fist into her face through the burlap bag.

Everything went black as her brain screamed his name. *Caleb Smoot.*

Chapter Twenty-Four

Two hours later

"Colonel, it's not like Bethany to be gone this long. I have a bad feeling," Aunt Theo whispered in his ears alone. He noticed Grandmère and Smith both taking turns and watching for the door to open. An icy feeling shot through him. *After what Smith had just told them, how could he have let her go by herself?* Matthew quickly excused himself and went to his room. Rummaging in the bag of his things that Bethany had hidden beneath his bed, he found his pistol and checked it. He left the room, nearly at a full run, when a voice behind stopped him.

"Let me go with you, Colonel," Tobias Smith said, getting up. "I know what you are thinking. If Caleb has her, I may reason with him. I would like to spare us any more bloodshed. He will listen to me."

Matthew stood there—his head full of emotion. He had never seen Smoot before but had smelled him. The thought of that man . . . of any man . . . touching Bethany made his blood boil. A red haze colored his vision. "Fine," he said, never turning.

The two men stepped outside, and Matthew called for Dandie, hoping the dog would come running with Bethany right behind her. No dog emerged. The door opened behind him and Grandmère came out with her shotgun. He recognized the gun as the one Bethany had placed under the seat of the boat. "I'll check at the dock. I swear, if he hurts my granddaughter, he won't live to tell about it," she declared, cocking the gun.

Matthew realized at that moment where Bethany got her backbone. The woman never backed down and never gave up. He counted on that—she had to be all right. But the sick feeling had taken hold of his gut and the haze had gripped his vision. If Smoot hurt Bethany, nothing Smith could say would save him. He glanced at Tobias and noticed the man's face had gone pale. Odd.

"I saw a garden earlier today, and Bethany and I were heading there, just before you arrived. I am going to check that, first," Matthew said. His body thrummed with tension and his head ached. *Where was she?* He heard Grandmère calling Bethany and Dandie in the background and instinctively knew the outcome would not be good if she found Smoot, although he might have a better chance of survival than if Matthew found him.

The two men raced across the bridge and followed the small stream to the garden he had seen earlier. He saw Mr. Duplantis hailing him down and carrying a bottle of something. He scanned the area—but didn't see Bethany or Dandie. Smoot would not have wanted Dandie—especially since the dog nearly bit off his ear. Desperate, he called out to the little dog, rewarded by a small whimper. Panicked, he searched everywhere, finally seeing the small white dog laying curled up beneath a tall shrub, covered by pink blooms. Her head was bleeding. Shoving his gun in his pants, he picked up the small dog tenderly. Bethany would want her safe.

"Come on, let's take her to Grandmère," Smith said.

Matthew looked at the man, realizing that he was angry with him. Smith had warned them, and despite the warning, he had allowed Bethany to wander off by herself. Yet he was directing anger at Smith. It was wrong. "That is a good idea. Talk to me, Smith. You know this area better than I do. Where could Smoot have her?"

"I've been thinking the same thing," Smith said.

"Wait!" Mr. Duplantis called.

The two men stopped and turned as Duplantis halted a safe distance from them.

"I saw a man rowing a boat about an hour ago."

"Did you see where he went?" Matthew asked, realizing Mr. Duplantis would not have seen Bethany. She probably was in the boat's bottom. He bit the inside of his cheek, something he did when he needed to control his emotions.

"I did. The boat is still there." He pointed across the water to the canopy of cypress trees. "You can barely see it. When I was young, there was a cabin up there in the fields. It's probably hidden by trees." He looked at Dandie, limp in Matthew's arms. "May I?" he asked, showing he wanted to touch the dog. Matthew remembered what Bethany had told him and nodded, placing the dog on a soft surface of grass and stepping back.

Mr. Duplantis came over and, with the small bottle of water, bathed the dog's face and held it up, giving her water. "She looks to have been kicked." He leaned over and listened for her heart and felt her stomach area. "Her breathing sounds like it's getting stronger. I think she must have been knocked out. Miss Phillips loves this dog. I have never seen her without her puppy."

"Climb the small path of rocks under the tree limbs. He may have done that. There are snakes in the area—deadly moccasins and rattlesnakes, so be careful. They hide under the low brush."

"How do you know about this cabin?"

Mr. Duplantis looked up. "The cabin was a hunting cabin maintained by the Bellovere family years ago. My grandfather was the groundskeeper here. As I child I did not have this . . . disease." His voice grew sad. "Occasionally, I would play near the cabin while he worked. The area was not overgrown, and it was a fine piece of property. It was grand looking down at the plantation, seeing the beauty of the gardens and the house." He stood and stepped back. "Thank you for letting me check the dog. I heard everyone calling for it and feared something awful had happened. I think she will recover. Her grandmother will know what to do for her."

"Thank you, Mr. Duplantis. If he is holding her up there, you have saved us hours of searching."

Matthew gingerly picked up Dandie and held her close to his heart, willing her to be better. "Girl, I know you gave everything you had to protect Bethany. I will find her," he said, feeling his eyes fill with tears.

"I know the area. Mr. Duplantis is right. We will need my hunting knife," Smith said, opening his vest and pointing to the leather-sheathed knife. "If you have your boots, perhaps you should put them on," he suggested.

Matthew nodded. "I apologize for behaving badly towards you, Smith. I know you care about Bethany." The man winced. "I am angry at myself for letting her go alone." Matthew glanced down at Dandie and noticed she seemed to look a little more alert. The house was in view. Grandmère and Aunt Theo were making their way towards him.

"Did you find her?" Grandmère said as she got closer.

"No, but we found Dandie," he whispered. The dog was holding her head up but looked weak. "Mr. Duplantis listened to her chest and thought she would recover. Smoot kicked her in the head."

"Mr. Duplantis knows animals. I'm glad he checked on her. Bring her inside," Aunt Theo said, holding the door open.

"Duplantis saw a man rowing a boat earlier. The boat is still docked," Smith said, pointing in the water's direction. "It's across from the Duplantis' dock."

"We think he's holding her in the cabin up on that hill."

"Be careful. Take our walking sticks, in case you come upon snakes," Grandmère said, grabbing the sticks from behind the door. "We will be here, waiting."

They heard Dandie trying to get up. "Go on," Grandmère urged. "I'll take care of the dog. Bethany would not want her up there. We keep the fencing in as good shape so we can keep the gators and snakes at bay," she added.

"I'll bring her back, "Matthew promised, heading to his room, and returning with his boots, planning to put them on in the boat.

"I know you will." Grandmère smiled through tears. "Find my girl."

"Wait, let me help you with those boots. You will need them," Grandmère said, pointing out Tobias' leather boots.

A few minutes later, the two men were heading out the door, hurrying to get to the other side of the tributary and not knowing what they would find.

>>><<<

BETHANY TRIED HER best to breathe. Her face felt like it had exploded. She tasted blood on her lips. *Surely, they would miss her by now. But would they even find her?* Bethany did not know where she was. *How would they?*

Dandie! The thought hit her cold. Her dog could be dead. If she ever got a chance, she would repay Smoot for his cruelty. Closing her eyes, she prayed they would find her dear puppy was still alive, hoping her mother was watching over her.

"Is anyone here... anyone, at all?" Her muffled voice didn't help. She listened, unable to hear or see. It made her realize how Matthew must have felt for those long, hard weeks when he could see nothing. How terrifying. She could barely see light through the thick black bag. It was filthy. Noticing the rag was not tied around her face, she spat it out, gasping and trying to breathe fresh breath where there was none. "Help," she yelled, as loud as she could.

They had bound her hands and feet, with a bag tied around her neck—it was loose enough that she could breathe, but not loose enough for her to free herself from it. Stressed, she closed her eyes and laid back on the floor, her chest heaving from exertion.

"Help!" a garbled male voice shouted from somewhere nearby. "I cannot breathe," he cried.

"Truly sorry, but I am slightly tied up here," she said in a huff. *Was that Smoot? What had happened that he was yelling for help?* Then it hit her. Snakes. This cliff was known for them—so much so, it was sometimes called Snake Hill. *Smoot had dragged her up here. He deserved what he got.* Her body quaked with fear. She could not see them and prayed that she was not near one. All she could see was darkness. Bethany needed to think. Smoot obviously had succumbed to panic. The man certainly would not have his way with her, as he had threatened. She wanted to laugh, and might have, had the thought not terrified her. How had this day gone so badly?

"Keep your breath shallow," she finally said, not really caring if he heard her. But her conscience was clear. She had helped him.

Thankfully, it wasn't hotter. That would certainly mean more snakes. The bayou was beautiful, but it came alive with danger in the summer. She was used to the dangers, but not with her head wrapped in a bag with a foul rag.

"I'm sorry," Smoot cried out, his voice growing faint. "Please, someone help me," he panted.

"You are slime, Caleb Smoot!" Bethany ground out, angry that she was in this predicament. "And you are a coward with no regard for others. You hope to trade another human being so that you won't face the punishment for what you did."

She had worn her voice out, crying for help. *How long would it be before they missed her?*

Time dragged before she finally heard voices. "Help," she called, barely able to hear her own cries. She was frightened.

"I see the cabin," a male voice yelled from a short distance away. "The door is open."

It was Matthew's voice. She could hear him and Tobias. They had come for her!

"Smith, here's Smoot. I'm going to check for Bethany."

Bethany could hear Tobias talking to Caleb Smoot, telling

him to calm himself. The man was still alive. *Of course, he is.* Grandmère would help him.

"Help me. I'm over here," she called out, in a raspy voice.

"Bethany!" Matthew clawed at the ribbon that tied the bag closed. Frustrated, he ripped it open and pulled it off her head.

She gulped huge gulps of air with tears flowing down her cheeks. "You came for me."

"I DID. WE both did." Matthew looked back at Smoot and Smith. Out of the corner of his eye, he saw a large, dead snake where Smoot had been. Matthew did not know what type of snake it was but realized Smith must have killed it. They had not been kidding about the dangers here.

They finally got Smoot down the hill and into Smith's boat, while Bethany rode with him in Smoot's stolen canoe.

Grandmère met them on the dock and, after hugging Bethany, followed Smith and Smoot into the house. Holding hands, Matthew and Bethany strolled back to the cabin. He had wanted to kiss her, but she refused him. "I smell terrible, even to myself. I need a bath so badly."

As she walked into the house, Dandie walked slowly over to meet her, and she reached down to pet her. Seeing her dog's bruised and bloodied face, her temper flared.

"Caleb Smoot," she called to him.

"Yes," a whiney male voice returned.

Bethany walked over to Caleb, who stood near the dining room table, waiting for her grandmother to help with his swollen leg and arm. He had been bitten twice. Served him right. "I owe you something!" Looking him in the eye, she hit him in the face as hard as she could. He fell back, knocked over the chair and landed on the floor, staring up in disbelief at her.

No one said a word for a long minute.

"That's my girl!" Aunt Theo finally quipped, clapping.

"I will help you with a bath, child. I think you need it," Grandmère finally said.

"I will stay here and direct Caleb's care. Tobias and the colonel can help me," Aunt Theo said cheerfully. "There's a small bottle of ammonia in the cabinet, Tobias. We will need it. Matthew, can you bring me the roll of muslin strips from the linen cabinet in the hall?"

"If you wanted to tangle with a snake, Caleb Smoot, could you not have done it closer to home and left my people alone?" she asked angrily, pouring the ammonia into the snake bites.

The man screamed and writhed in pain. Matthew doubted anyone cared. Even Smith, who seemed to care about Smoot, seemed immune to his whining.

The older woman soon had Caleb's hand and foot bandaged.

Matthew wondered how Bethany was doing. She had been gone for a while. He thought about the day and how it had spiraled from being the best of days into something he could barely describe. He was engaged—something he had never thought much about before. Suddenly, he realized they had told no one about being engaged.

A knock sounded at the door and Matthew went to answer it—leaving Smith to handle Smoot, ensuring the man could not cause any more trouble. Walking into the parlor, he saw Edward Sinclair standing there.

"I knocked a few times, and finally opened the door, afraid something had happened. Placing his bag near the door, the older man extended his hand. It's nice to see you up and walking about, Romney," Sinclair said.

Matthew noticed Sinclair's somber tone. "I am feeling pretty good. Has something happened?" Matthew asked, studying the man's eyes.

Male voices drifted from the dining room. "It sounds like you have company. Did I pick a bad time to come?" he said, attempting to be jovial.

Matthew noticed he had not answered his question. "No. Not at all. It's good to see you," he replied. "Come on back. Grandmère is with Bethany, but Aunt Theo is in the dining room."

"To your question. I have news, but perhaps we should wait until later," Sinclair said, nodding towards the company.

They walked into the room and were met by Tobias. "I believe it would be best for Caleb to leave with me—tonight. I do not want to risk him causing any more of a stir. And I believe the snakebites are under control enough that if he sits quietly, we can make it back before too late."

"You have already discussed it with the women, I am assuming." He would be glad to see the men leave. "Let me make introductions." He turned to Sinclair. "Edward Sinclair, this is Tobias Smith, a friend of the family and the proprietor of the Trading Post near Miss Phillip's home. And this is Caleb Smoot, a local that lives near Miss Phillips."

"Caleb is my half-brother on my father's side," Smith said quietly, causing everyone to look in his direction. "He is older, so most people don't realize we are related. I need to think of something to keep him from doing something desperate, again." He extended his hand to Matthew and to Edward Sinclair. "Good luck, Colonel Romney. I hope you make it back to your homeland soon and safely."

Understanding shot through Matthew and Tobias Smith rose in his estimation. He had wanted to save his brother. Matthew locked gazes with the man and clasped his hand, shaking it. "Thank you, Smith, for everything."

"Yes. She is my friend. I care about her, as I realize you do as well," Smith said, smiling at Matthew.

"Yes. I do." Matthew said. He turned to Edward Sinclair. "Sinclair is a family friend," he added. He realized Sinclair was a lifeline to his family.

Smith turned to Grandmère. "May I leave the extra pirogue and pick it up later? I think it's best I get Caleb home, and I can easily take him in my canoe."

Grandmère smiled, agreeing. "Of course, Tobias. Anything you need." She whispered, "I will continue to think on your half-brother's situation."

Tobias thanked her with a hug. Then, he and his half-brother said their goodbyes and made their way to his boat.

Matthew smiled, listening to Grandmère continue to give directions to Smoot. She warned him against drinking with his snake bites, explaining alcohol could make it easier to succumb to the poison. It was good his half-brother heard it, he thought. Otherwise, Matthew was certain Smoot's cure of choice would have been a bottle of whiskey.

Sinclair settled in and helped prepare for dinner. It delighted Matthew to see how easily the man had become friends with the family.

By supper time, Grandmère's medicines had worked their magic on the dog. It was easy to see Dandie had returned to her old self.

Smiling, Matthew gently tapped his glass, gaining everyone's attention before walking to his betrothed and putting his arm around her.

He turned to Grandmère. "I hope you will forgive my lack of manners. However, I can withhold my good news no longer." He looked at Bethany, whose green eyes sparkled in his direction. "Bethany Phillips has made me the happiest of men and agreed to become my wife. Over these weeks and month, now, I have found myself quite taken with her and cannot imagine returning to England without her by my side." He looked at Aunt Theo and Grandmère. "I realize your homes are here, but I would very much love for you to consider coming to live with us. Failing that, I assure you we will visit as often as possible." He looked at the stunned group, momentarily afraid he had overstepped considerably.

Abruptly, Grandmère stood and raised her glass. "To my future grandson." Her eyes glistened with unshed tears. "I had never imagined my Bethany leaving us—however, we had never imagined her meeting her husband under these conditions. My sister and I welcome you to our family." She reached over and hugged her granddaughter. "I had my suspicions that things were developing, so my heart had conditioned itself, Bethany. He is a good man. Your mother would be so proud of you both." She looked back at Matthew, sitting next to Sinclair. "As for travel to England, Theo and I had even discussed that. We did not know whether this would materialize." She winked at Matthew. "Give us time. We would like to join you, but it may not be immediately."

"Congratulations, Romney. Your family will love her. I am sure," Sinclair added, holding up his glass and joining the toast. "I have never had Creole crab and am quite looking forward to it."

"I cannot believe you have shared our country for so long and have missed a crab boil. We will rectify that immediately," Grandmère reproached playfully.

It was after dinner when Sinclair finally approached him. "Can we talk, Romney?"

"Yes. I had expected something was amiss," Matthew said, absorbing the strained look on Sinclair's face.

The two men went to the parlor. "I have some important news from home and hate to tell you this on the heels of your wonderful news. Yet, I fear it cannot wait," Sinclair began.

"Is everyone well?" Matthew asked.

"I hope so. A missive was waiting for me. Your parents are beside themselves with grief, thinking you dead. I felt it was very important to let them know I had found you and that you are safe."

Father had been proud of his military accomplishments, taking comfort in his officer status, and thinking that he would return from this war. He would have a surprise when they returned—a wife. "Thank you, Sinclair. That should ease their minds. It pains me they thought me dead, although if not for Bethany, I would surely have been."

"Your father will love her. He will be proud that you have found someone like Bethany," Sinclair replied.

Matthew hugged the man and allowed the tears that had accumulated to fall. "I appreciate everything you have done, Sinclair. Thank you for finding me."

"My help is not over with. I am going to find you a way home. I hope you don't mind, but I sent word that you would make your way home and speculated it could be from one of the northern ports. I will escort you there."

"No, I do not mind, at all. I want to return home soon. Will you return with us?" Matthew asked, studying the man.

Sinclair shook his head.

Matthew recalled the woman that Sinclair had mentioned before he left. The one that had taken care of him when he fell ill and realized he may stay because of her. He understood.

"Do you think we can find a way home from New Orleans?" he asked, mulling over thoughts.

"That's very possible," Sinclair returned. "I can check."

They returned to the dining room, and he pulled Bethany aside and told her about the message Sinclair had sent. "I understand, Matthew," she said. "My family would be consumed with grief if they thought me dead." She raised her eyes to his face. "I suppose you want to leave soon."

"It will thrill your parents to get you back," Aunt Theo said. "As much as we hate to see our Bethany leave us, you have provided wonderful options." She smiled, bemusedly. "Angelica and I are thinking about your offer. I know how to get you home. And it may be quicker and easier than making your way to Massachusetts."

They all looked in her direction. "Johnny's father, Dom Roeux, may be able help. We will have to wait for his return, but he usually returns at the end of the week. He is the quiet type that always lends a hand to help his neighbors. We are like family here. Let me speak with him. Recently, he went to work for his good friend in the city. His friend is Jean Lafitte."

CHAPTER TWENTY-FIVE

Late Summer

THEY WOULD SOON be married, and the thought both excited and relieved him. Since they had announced their engagement, they tried to make the most of every day they were still here, and discussion only briefly touched on their leaving. Finding passage home had been no simple affair, as the war between their two countries had only ended a few months past. Dom Roeux confirmed that the transatlantic voyages back and forth to England had been slow in resuming. However, ships were docking from other countries and he felt sure they would find passage for them soon.

Matthew focused his attention on Bethany's family. He worked on whatever Grandmère and Aunt Theo said needed fixing in the house, as well as in the house where Bethany had taken care of him following the battle. He enjoyed doing it, as it kept his mind focused, even though he had never done handy work before. However, he caught on quickly and even designed Grandmère and Aunt Theo a round, turning shelf. It was a proud moment when he showed them how it worked. It allowed them to spin the contents around and select the spice or whatnot they needed. Their elation had been balm to his heart.

Bethany had spent these last several weeks helping her aunt

and grandmother with their gardens, and with anything else she could think of. She and Grandmère turned the soil, pulled weeds, and seeded and tended the crops. Herb gardening had been her domain, and until now, Matthew had not realized how much her family counted on her. However, they were opening a new chapter to her life and could not wait.

"Bethany. Are you out here, love? We have visitors," Matthew called to her as he walked two men towards the back garden area.

"I am on my way, Matthew," she said, brushing the grime off of her skirt and wiping off her hands.

"Mr. Roeux brought the priest with him," Matthew said, walking her into the house. They met the two men in Aunt Theo's parlor.

"Bonjour Mr. Roeux," she said, extending her hand. It was Mr. Roeux and a local priest. Roeux had returned home two days ago and offered to help them gain passage to England on a merchant ship when he heard of their plight. His friend was heavily involved with trade in and out of New Orleans. It had not hurt their chances that her Grandmère and Aunt Theo had helped Johnny through the fever only this past summer. Mr. Roeux brought the priest of his family's church.

"Bonjour, Miss Phillips," he returned. "This is a family friend, Father Hebert. He has agreed to perform the ceremony tomorrow."

"*Merci*, Father Hebert. Thank you!"

"I heard you had considered the romantic option of a shipboard wedding but chose to be married before boarding." He smiled. "I feel honored to conduct the ceremony," the priest said.

"Getting married before the trip makes sense. Grandmère and Aunt Theo can attend, as can Johnny and Mr. Duplantis, and other friends that mean so much," she replied.

It would also make the passage easier—*not to mention more exciting*, Matthew thought, willing his body to behave and not react to the thought of Bethany's lithe, beautiful body.

"Mr. Roeux, have you been able to determine which merchant ship we will be on?" he asked.

"Yes, Colonel. I have discussed this with Lafitte. He has a ship in mind and hopes you will be most comfortable: *The Rising Tide* will be perfect. The ship will transport mostly cotton, tea, and tobacco products. There should be plenty of room," the man responded.

"That sounds wonderful. We do not know how to thank you. Of course, I will reimburse the good captain for our passage." Finding a boat that would take them to England had been difficult, and with Mr. Roeux helping them, it seemed a better idea to sail from New Orleans. With the onset of spring, the Atlantic had been more difficult to cross. Voyages could average as much as fourteen weeks or more, or as few as eight weeks. Matthew could not believe he could be home within a few months—possibly sooner, depending on the route taken. He understood the Atlantic in the summer could be quite violent, so the captain may have to sail around problem areas, which could add time.

Roeux gave a quick nod. "He has agreed to your offer. The ship sails two days hence. I should warn you that the route will not be direct." He looked down at Dandie, who had walked up smiling and wagging tail. "You must leash your dog when she is out of your cabin. He doesn't want her running about the ship. There was no additional cost for her." He smiled at the dog. "My son has asked for one like her. He will miss you, Miss Phillips."

"I will miss Johnny very much. He has agreed to walk me down the aisle, tomorrow," she said.

"Does this merchant ship have room for an additional hand?" Matthew asked.

"Jean said this merchant was not the right ship. However, if your friend, Smith, will bring his half-brother to Lafitte, there is another merchant ship that needs to replace some crew. They also leave in two days," Roeux detailed. "The captain is one that will not tolerate lazy work."

"I caught the last of what you mentioned. It is glorious news. But any date would be too soon," Grandmère said, wearing a smile as she stepped from behind Matthew. "Thank you, Mr. Roeux. By the way, Tobias Smith may be very interested in speaking with him."

"I will speak to him. Lafitte has also issued a directive to the captain of your granddaughter's ship that she and her husband be treated *very* well." He beamed, clearly proud of his arrangements.

At dinner that night, they discussed all the arrangements with Sinclair: "That means you may arrive by Christmas or shortly thereafter, depending on the speed of the wind."

The next day

TODAY WAS HER *wedding day*! While it thrilled Bethany to marry Matthew, she wished her mother was with her. She would love him. He was the most handsome man Bethany had ever seen, and his presence could make her giddy, comfort her, and stir a depth of feeling that made it difficult to breathe. She sensed she was at her best with him and cherished every minute they spent together—the touch and feel of him, and every kiss—kisses that sent wicked pulses to her toes. She loved him and she ached to tell him—but could not bear it if he could not return the sentiment. So Bethany kept her feelings to herself. It was better not to say it . . . *first*. Her mother had always pointed to actions. And if Matthew's actions spoke louder than words, she knew he cared deeply for her. *Was it love?*

Everything he did was for her, about her, and with her. With their worlds about to join, he had embraced her world—even the most frightening aspects, like the alligators—and *thrived*. He had embraced her world blind and embraced it sighted. She planned to embrace everything about his—even the alligators, *or the scariest creature in his world*. According to Matthew, the scariest creature in his world was Society's gossip. In her mind, this conjured up a rotund, bespeckled lady with a bird on her velvet hat and an excessive amount of rouge, who appeared without warning. She giggled. She would be the Viscountess Longueville, a title with a lifestyle that she knew nothing about. As she thought about it, perhaps the alligators in his society were more frightening.

She stared in the looking glass at the white spotted muslin dress. Her grandmother had transformed an older dress of her mother's, which had included shortening the sleeves. The bodice and short sleeves were lined in white linen, and a white satin ribbon gently cinched the bodice and the empire waistline. Reaching down, she picked up the small bouquet of pink anemones, white roses, and baby's breath that she had picked from Aunt Theo's gardens and tied a piece of white ribbon around it to match her dress. A chemise was her only undergarment, having discarded the thought of petticoats and silk stockings. She slipped on matching white slippers and checked her image. Grandmère had done a brilliant job with her hair, pulling it into a soft cascade of curls that flowed haphazardly about her head. The delicate pins and pearls attached to her hair were her only adornment.

"Are you ready, Bethany?" Grandmère stood in the open doorway, dressed in a pink linen sundress, a wide-brimmed straw hat, and matching pink leather flats. Aunt Theo walked up behind her in her lavender dress and straw hat. They had decorated her walking stick with a small daisy chain that wrapped around it.

"I am." She looked down at her small dog. Dandie had a collar of daisies that matched the ones on Aunt Theodosia's cane. "Ready Dandie?"

Her Grandmère gave her an adoring look of approval. "Your mother would be so pleased for you," she said through misty eyes.

Dandie gave a quick bark.

As they walked to the door, her grandmother leaned over and

whispered. "I prepared Matthew's bedroom for you, and I added some darker curtains."

Bethany colored from her head to her toes.

"Truly, I'm sorry. I had not meant to embarrass you—only to let you know I've cleaned the room and made it more comfortable."

"Thank you, Grandmère," she murmured.

The three women and the little dog walked to the door, where they met a dashing young man, ready to escort the bride down the aisle.

"Hello, Johnny," Bethany greeted him, smiling.

"Miss Bethany, I am to give you to the colonel, as long as you promise to visit. Your man is waiting in the garden."

Bethany nodded through tears. "You are very dear to me. We will always be friends, Johnny."

"Thank you, Miss Bethany. I feel that way fer you."

As they walked through the back gate into the garden, she spotted Matthew. He wore his regimentals—the jacket she had mended. He looked spectacular. Bethany's legs wobbled.

Father Hebert stepped in front of the large white gardenia shrub ensconced between green-leaved camellias.

Johnny held out his small arm so she could loop hers within it and together, they stood in front of the preacher. "Who gives this woman to marry this man?" Father Hebert asked.

"I do," the young man said proudly, and placed her hand in Matthew's before turning to leave. Dandie stepped to the left of the couple and watched.

The vows were said, and they were pronounced man and wife.

Matthew brought Bethany close and lifted her chin with his gloved hand. "My sweet Bethany. Finally, you are mine."

He leaned down and kissed her lips gently, sending shivers down her spine and butterflies taking flight throughout her body.

"Are we ready for this?" he asked.

"We are." She was ready for this man.

The couple faced a small group of their friends and family—Aunt Theo, Grandmère, Johnny's parents, and Mr. Sinclair clapped and whooped for them. Mr. Duplantis and his small family stood a few feet behind them, clapping. Matthew and Bethany rushed through the handfuls of lavender seeds thrown at them as they ran to the house where her grandmother had prepared a wedding breakfast to celebrate. She had sent a similar meal to the Duplantis house so they could celebrate alongside them.

Two hours had passed when her husband squeezed her hand beneath the table. "Let us slip out and make our own celebration. I can wait no longer to make you mine."

Heat rose up her neck. Grandmère had told her to trust her husband and not to be afraid of the wedding night. *Relax and enjoy, she had said.* Bethany took a deep breath, hoping to accomplish that. "Should we say goodbye?"

"No. I think they will understand," he said, pulling her up with him.

Dandie gave her a questioning look as they left. Seeming to understand they did not invite her, the small dog sprawled out and stayed by Grandmère's side, as her grandmother continued her conversation with Mr. Sinclair.

ALONE AT LAST, Matthew carried his new bride over the threshold to the bedroom, opening the door with a free arm and kicking the door closed with his foot, before carrying her to the bed. A small candle burned on a table near the bed, emitting the soft smell of honeysuckle.

Sweeping back the mosquito netting, he secured it, before propping a pillow behind her back. Carefully, he laid his wife on the crisp white sheets. Someone had already changed the curtains out for darker ones, cutting back the light and effecting a level of privacy in the room.

He glanced at Bethany and was taken in by the wonder he saw in her face. She watched him as he sat in a wooden chair and pulled off his boots. After discarding his very hot regimental coat, he cast off his white breeches and opened the neck of his shirt. He came to bed wearing only his smalls and his shirt.

The fresh scent of honeysuckle stirred his need. Gently, he lifted her hand and, with his thumb, rubbed the inside of her hand in little circles as a lazy smile warmed her lips.

"Shall I stop?" he asked, his voice husky.

Bethany closed her eyes. "No, please do not stop." A smile lifted her lips.

Matthew bent and gently brushed her mouth. With more force, he kissed her, his teeth nibbling gently on her lip. Gentle coaxing from his tongue gained him entry, and she pulled back her neck to give more room, seeming to enjoy it as his breath heated her neck.

As he kissed her, he loosened her dress, pulling it over her head and leaving her in her chemise.

"The rest of the day and the night are ours to spend at our leisure—until hunger persuades us to gain sustenance. What better way could there be to spend our time?" His breath gently fanned her ears.

He gently slipped her sleeves from her arms, exposing her breast. "Allow me to warm you, wife."

"Matthew," she murmured, wrapping her hands around his neck and pulling him closer.

Matthew reveled in the feel of her hands gently touching his neck and combing through his hair. His head dipped, and with his teeth, he pulled the shoulders of her chemise away from her, freeing both breasts. Bethany moved her head back and gave a guttural hum as he gently pulled one breast into his mouth, licking and suckling before moving to the next one to give it equal measure. Lifting his head, he moved to her mouth, kissing and nibbling her lower lip as his hand worked her moist folds. "I want you," he whispered against the lobes of her ear, sending prickles across her shoulders and into the base of her skull.

BETHANY HAD NEVER experienced such delight coming from her body. Delicious waves of feeling throbbed through her arms and legs, pooling in her core. She gasped, unable to comprehend what she wanted, only feeling an uncontrollable wave of desire. Pulling his head back to her breasts, she reveled in the warm wetness of his mouth. He wet his fingers and touched her nipples, blowing softly to pebble them beneath his touch.

"My insides feel tingly," she gasped, trying to explain her insatiable desire.

"I want to please you, first," he breathed in her ear. "However, my desire to join with you is almost intolerable," he whispered. Lifting himself, he adjusted himself over her, with his fingers probing her moist core.

Bethany inhaled as her body both convulsed and craved his attentions. His lips covered hers and their tongues swirled with tides of desire covering the insides of their mouths between heated breaths. She squeezed her eyes closed and clung to the sensation of being detached from her body.

"I think you are ready," he said between pants. "My love, I will take my time, but you will feel a slight pain. I promise it will get better," he exhaled, his words enunciated slowly between heated breaths.

"Yes," she said, unsure of what pain he spoke.

He entered her and stopped, causing a piercing pain that lasted for only an instant. She struggled to get her breath before he began once more, moving slowly, inciting her own body to respond to each of his movements until their bodies exploded together.

"I love you, Matthew." The words burst from her lips.

He rolled off her and they laid side by side, panting. Bethany pulled his arm over her head and curled herself against his side, softly running her fingertips over the puckered flesh of the wound that had brought them together. "I had never imagined making love could be so wonderful."

Matthew raised up on his elbow and stared into her deep green eyes. "I never thought to marry until I realized that I could never be whole without you by my side. I love you, my dearest wife," he said with a ravenous look in his eyes. "There will be much to look forward to, including this night, which is still young."

They made love again until they succumbed to exhaustion. Bethany tucked her body into the curve of his and closed her eyes, falling asleep at last.

Epilogue

*The morning of
December 31, 1816
Kent, England*

After almost a year at sea and several days traveling in a carriage across England, Matthew, Bethany, and Dandie were but hours from their home. Their voyage home had turned into a disaster, but thankfully, everyone was safe.

"The carriage is ready, darling," Matthew said, pointing to the black-lacquered carriage that had just pulled up to the inn. "We should be home in a few hours. Normally we might have pushed through, but in your condition, I felt it best to stop."

Bethany smiled and held out her hand for her husband to help her into the carriage. They had spent a day in London to find suitable clothing. Thankfully, the small modiste's shop and the tailor across the street had assisted. Bethany was almost four months pregnant. Not only would she be meeting his family and friends for the first time, but she would meet them *enceinte*.

For the first few months of her pregnancy, she had feared she would give birth on the island. Thankfully, England would be the baby's birthplace.

"Thank you, Matthew." She patted her lap. "Dandie, jump up here, girl. You can curl against me and share the heat." The dog gave her a smile and jumped up on the bench next to her.

Matthew jumped in and sat next to her. "I thought you might like to stretch your legs," he said, grinning. "Dandie will not need the leg space."

"And I am looking forward to my beautiful wife sleeping in a soft bed for as long as she wants."

"Mmm . . . that would be good," she said dreamily as she laid her head against his shoulder. She reached into her pelisse and her gloved hand found the smooth white crystal Aunt Theo had given her. It had worked its magic, although not as she would have imagined. They were all safe.

"I find myself nervous, now that we are this close to your home," she said. "You sent a letter to Mr. Sinclair and to Grandmère, right?"

"I did. Do not worry. Sinclair would have gotten word of our rescue," he replied, distractedly glancing out the window.

"I am glad we are together," she whispered from his shoulder as she dozed, thinking back to the day they left home.

Their trip started the same as most. The trunks carrying their belongings, including the small, tufted bed that Aunt Theo made for Dandie's voyage home, were taken aboard the ship while the small family said their goodbyes.

Aunt Theo pressed a clear crystal quartz in the palm of Bethany's hand. "For luck," she said with her eyes full of tears.

Bethany closed her fist and squeezed her eyes closed, determined to remember these moments and not cry. The tears came anyway.

"Bethany, I put together this small satchel of medicinal herbs and rolled some dressings. You understand it all, so I labeled nothing but the small vials. I hope you will never need them, but it comforts me you have them," her Grandmère said.

Her body quaked with unshed tears.

"Do not cry. Aunt Theo and I plan to come. I just have to convince her of the merits of living there. It'll be our grand adventure," the older woman said, soothing the tears from her granddaughter's eyes. "I love you, Bethany." She kissed her cheeks. Grandmère walked over to

Matthew. "Take care of my girls," she said, kissing him on the cheek.

"I will. I promise," he said, taking a quick swipe at his eyes.

Grandmère leaned down and kissed Dandie. "You be a good girl. Take care of Bethany and mind them, Dandie."

The dog waggled her rear end and grinned back, signaling she was ready for the adventure.

One more face worked its way to the front. Johnny brought a small bouquet and a bone. "This is for you, Miss Bethany. And this 'ere bone is for Dandie." Big tears rolled down his cheeks. "I will miss you all." He looked up at Matthew and saying nothing, wrapped his arms around her husband's waist. "I will say a prayer for you to have a safe trip," he said through tears.

A whistle blew on the ship behind them. "It's time to go, Aunt Theo, Grandmère, Johnny. I will write—to all of you."

Mr. Sinclair stepped up to Matthew and shook his hand. He handed Bethany a small package wrapped in brown paper. "Bethany, I think you will find the gift useful," he said gently. Turning to Matthew, he said, "Write me when you get there. If I do not hear from you, I will send the British navy to find you."

"You would find a way," Matthew laughed. "I will write as soon as we arrive. I promise."

The older man gave a quick nod and stepped from the loading area. He stood there with her family and Johnny waving at them. Matthew held her close until they could no longer see them.

"We should be home in a half-hour, Bethany." Matthew's voice penetrated her dream.

"Mmm . . . I am ready to meet everyone," she sighed, lifting her head and smiling. Seeing more road ahead, she settled her head back on his shoulder and dozed.

A week out of New Orleans had seen their ship blown off course, tossed furiously in the waves of the ocean until finally finding purchase on the jagged, rocky coast of a seemingly uncharted island.

The ship's crew had tried their best to repair it, but they needed more wood than they could find. They spent months on the island, at first trying to patch the ship, until finally, hoping a ship would find them—as long as it wasn't a pirate ship.

The weather had been much milder than in America. It never grew cold. By Bethany's calculation, they spent almost nine months there. Had she not made strikes on paper for each day, she might never have realized.

Matthew became their de facto leader—a nod to his position in the military, Bethany assumed. And she treated illnesses and injuries. As her satchel of herbs depleted, she quickly found substitutes or replacements. Turtles, alligators, fish, and wild boars were plentiful, but they found no sign of humans—or even a sign that humans had ever been on the island.

Dandie made herself useful, immediately alerting everyone anytime she heard a boar. She never even saw a snake, a blessing as far as Bethany was concerned.

It had been Matthew and Dandie that spotted the ship. It was a British frigate, and it appeared their luck was finally turning up. But luck is a matter of opinion.

The ship had been sent to find any sign of their lost vessel. When the British Captain Horatio Greene found the lost ship and their crew, unharmed on an island, the man was beside himself with joy. It was then that Bethany knew Mr. Sinclair had made good on his promise to send it. The captain had a message for Matthew and handed him a missive from the Admiralty. It was from the Duke of Dorman—his lifelong friend.

"What's wrong, Matthew?" She had asked when they got to their room.

"My father died unexpectedly," he said as tears coursed his cheeks. "My uncle, Baron Longdale, has identified himself as guardian for my younger brother. He had even requested that Sinclair stop searching for me, thinking they had never found me. It is very important we get to England."

Bethany was speechless. Matthew's father had died, and he had never said goodbye.

She felt the road change from smooth to loud and crumbly, as if they were riding on crushed rock or shells, waking Bethany from her sleep. "This is to be a surprise, right?"

"I thought about sending a note but decided it would be

better to surprise everyone. I hope they are home, and we are not the ones surprised," he said, laughing.

As the carriage pulled up front, a liveried footman hurried down to open the door.

"Lord Romney, welcome home," he said, bowing.

Bethany saw her husband wince at his new title, an acknowledgment that his father was gone.

Matthew directed the trunks and took her hand, helping her from the carriage. "Welcome home, my beautiful wife. You are now the Countess Romney and will be afforded any luxury you wish."

"You of everyone should know my needs. Besides you, and Dandie, and this baby," she patted her belly, "I need very little. My only desire is a soft bed," she replied.

As they approached the top step, the door opened, and a tall graying man stepped out. His eyes widened when he saw Matthew. "Welcome home, my lord!" The man's eyes watered.

"Myers, let me introduce you to my wife, Lady Romney, and our dog, Dandie," he said, acknowledging the small dog's place in their home. He took Bethany's pelisse and handed it to Myers.

"You picked a fine day to come home. Your family and some of your friends are in the drawing room."

"Everyone?" Matthew asked. "All at the same time?" His voice sounded incredulous.

"Yes, my lord. They are preparing for the New Year's Eve celebration."

Matthew held out his hand and Bethany placed her hand on his arm. She had immersed herself into the etiquette, learning as much as she could from a book Mr. Sinclair had given her, and hoping that she would not embarrass herself or her family. Self-consciously, she glanced down at her emerald-green muslin dress. At almost four months pregnant, she felt lucky enough to see her toes.

They walked into an elegant, red- and gold-appointed room and were met by surprise. "Matthew," Lady Alice Romney, dressed in black silk, rose from the burgundy sofa and met her son at the door. She threw her arms around his neck, hugging him tightly to her. When she pulled back, he nodded towards Bethany.

"Mother, allow me to introduce Bethany, my wife."

There was a moment of silence as the woman digested what she had just heard.

"I have a new daughter," his mother effused. "Welcome to the family, Bethany!" The older woman hugged her, giving her a kiss on the cheek.

Suddenly, the room erupted in talking, with everyone coming to their sides and talking at once. Each family member pressed to meet her and get to Matthew. Dandie barked to make her presence known as she tried to protect her mistress from an avalanche of people.

Matthew put his arms around Bethany and led her to the couch, showing she should sit. A beautiful red-haired woman with green eyes and a young man of maybe ten years came up and introduced themselves.

"Bethany, I'm Charlotte Clarendon, Matthew's sister."

"And I'm Jason, Matthew's brother."

A tall man with shortly cropped brown hair walked up. "I am Evan Prescott, The Earl of Clarendon—Matthew's friend and Charlotte's husband."

Bethany laughed softly. "This is Dandie." She patted her small dog on the head and watched her edge closer. "We are so very glad to meet you."

Myers came to the door and cleared his throat. "My lord, The Duke of Dorman and the Marquess of Banbury have arrived."

Moments later, two footmen arrived with a tray of refreshments.

A small bell tinkled, drawing everyone's attention. Lady Alice Romney addressed her family.

"We have so much to celebrate as we enter this new year. Not only has my son returned to us, but we welcome a new daughter to the family." Dandie barked. "And her beautiful little puppy, Dandie," she smiled. "I know we have overwhelmed you both, but we have so many questions and so much to tell you. We had heard you were on your way, but had no notion of when to expect you," she said. "Honestly, I had thought I lost you, again." She swiped at a tear.

"Mother, we would have been here almost a year ago, but had the most fantastical trip home you could ever imagine."

Bethany looked over at her husband. The men had served themselves a glass of brandy and made themselves comfortable as Matthew began to relate the highlights of his last two years. It was wonderful to watch him interact with his family and friends—to watch him laugh.

"Remind me to limit my travel with Romney," the duke said, raising an eyebrow in amusement.

"It was an adventure. However, I cannot consider it a misadventure," Matthew said, jovially. "I have one small announcement to make."

Everyone became quiet.

"Besides being lost from the battlefield, helped by a beautiful angel, escaping an alligator while blind, surviving yellow fever, and being lost at sea?" Banbury interjected with a guffaw.

Everyone snickered.

"Besides that," Matthew returned with a grin. "I am to be a father in five months."

Dorman raised his glass. "Romney, we are grateful you have returned." He turned to Bethany. "Welcome to the family, my lady. By now you must realize nothing ever happens halfway with our friend." They all hooted. "To Romney and his lovely wife. We are grateful to have our Earl of Excess back among us."

About the Author

Anna St. Claire is a big believer that *nothing* is impossible if you believe in yourself. She sprinkles her stories with laughter, romance, mystery and lots of possibilities, adhering to the belief that goodness and love will win the day.

Anna is both an avid reader author of American and British historical romance. She and her husband live in Charlotte, North Carolina with their two dogs and often, their two beautiful granddaughters, who live nearby. *Daughter, sister, wife, mother, and Mimi*—all life roles that Anna St. Claire relishes and feels blessed to still enjoy. And she loves her pets – dogs and cats alike, and often inserts them into her books as secondary characters. And she loves chocolate and popcorn, a definite nod to her need for sweet followed by salty...*but not together*—a tasty weakness!

Anna relocated from New York to the Carolinas as a child. Her mother, a retired English and History teacher, always encouraged Anna's interest in writing, after discovering short stories she would write in her spare time.

As a child, she loved mysteries and checked out every *Encyclopedia Brown* story that came into the school library. Before too long, her fascination with history and reading led her to her first historical romance—Margaret Mitchell's *Gone With The Wind*, now a treasured, but weathered book from being read multiple times. The day she discovered Kathleen Woodiwiss,' books, *Shanna* and *Ashes In The Wind*, Anna became hooked. She read every historical romance that came her way and dreams of writing her own historical romances took seed.

Today, her focus is primarily the Regency and Civil War eras, although Anna enjoys almost any period in American and British history. She would love to connect with any of her readers on her website – www.annastclaire.com, through email – annastclaireauthor@gmail.com, Instagram – annastclaire_author, BookBub – www.bookbub.com/profile/anna-st-claire, Twitter – @1AnnaStClaire, Facebook – facebook.com/authorannastclaire or on Amazon – amazon.com/Anna-St-Claire/e/B078WMRHHF.

www.ingramcontent.com/pod-product-compliance
Lightning Source LLC
LaVergne TN
LVHW011934070526
838202LV00054B/4644